CW00434630

THE CASE OF VULCAN

Secundus Sulpicius Book 2

©Copyright – Francis M Mulhern

In writing this book I have attempted to be as true to the time period as possible. However, invariably the telling of a story requires some frames of reference for the reader to ensure consistency. As such I have used some terms such as hours, minutes, miles, some 'modern' swear words etc. to enable the action to be positioned and understood by a modern reader. I write in UK English so our cousins across the pond may find a few words appear differently to that which they may be accustomed to.

In researching the book it was also clear that there is no definitive nomenclature for the road systems in the City of Rome from this period and so I have used more conventional names where necessary even though they may not have been named as such within this time period and were introduced much later. In this way I hoped to be able to give life to what was a growing city and allow the reader to understand the world in which Secundus may have lived.

I have also included temples and other historically significant sites which give a flavour of the diversity of sacred and religious sites that are known to date. I may have missed some and I may have added them in the wrong location if the details of their exact position could not be found in my research. I have attempted to include some historical facts and information which I present to support the thinking of the period and included supposition of knowledge as opposed to confirmed understanding of developments form the period, especially related to Greek (there was no Greece at the time period, just a collection of states) history and associated awareness from the time period.

Contents

Map 1:

The hills and roads of Rome in the time of Secundus Sulpicius Merenda. Picture copyright © Francis Muhern

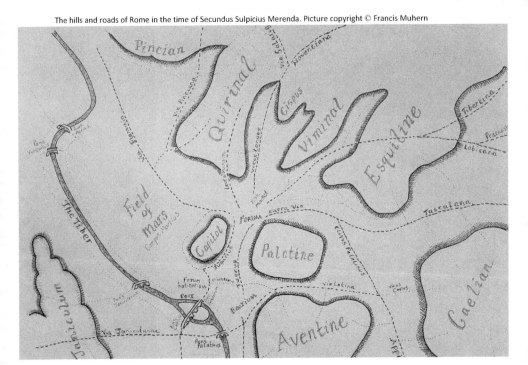

I

It was big news so I wasn't surprised that Milo was in my face fishing for gossip from the moment I arrived at his roadside eatery.

I'd tried to ignore him, slurping my soup noisily and giving him my sternest frown as Graccus sat back and rubbed vigorously at a red lump on his arm. I looked at it with disgust as my friend licked his finger and wet the sore-looking area, rubbing his finger up and down to leave a trail of saliva over the bite. He proceeded to pick up a lump of bread and tear off a chunk which he then offered to me. I shook my head slowly with a glance to the wet patch on his arm, the bread and the soaking finger. At that moment I lost my appetite.

"Come on lads you know more than you're letting on," drawled the food-seller, exasperated at our silence and with his thick eyebrows dancing in disbelief whilst he waited for us to answer.

"We don't know anything Milo, honestly," I replied to his intense stare. "I've just come back from Laurentina so I missed the fire." I was waving my arms and shrugging my shoulders as I continued. "I haven't spoken to my father yet. He's been in meetings with the Senate all night and didn't come home. I hear all the officials are chasing about like flies around shit. It's a big problem but it's not *my problem* and I don't have any news for you," I added with a further glance at his disbelieving face and jumping brows. "And it's not a problem that I particularly care about either. You probably know more about it than me."

Graccus upended his bowl and licked at it for a moment as Milo sighed heavily and rolled his eyes. We were obviously not the purveyors of red-hot gossip that he'd expected when he greeted us with open arms and ushered us to the best table in his street-front food shop. To be fair the best table was the one out of the late morning sun under a rickety roof and containing less of a swarm of flies than all the others. It was becoming our *usual* table and we were probably his most regular customers.

"Well I can't believe they got away with all that treasure." Milo was shaking his head but watching us with the intensity of a hawk in case we gave any indication that we knew more than we were giving away. "I heard that there were five ingots of silver and thirty of iron and bronze at least, but they left some of the iron. Too much to carry I guess?" His knowledge of official records seemed accurate from what I'd heard from Graccus just moments earlier. My friend looked at me sheepishly above the lip of his bowl and I held back from a sigh lest I turned into my mother and started to wag a finger at him. "How can they have made off with that much without anyone seeing them? And why burn the place down? And that poor priest, he died a hero's death trying to save the Temple. Poor bastard."

He was walking away as he spoke, a customer approaching.

I continued eating, wondering if he would come back before I had a chance to speak to Graccus.

I'd sent Micus ahead to get Graccus to meet me here as I was only just out of my bed after a long journey overnight and a lie-in till almost Meridiem. In honesty I didn't know much more than Graccus had already said to me before Milo arrived with his questions, which from the sound of it was the topic of gossip across the city. I yawned deeply. It was strange that I'd slept so well but still felt as if I needed to go back to bed for a few more hours. I'd heard the news of the fire from my mother shortly after my arrival at home, she was up late drinking with a new friend from the Temple of Minerva, a lady who lived on the Vaticano whose family grew olives and also seemed to have a passion for Bacchus' water. Through mouthfuls of the green berries my mother and her friend had explained that the Temple of Vulcan at the foot of the Capitol Hill had been raided the night before and a priest who was guarding the site was killed before the Temple was set ablaze.

My father had set his team, Scavolo as their leader, onto the case immediately and had hardly returned home since that moment. This was a *big* problem, a religious institution attacked, robbed and a priest killed. It was state funds that had been taken, so it was everyone's problem to some degree, however small. So far, according to Graccus, they had found no clues to why the temple had been burned to the ground and what treasures had been taken. I assumed Milo knew that too as I looked to my friend, soup on his nose and chin as he placed the bowl on the table.

"Tell me again Graccus," I asked, stifling another yawn, "What do they know so far?"

To his credit he looked across to see if Milo was listening, which he wasn't.

"Novius said this morning that Scavolo has been bashing heads to get information but the priests of Vulcan are like mutes, they have nothing to say."

I knew what he meant, they were a strange order, one of Rome's oldest and said to have started their cult at the time of Romulus but also notoriously close knit and difficult to work with. To join the order you had to give up all formal rights beyond that of citizen and live a basic life, despite the fact that they usually held vast sums and treasures in the vault of their temple. Their uniform was a dark blue tunic with gold thread at their necks and they maintained a very simple life, farming their small plot of land, devoting their days to praying to Vulcan, helping their devotees with legal disputes and completing prayers and sacrifices. It was the sort of thing I'd dreaded when the priestess of Minerva, Fucilla, had suggested that I had been granted a goddess-given power to find the killer of her daughter. My fear that I might end up being forced into some kind of priesthood had kept me awake for nights, with the face of her daughter, and my own dead wife, staring back at me as I slept.

The priests of Vulcan followed the old ways, shunning modern ceremonies and sticking to the humble rites which focused on the aversion of harmful fires. I smiled, that one didn't seem to have helped them in this case as the place had been gutted from what I understood. Apart from that, the main duty they'd held since the time of Romulus, and the one for which they were most renowned, was to receive all the metal spoils of war which they melted down into ingots and handed back to the State and citizens as and when there was demand. To this end they had contracts across the city to smelt their goods and stored all of the ingots in their own vaults until they were collected. That was simplifying what was an institution in Rome but in essence the Temple kept a small fortune in a sunken strongroom, with iron bound doors and a guard or two. This break-in and the theft of the treasure had caused a major uproar as much for the robbery as the burning of the site. The fact that one of their priests had been killed in the robbery had caused as much of a stir as the theft of the silver and bronze.

"The priest who was on guard that night was killed and they took all of the precious metals and about half of the iron," finished my friend as I looked to him and held back another yawn.

"How? What did they do to get all that metal out of the temple?"

"That's the problem, nobody can tell."

I let out a huff.

"What do you mean nobody can tell? There must have been a fair few of them, carts and horses to move that much metal?" Graccus was lifting his shoulders and moving his head from side to side to suggest that nobody seemed to have an answer, particularly him. "Someone must have seen or heard something at least, you can't move that much stuff in silence?"

"Ghosts in the night. That's what Scavolo said."

"And the priests? I thought they slept in the Temple?"

"yes they do but the priest who died was left as a guard. The others had been on a vigil at their sister Temple near Ostia and came back to find the place ablaze."

That seemed like a convenient occurrence and I huffed at his words and rolled my eyes.

"Well, I don't give a shit. Who cares if a few bars of bronze and silver have been taken," I said promptly. "I have better things to do now," I said to his sad eyes. "*What?*"

"So it's true. You're not coming back?"

The tone of his voice made me realise that he was still my client and that he'd been offered a job at the Temple on the basis that he was supporting me in whatever I did for my father. Since I'd suddenly gained a wedding proposal from a socially superior family and a new farm a few miles out of the city I hadn't given this any thought.

"Anyway, who says I'm not coming back?"

I'd spoken more cheerily than I felt as the last thing I wanted to do now was slog my guts out with that bastard Scavolo looking over my shoulder and telling me I was a prick every few minutes. My future was set and I was looking forward to greeting it with open arms, basking in the gaze of Minerva and Janus as my new patrons.

"Philus."

"*Philus?* What does that prick know?" I slapped my friend on the shoulder and gave him my broadest smile. His glum countenance suggested that he didn't believe a word I was saying, which was probably true. I really did need to engage a new tutor to improve my ability to take the patrician stance of holding little or no emotion in my face or bodily expressions.

"More?" I was pointing to the bowl of soup to distract him.

With an expression of utter despair my friend shook his head and stood to leave.

"No, I have work to do. Scavolo has me scribing some of the reports from the fire, with Novius and Pemptor. I best get back before he starts looking for me."

Graccus turning down another bowl of soup indicated the depth of his despair. My jaw fell slack as he said goodbye to Milo and then slumped off up the hill, shoulders sagging and head down. I was watching him shuffle along the steepest section of the Clivus Capitolinus in silence, not quite sure what to make of it when Milo came up and sat next to me, elbows on the table and head down. I edged away at his familiarity and gave him a look of distrust.

His head turned towards the hill and he watched my friend for a few seconds before speaking. "Graccus has been talking about you coming back and solving this case all morning," he was shaking his head as he looked at the forlorn figure that was now turning the corner towards the Temple of Jupiter Optimus Maximus. "He's been really excited that you could solve it."

His shaking head continued to admonish me without saying it directly as I bit my lip. He gave me his broadest grin.

"Anyway, prick can't do anything on his own can he? Heard he ballsed-up your last investigation," his eyes were conspiratorial now as his eager face stared at me and his teeth showed though his grinning lips. "Probably lose this job too if you're not around. You going to get on this case? *More soup?*"

He'd assassinated my friend, tried to get some gossip about my actions and moved to selling more of his food faster than my mind could keep up with his furtive eyebrows.

"I have no interest in the problems at the Vulcanal," I said angrily, giving the Temple its local name. "Why do I care if it's burned to the ground and everything taken? I couldn't give a fig for those priests, they probably stole it all themselves to go whoring."

Milo stood urgently and looked down at me for a moment with concern written across his face.

"You want to watch it cursing the priests and the temple out loud," his beetle like eyebrows danced again as he spoke and his hand rose to his chin.

I glanced to him, a modicum of fear shooting through me at my mistake and I turned to see Graccus' heel disappear around the corner. Had I said a curse out loud which would come back to haunt me? I decided I better make a devotion to the gods quickly.

I watched Milo return to his urns and shook my head at my own insecurity. I really couldn't give a shit about the temple of Vulcan and its priests. Things were on the up for me and I was looking forward to a bright future. Let that prick Scavolo solve this case, I had absolutely no interest in it whatsoever. I'd make a small devotion, but with Minerva, Janus and Jupiter all looking after me, I was sure it was all fine. It really didn't interest me at all. I sat back and closed my eyes, smiling at my luck in finding the dead girl, Lucilla, and the positive change it had made to my life.

II

I stood at the burned-out Temple two hours later, Graccus fidgeting nervously beside me with excitement. I was mentally kicking myself for my stupidity. I really shouldn't have cursed out loud, what a prick. A squint-eyed guard looked me up and down suspiciously, his grey beard suggested he might be one of Scavolo's old soldiers and I waved a docket at him, my official permit.

"Secundus Sulpicius?" he asked through a mouth of broken teeth that he'd gained from some campaign somewhere.

I nodded.

"Great!" he seemed really thrilled to see me.

His evident joy matched Graccus' elation when I'd sought him out soon after my father had barged into my room at home and almost dragged me by the scruff of my neck back to the Temple of Jupiter in a complete frenzy of panic. Even my brother had been shouted at to follow us. Sul had asked what was happening, fearful that my father might have a seizure he was in such a state of anxiety, anger and shock. 'Just get a move on', he'd shouted as we asked several quick questions to his retreating back.

"Follow me," said the old soldier, bringing me back to the present. He picked his way over the yard, hard-packed earth with several small vegetable plots which were well-tended and seemed not to be damaged in any way despite the carnage of the fire which surrounded them.

As we closed on the Temple I noted the sacred Lotus Tree within a small low-walled area. The base of the tree contained gifts from the locals which were arranged in neat piles, probably as offerings to the god. The fruit of the tree was said to be medicinal and caused drowsiness from which visions of greater glory came to the chosen priests and elders. It wasn't a large tree but the green fonds were healthy and bright, which was linked to an old story that Romulus himself had planted the tree and said that as long as it thrived, Rome would survive. I doubted it, but these priests clearly kept it in excellent condition so that Romulus' prophecy remained true to this day.

"Athitatus!" the guard was calling to an old man, bent at the shoulders and slightly crook-backed. He was picking through rubble, as were several others dressed in the blue of the priestly order and moving the stones that they could salvage into a pile on the left of the remains of the building. As the old man turned his heavy-lidded eyes to us I took a moment to glance around the scene.

The Temple had been a small affair. I'd passed it several times without recourse to the building, and I'd attended the Vulcanalia festival late one summer when my father had spent a small fortune to be a guest of honour to get his name known amongst the local tribes who voted for minor official positions.

Pay the plebs and the plebs will pay you back I remembered him saying at the time as he'd used the last of our ingots, and borrowed several from his patron, to buy favour in his relentless desire to rise up the ladder of Rome's officialdom. Well, it had certainly worked out for him. The walls of the Vulcanal had been built of light Tufa, hard-wearing blocks of porous stone which were commonplace in many of the early sites across the city. These were still in-situ in a rough square on which had sat the wooden struts that held the timber and slate roof. This had collapsed inwards in the fire and lay in heaps around the large stone altar which we could see had been mostly cleared of rubble. A patch in front of the altar had been totally cleared and I knew that was where the body of the dead priest had been found. I saw the iron ring Scavolo had mentioned his body was near and peered at it, thinking that I needed to get a closer look at the location the priest had been found dead.

"Are you the man from the Temple of Jupiter?" asked the crook-backed priest, his sunken cheeked face turning to me with intelligent eyes.

I noted the dirt on his clothes and the gold ring on his left middle finger as well as the golden thread at his collar circled in a pattern of squares that reminded me of a lesson from my military training in the basics of designing a marching camp. His hands showed that he was used to manual work, a few hard callouses evident, which reminded me that the temple didn't have any slaves so all the farming and tending to the site was done by the priests alone. It was, indeed, a strange cult; why do the work when someone else can do it for you?

"Secundus Sulpicius Merenda," I announced myself with a stiff nod. Now that he was in front of me I noticed the quality of the tunic he wore. It was a very good standard of cloth and I was surprised he was wearing it to do this manual work.

His brows rose for a second as I stared at his garment before he spoke. "Merenda?" His memory was working and he allowed a smile to creep into this clean-shaven face, his skin browned from outdoor work.

"The Quaestores son, we are honoured."

His voice suggested they weren't, but I ignored the half-jibe.

"Did he send this lad to help us clear up?" He was looking to Graccus, whose nose was wet and his eyes nearly popped out of his head at the thought that he might be set to work on picking rubble.

I let the suggestion hang for a brief moment to make Graccus think I was considering it before I replied. "Unfortunately not, this is my assistant Graccus Porcius. We're here to support Scavolo in understanding what happened here. Get them to help," I said this with a flick of my chin towards the crowd that stood watching from the roadway. To be fair most of them were either old men, flocks of brightly dressed women come to spend the day watching the men toil and children who looked bored, one of them pissing against a wall. The head priest looked Graccus up and down with a look of frustration before disregarding him and following my head movement.

His lips pursed and his eyes narrowed to a scowl before he shook his head.

"I'm not having those bastards on my land."

It was said with force and I was surprised by his reaction, but I did understand what he meant. Scavolo had told us that local boys had been scouring through the rubble the night before and removing any valuables they could find in the still hot detritus of the building.

"Caelius!" called Athitatus, "come over here and show these men to the strongroom. But then come straight back and help with the rubble."

"I can send some men to help if you need them?" I said to his retreating back.

"Your man Scavolo promised the same but no-ones turned up yet." He mumbled some sort of expletive and the men around him gave me dark looks before turning back to their work. He was a friendly sort. Maybe I needed to pay my respects to Vulcan to ease my passage in this latest mystery after my outburst at Milo's, which the god had clearly heard and was punishing me.

I made a note to do so.

Caelius bowed with a bright and welcoming smile, his face as clean shaven as his leader. "Masters," he said in a soft voice as he bowed. He had dark brown eyes and long hair, flecks of grey starting to show, which was tied into a single strand that ran down his back. "This way please," he was already picking his way across some of the burnt-out shell and moving towards what would have been the rear of the building. I looked left and right as we followed, not sure what I was looking for but looking none the less. Graccus tripped on a stone and cursed under his breath and Caelius turned a baleful glance to him. I apologised for his stupidity. Graccus wiped his wet nose.

We came to a steep stairway which led into the ground, deeper by a half than the height of a man. The iron gates stood open, the remains of a chain and lock pushed to the side.

"Did they smash this with a hammer?" I asked, which received a nod and raised eyes as it was such a stupid question that a child could have guessed as much. It was clearly what had happened. I ignored his expression but noted I should think twice before I speak lest I look like a dimwit. The steps had been cleared, as had all of the contents of what had been within the walled strong room below us. I knew that Scavolo had moved the remaining iron, some of it was still hot according to Novius, to the vault at the Temple of Jupiter. The Flamen Vulcanalis, Athitatus, had made them account for every ingot despite losing the rest, which Scavolo had apparently shouted at him as they moved the iron. Typically Scavolo wasn't making any friends in the completion of his duties. I stepped down into the darkness and looked around. It was a dank square about four strides long and wide. I touched the rear wall, it was cold but solid. The heavily flagged floor was covered in ash and what remained of the roof that hadn't been cleared when the ingots were removed. I stamped about, there didn't seem to be any loose stones.

I stood for a moment and remembered why I was here.

****

I'd strolled home from Milo's, my belly warm from the soup, with thoughts of the farm and Fabia racing through my mind. Life was good. Minerva was looking down on me with a benevolent smile. I'd stopped at the Temple of Vesta and paid a libation to the spirit of Perdita and asked for her permission to seal my marriage and future with Fabia, as one should do, and everything seemed perfect.

The land we'd purchased in Laurentina was fantastic, rolling pastures, a half-decent farmhouse that Fabia had sketched developments to. She really was a whirlwind of action. Her maid was an old hag who kept us apart, clearly sent to do so, but I'd managed a quick kiss after we had a few moments alone early one morning. She was playful, happy. I'd thought Minerva and Janus really had conspired to give me a great new beginning and I'd dropped a coin at each of their respective sanctuaries on my way home too, adding a coin for Vulcan just in case he was watching and listening to my derision earlier at Milo's; you had to be careful.

And then as I lay down on my bed to sleep away the afternoon my father had burst into my room, Scavolo at his side and they'd gripped my toga and literally dragged me out of the house and into the street shouting that I needed to help them solve this case or the gods themselves would be stamping on our heads and kicking our arses into the gutters before shitting on us.

We'd raced to the Temple at a forced march. I was out of breath as we'd almost run up the long slope of the Capitol Hill and my father had given me the bare bones of the problem we now faced. Three days before the fire his patron, Fusus, had been moving his wealth between the Temples as he was about to invest in two large transport boats to bring grain from the north to sell in the city. He'd placed an order for these with a reputable boat-builder at Ostia who was a distant cousin and as such was family. He could be trusted, or so they said. His men had moved fifty ingots of silver and twenty five of bronze to the Temple of Vulcan two days before the fire and every scrap of it had been lost to the Temple-thieves.

It was a staggering amount of precious metal, enough wealth to buy more than half of his farms and the loss of such a sum could ruin him if the news got out. It was a disaster. On top of that problem he had then called all of his clients together and told them that he would be calling in every one of his loans if he could not find the thieves and retrieve his stolen goods. With a finger pointing to my father he told him to scour the city to find the bastards who'd taken his treasure or he'd be the first to repay the loans he owed.

Scavolo, striding purposefully at my side and not even out of breath, told me that it was too much of a coincidence that a fire had broken out at the Temple and the treasures stolen on the same night and that there had to be a link. That was clearly the case, even the village idiots would surmise that much. Another issue, he said, was that my father couldn't afford to re-pay the loans he owed to Fusus as he'd spent it all on getting the magisterial post he held for this year. I'd almost stopped at that point, as had my brother, both of us having slack jaws and wide eyes as we realised the implications. My brother's place on the Cursus Honorum was now at risk, it was a costly system to keep yourself in the public eye and so was my marriage to Fabia and new land-owning future. If my father had to call in all his clients loans to pay back Fusus then the marriage would be off as we would be disgraced in the eyes of his social equals.

And then to add to this my father said that we all had to swear to secrecy because if the news got out that Fusus had lost the majority of his fortune he'd be ruined and by consequence we'd be ruined. The dice were rolling badly and I could see nothing good coming of this. I cursed my stupidity at saying that I didn't care about the Temple of Vulcan to Milo. The god of fire was very clearly angry at my dismissive comments and my curse.

I was in shock.

Vulcan had heard me cursing the dead priest, I was certain, and his hot steaming piss was raining down on me in his ire. It was a disaster of the highest proportions. I was such a fool to have spoken my thoughts aloud and I cursed myself again for my folly but I bit my lip and didn't share my unfortunate outburst with Scavolo or my father.

We'd arrived at the temple and moved to my father's room where we were greeted by several frightened faces, Agrippa Furius Fusus, the man who had lost his fortune in the fire at the fore of them, his usual cool brown eyes glaring with fury. "Ah, Merenda. About time" he said critically as we entered. I was unsure which of the three of us he meant but he was evidently directing his voice at me. I noted that the room was full of his clients, men I knew as social equals to my father or of higher standing and every one of them gave me the haunted look of condemned men who expected the noose to drop in front of their eyes at any moment. I swallowed nervously.

****

Graccus spoke from above and brought me back to the moment. "Anything?"

I was waving away his question as I came back up the steps. "Caelius, can you tell me what you know happened on the night of the fire?"

"We've already told your man Scavolo," he said, bristling at the memory.

I gave him my best smile. "Assume I know nothing and that Scavolo hadn't been here and stamped across your sacred grounds like the oaf he is."

My suggestion that my former boss had been heavy-footed brought a slight change in his facial expression before he glanced across to the Flamen, the head-priest Athitatus, it was almost imperceptible but I caught it.

"We returned from the Temple at Ostia late at night and were met by locals who had seen our candles and came to warn us that the temple was ablaze. Some others were attempting to throw water on the burning wood and steaming stones but it was too late by then, the majority of the building was gone."

He was almost in tears but it was such a poor answer I urged him on with another question. "What hour was this?"

"An hour before dawn." He was very precise. I nodded and let the silence stretch as I gazed at him. He had large, baggy, eyes and a round face perched on a thin neck. I realised that he wasn't as young as I first thought, with few lines on his face but enough age to consider that he used creams and goose fat to maintain a look of youth, like some of the women did. His neck gave him away, lined skin stretched into his open tunic. It was hot work moving the rubble and a sweat stain showed on the lip of the garment. He played the game well and looked back at me with a fixed expression, clearly not used to long speeches. I wondered who his tutor was as I started to wilt in the silence, turning my head to the steps as if I was considering some deep thought whilst inside cursing how shit I was at this investigating job.

"And your priest who died in the fire, what was his name?" I noticed that he'd not mentioned him in his description a second before. It caught my interest.

"Titus," he replied.

A good name for the man, I thought, as the Temple was dedicated by Titus Tatius an old Sabine King centuries before. I wondered for a moment if the priests all took new names or maintained their old family names when they joined the cult.

"And he stayed behind to guard the Temple?"

His eyes betrayed him with another glance to the Flamen. "He did. He has done so often recently," he said shortly. "Have we finished here, I am needed," he lifted his face to reveal a false smile.

"May I see where he died?"

The question caused a confused glare but he acquiesced and led us to the altar, where he bowed and so did I, following his lead, which he noticed and pushed out his bottom lip in acknowledgement of my reverence to the sacred altar.

"He was found here," he touched the ground with his foot, almost kicking at the spot as if the man's body still lay there. It seemed an odd gesture but I said nothing.

The space was at the right tip of the altar and cleared of detritus where possible. The remains of burnt clothing could be seen where it had stuck to the ground in the heat, along with a dark spot on the flagstones which may have been from a pool of blood but equally could be something else. The stain caught the edge of the altar and was about as wide as my forearm and almost the same in depth and seemed contained to this small area. Above this dark spot the remains of a thick rope hung, charred and blackened, from the iron ring where the animals would have been tied before being sacrificed. I touched the rope gently as I crouched and looked around the area, searching for anything out of the ordinary. I could see nothing remarkable but spent a short moment looking at the edges of the rubbish that had been piled up around the space, likely thrown aside by Scavolo and his men. The space was roughly the size of a man but the shape that they'd made moving his body picked at my mind.

14

I glanced to the altar, then back to the main door, a good fifteen strides of open space. The stairway to the strongroom was a further eight or ten steps behind the altar to the left. I considered this for a moment. The story said that he was defending the Temple, and I guessed that they'd pushed him back against the altar, which is where the poor man had made his last stand.

"Was anything else taken other than the ingots?" I asked as I lifted my chin back to Caelius. His confused look suggested he didn't understand my question so I stood and asked it in a different way. "Was the statue of Romulus taken?"

He appraised me through narrowed lids and a tight mouth, clearly seeing that I knew my Temples and their treasures. In truth it had only just come to my mind as I looked at the altar and saw the carved figure of Romulus with a hammer and an anvil, one of the motifs which circled the altar. It was a memory from my lessons years before. My tutor made me recite the names of each Temple and their gods and this had sprung to mind as I ran my sight along the stone. Yet again I was surprised how much the man had taught me as I believed the man and his lessons had been as much use as a two-legged donkey.

"No, the statues came with us to Ostia," he said pointedly. I understood his words as the other local treasure was a statue of Cocles which was given to the Temple a hundred years ago when it was said a further Temple to Vulcan on the Field of Mars had been closed and moved to this site.

"Thank you," I said in reply. "And may I say how sorry I am that your friend died in this tragic incident," I added quietly.

His chin lifted. "He wasn't my friend," he spoke the words under his breath before he realised he had done so and then stiffened with a dark glance in my direction.

I tried to show no reaction.

"I must go, the Flamen is calling," he announced loudly.

I turned to see the Flamen's back bent over a large piece of wood so his claim was unlikely as I had heard nothing. What nerve had I touched with that comment? Caelius bustled away swiftly and left us standing by the large altar with an image of Romulus and Vulcan wielding hammers in a fire pit standing proud despite the damage that lay around us. I looked back at the space left by the dead man and wondered if I'd missed something here so stood silently for a moment to allow my mind to consider what might have happened.

"He was as friendly as the head priest." It was Graccus whispering at my side. He was right, they were an odd bunch.

"What did the report say happened?" I asked. "Was there any detail about the trip to Ostia and the timing? I'm sure Scavolo asked."

"I didn't scribe them but I'm sure they're all written up by now. I think Scavolo and Novius were doing them."

I nodded but was surprised that the two men would take that duty, this really was an important task. Then I had a thought. "Let's spend an hour helping out here Graccus. They look like they need a hand and we can get close to them and ask some of those other priests some questions, see what they have to say. Get some of those locals to start working on the areas there." I was pointing to a pile of roof slates that had slipped into the space outside the Temple and likely held no hint of treasures which they could steal. "I'll tell the Flamen that we're helping, see if it warms him up a bit."

III

It was thirsty work and we'd not been offered a drink for the whole time we helped at the Temple, Graccus cutting his hand on a sharp slate and wiping his nose so often he looked like he'd been kicked by that horse in the Forum when he spoke to Hastius. I grinned at the sight of him.

We were back in the Temple after the trudge back up the hill to our room, both sweating slightly as the sun had beaten down on us until late in the afternoon. We drank cool water and then watered wine from Ducus' farm which I had labelled clearly and placed in a locked cupboard to keep thieves, well Scavolo, away.

"This is nice," I said to Graccus.

"Getting pissed on the job isn't going to help you sort this fucking mess."

It was Scavolo, timing impeccable as usual. He entered, stared at our drinks and then dragged a chair across noisily before sitting and crossing his arms.

"What have you learned?"

I pushed the reports back across the table. "You need to get your men to ask better questions," I said. "These are rubbish. I can't understand them. They make no sense." It was true they were nonsensical gibberish.

"Are you stupid?"

He gave me that stare which made me take a sharp breath and open my mouth to reply before I realised what he was saying. He beat me to the explanation to rub in the fact that I was as dim-witted as the fool at the Lupercalia festival who had fallen into the river and drowned.

"We can't write down the real story you prick. What if it gets into the wrong hands?"

He was continuing to express his displeasure at my idiocy through a shaking head and grinding teeth. "Do you understand that *everything* that is at stake here, lad? Not only *your future* but mine and every member of the team at this Temple too. We're all tied to your fucking family, so you better get your head from up your arse and start thinking straight. Drinking that shit won't help."

His blood was up and I felt the rebuke like a kick to the balls.

My hand was halfway to my mouth, cup of wine waiting to be drunk but the anger in his voice stopped me dead. Yet again I had failed to realise all the points he was implying. Of course it was personal. He was my father's man. He had this commission because my father did. His family probably had loans to my family which would be recalled if Fusus' treasures were not returned. Ruin for us, ruin for him. I let the cup drop back to the table.

"Get it now do you? Good. You better not cock this fucking thing up, lad. There's more to this than you can imagine."

I took a long breath. "I'm sorry Scavolo. I won't let you down."

"If you want to be shagging that pretty girl of yours on that farm you better not," he responded in his typical base manner. "What have you learned?" It was a command.

"Not a lot yet," I started. "They closed up like vultures on a fresh carcass. The Flamen didn't want to speak to us, but a priest named Caelius let slip that the man who was killed by the thieves, Titus, wasn't much liked. I need to get more information about why."

Scavolo nodded at this small scrap of information. "Has Novius looked at the body? Is it still here?" I asked with sudden interest. Scavolo frowned but said that it was and he had. "How did he die?"

Scavolo looked at me as if I was an idiot. "Several stab wounds to the chest," he said in reply. "Looks like the prick wasn't even armed, or if he was they took his spear."

I nodded. "There was a dark area near the altar, was that where his blood had pooled and burned?"

The ex-centurion pushed out his bottom lip to suggest he hadn't seen this, his interest now piqued. "Graccus, get Novius and bring him here," it was another order. He turned back to me with a gesture to continue.

"The gates must have taken some time to open based on the size of that lock and chain." I was thinking through what I'd seen. "I don't know how the noise didn't wake the houses closest to the Temple."

"I thought that too but I got Manius," one of his men "to stand in the vault and shout whilst I went to nearest house. I counted fifty eight steps and I couldn't hear a thing after twenty five. With a roof and thick walls between them it could be possible that nothing was heard."

I agreed, thinking that I wouldn't have thought of that and re-appraising his efforts which had sounded like he and his men had tramped all over the site like a herd of bulls from what Caelius had said to me but had clearly been more organised that I'd given him credit. The Temple was almost in the centre of the road and the closest houses were quite a distance, he was right.

"I haven't spoken to anyone who lives near the Temple to see if they heard anything, that's why we came back, to check out their stories from your reports before we went back to find holes in them."

"Good idea," he said, his demeanour now calmer than when he'd arrived. "I'll tell you what we know when Novius gets here." He urged me to continue, taking my cup of wine from the table in front of me and drinking from it.

I ignored his lack of etiquette, I was above such things but I gave him a stern glare which curled his lip. "Caelius the priest seemed frightened to speak and when I asked him if any other items had been taken beyond those in the storerooms he said no."

"What items?" asked Scavolo with a frown.

"The statues," I replied, his blank face looking back at me. "The Vulcanal has two bronze statues sacred to the altar of Vulcan. They are highly prized relics. It seems that they took both of these with them to Ostia."

"Bollocks!" said Scavolo. "That doesn't sound right," he added with an appraising glance to me.

"Nevertheless we need to check if that is custom and practice or a one-off. I'm sure you've already surmised that it was an inside job?"

"Of course we fucking have. And of course it was. We just can't prove it yet. Those bastards are tighter than a new whore and not letting anything slip," he said angrily, his emotions tipping over in his evident frustration at the lack of anything worthy of further investigation. He took another deep drink of my wine and looked at the cup as he let the liquid roll around his tongue. "I had them all clamp up the minute we started asking questions and that prick Spurius Maelius turned up and started telling them they had nothing to answer to as they were out of the city at the time of the theft."

Maelius was a local politician intent on climbing the social ladder. He had a reputation for being the people's champion, something that many of the patrician senators disliked about the man but he also had enough money and power to hold many positions of strength across the city. He was also popular with the people and had many business interests which maintained his position as patron to a host of lower class wealthy citizens. Indeed he often intervened on behalf of the plebs in cases which needed additional patrician support.

"Why was he there?" I asked.

"He has a townhouse just along the Clivus Capitolinus," he answered, meaning the main road up the Capitol Hill. I nodded my understanding as I remembered this fact from somewhere deep in my memories. "And yes, I have considered that the bastard could be involved, it's close enough to move the ingots without too much trouble or noise. Though he'd need an army to take it up that hill in a short space of time and nobody saw anything like that. Not even the priests." He was brooding as he spoke. "But he's too well connected to link him to this without serious proof, I can't accuse him without something as solid as the Tarpeian Rock to throw him from."

"Not even the priests?" I'd frowned at those words as he'd spoken them and looked to him.

"They came back from the Sublician Bridge and through the Halitorium. If anyone had gone that way they would have seen them. They saw no-one?"

I understood now what he meant. The priests had walked back from Ostia and the main roadway was probably the direction anyone trying to get the ingots out of the city would have used. I sighed and looked to my cup as it was lifted again and the wine sunk, bastard.

"I need to get each of those priests alone and question them, but my guess is that the Flamen doesn't want that to happen. We stayed behind to help clear the rubbish as a way to get close to them and ask more questions," I explained, "but every time Graccus or I approached one of them he was on us like a dog on a bitch in heat."

That curled Scavolo's lip again.

Just then Novius and Graccus appeared.

"Ah!" Scavolo was standing now, pushing the chair towards his man.

"Got any of that?" asked Novius with a nod to Scavolo, his tongue licking his lips in anticipation.

Clearly drinking my wine on duty wasn't an issue for these two investigators. I waved to Graccus to get the key and fill a fresh cup, Scavolo holding out my cup for a re-fill.

"Novius, can you describe the body to me. How was it found, what marks did it have?"

I was starting to have an idea. There had to be something about the man Titus. His standing by the altar in defence didn't seem right. The doorway to the Temple or the open ground by the iron doors to the strongroom would have been a better place to mount a defence. Maybe he wasn't a fighter, but basic principles suggested that the right edge of the altar was not the best location and he would likely have fallen closer to the door or the centre of the room if he had no spear and had been taken early in the confrontation. Caelius had told me that he wasn't defending the relics which were the only other thing that was of likely value in the Temple, so why was he by the altar? Maybe he'd crawled there to touch the altar in the throes of death, although Scavolo had just said he had several stab wounds which didn't give me the impression he would be able to crawl very far.

Novius pushed out a lip before answering. "We found what was left of him just below the altar. Poor bastard must have made a last stand next to it," he said that with a slight twitch of his head. "He was lying on his left side with several stab wounds in his chest, through his ribs here," he was touching his right side as he spoke to show us the location of the wounds. "He's a bit of a mess though, pretty burned up and charred. Stinks," he said, wrinkling his nose.

I raised my brows. "How do you know he was stabbed there? Wasn't his body too badly burned to see the marks clearly?"

"Yes to some extent but he had a thick cloak over his tunic and some areas of his body weren't too badly burned. He was on the ground too and the area near the altar doesn't have anything which would catch fire quickly so he probably didn't burn until the roof fell on him by which time most of the heat of the fire had died down. It was probably the burning roof falling on him that caused his clothes to catch, and he was dead by then," he shrugged slightly as he finished speaking.

It made some sense.

He drank my wine.

"Was there a lot of blood?"

"Yes, a fair bit." Novius was touching his chin, then the top of his chest and face moving towards his left shoulder, "here, here and here" he added.

It seemed to fit what I was suddenly thinking. Was Vulcan guiding my thoughts, giving me a clue? If he was now starting to give me random thoughts maybe his ire was lessening. I needed to sacrifice to his honour if that was the case.

"It kept some of his robes from burning as well as most of the hair on the back of his head which is still intact," he lifted his hand to the left side of his head to indicate where he meant.

"Poor fucker!" said Scavolo, taking another drink. Novius followed him and I swallowed dryly.

"Did you see any other signs of a struggle? Anything at all? I didn't see anything except that dark patch on the floor which must have been his blood," I added this to jolt his memories to see if I was right in my quickly forming conclusions.

"Nothing," came the reply. "If he had a sword or spear they took that as well as we couldn't find it. There was a store of weapons behind the altar too, old gallic weapons which were gone as well but they don't know if the locals took them once the fire had cooled. That's what Athitatus told us," he answered to my questioning look.

"What else did you see? We didn't get much from the priests," I said with a glance to Graccus who was agreeing whilst re-filling both of their cups with my wine. I glowered at him so he sloshed a last drop in each and then returned the amphora to its cupboard. I heard the key click with some satisfaction.

"We checked the area around the Temple for tracks or marks but there was nothing of interest."

"How do you think the fire started?"

"A barrel of oil stacked at the back of the small kitchen was broken, cloth thrown on top from what we could surmise and set alight. Looks like they were the priests cloaks and gowns that were used to start the fire."

"Oil? That's convenient."

"The Flamen said they use the oil for cooking and keeping the oil lamps burning. You know what they're like with their morning rituals."

It was true, they welcomed the light of the day by brightening the temple with their flames. It was an old ritual and one which was celebrated akin the Vestals perpetual fire.

"How many of the local houses did you visit?"

He looked to Scavolo before answering. "We asked the crowds who were standing around, we didn't go knocking on doors if that's what you mean. Most of the locals were there though and they were happy to tell us that they'd seen or heard nothing before the alarm was raised."

I nodded slowly as I listened and thought about the scene.

"The Flamen was being a prick and wouldn't let us on the site at first until Scavolo told him we'd throw him in the Carcer for getting in the way of an official investigation if he didn't get out of the way. After that he and his men just clamped up. It was yes and no and nothing more than that. Bastards." He shrugged. "There's six of them, seven with the dead man. We checked the vault and then cleared the body away. They'd covered him with a sheet but kept out of the way as we started to move the rubble from around him."

"I say we get all of them and whip them until one squeals" said Scavolo.

I took a moment to respond, thinking through something he'd said which was burying away in my mind like a worm in the soil. "We can't do that," I answered, to which he simply huffed as he knew my answer to be true. I then said, "so they found his body and could have removed a spear or sword?"

"They said they left him alone and stayed back. He was smoking hot when they got into the Temple."

I closed my eyes to see the picture I had in my mind forming. The altar, the iron ring and the dark patch which could have been a pool of blood. No weapons. "Did you find any rope?"

"Rope?"

"There was a charred rope attached to the altar, the one they use for the sacrificial animals. Did you find any more of it?" he said not and I couldn't get to the point my brain was trying to shout at me so struggled for a moment as things started to line up and then slipped apart like two young lovers caught by the Master of the house.

Novius spoke again to light the way through the fog that was swirling in my mind. "There was a reed sheet under him." I looked up at this. "He probably sat on it or slept on it when on guard," he added to my confused expression.

Click. The piece I couldn't find hit me. "So how did he die on his bed if he was fighting to defend the Temple? Do you think he crawled to the altar after being stabbed?" It was an odd question but Novius understood what I was getting at.

"Not a chance if those stab wounds are anything to go by." He glanced to Scavolo again, who upended his cup and looked disappointed that it was empty.

"I need to see the body, I don't think he died defending the Temple."

The Temple was still being cleared, but now a small army of people were being cajoled into moving piles into that which could be salvaged and that which looked like it needed throwing in the river. Athitatus saw us coming and moved across to intercept us, his face dour.

"How can I help you gentlemen?" he asked with his thin arms across his chest to suggest that helping us was the last thing on his mind. His hands and robes were covered in dust and dirt and his face bore the marks of sweat having dripped down his forehead.

"We still have questions to which we must find answers if we are to find the treasures. You know what I am speaking of," I said in a whisper.

His face darkened. "No doubt you think we stole his treasure?" he answered with a growl. I didn't reply but took up my father's best stoic face and looked over his shoulder at the workmen moving piles of rubbish as if it was the most interesting thing I had ever seen. Graccus crossed his arms and his tensed features imitated a constipated goat as he tried to follow my lead.

"Follow me," he said this without looking at us and turned to march across the site towards the Carcer where he turned right and then sharp left onto a flight of steep steps cut into the side of the hill. After a short minute he rapped on a door and was greeted by a bright-eyed slave who immediately frowned once he noticed that his Master had guests.

"Water," snapped the Flamen as we entered his house.

I was struck dumb for a moment as I had assumed that the Flamen and his priests all slept at the Temple. Graccus' wide eyes suggested he hadn't considered that they owned a house either. The slave moved quickly and we passed closed doors in a narrow corridor before we arrived at a room which held a table with eight seats. A small window overlooked the Clivus Capitolinus and if I stood close to the window, which I did to confirm my suspicion, I could just see the remains of the Temple below with the temple of Saturn further along the road to its right. It was a well-appointed position and no more than a minute or two run downhill if the need arose.

"Sit," he ordered, clearly angry at the further intrusion to his day. "And ask your questions. We have nothing to hide but it is best to speak of them here rather than in the open."

I thanked him, ignoring his mood, and apologised that I had to ask as he knew my father's patron had lost a significant fortune through the robbery at the Temple. His expression darkened at my gratitude, which was obviously not meant. "Tell me why Titus was left behind when you went to Ostia?"

He seemed surprised by this question, clearly expecting another. "It was his decision to guard the Temple. He'd taken the role as guardian often in recent weeks as his dreams told him he needed to be there," he echoed what Caelius had told us.

"Was he an older man or younger?"

"He was twenty summers younger than me," came the quick retort. So he was older than all the priests except the Flamen, but I guessed not much older than my father. "He was strong enough to hold the door with a spear if that's what you're asking?"

I was.

"And did he have a spear or sword as we don't seem to have found one in the rubble." His eyes rolled, clearly a question he'd been asked before.

"Probably stolen by the plebs," he said dismissively. "You saw them. They've been back in the dark trying to steal anything of value, they even hacked at the altar itself last night from what Hector tells me, the bastards," he gave Graccus a narrow-eyed look to check that he didn't react to the slur.

I nodded, ignoring the obvious slight and pushing on. "Was there any sign that they'd disturbed the body at all, when you got back?"

His chin receded into his neck at this before he answered. "He was almost totally covered in rubble and the stones were still hot," he answered with a glare at my line of questions, assuming I was a dimwit by the line I was taking.

"So any spear or sword would have been under the rubble when he was killed?" His eyes widened and he was about to reply but I cut him off. "And did he often sleep at the foot of the altar? Is that what the priests do when they are on guard?"

He looked at me suspiciously now, realising that I was not as dim-witted as he thought. He stiffened and placed both hands on the table as he leant forward slightly. "Some do. I have done so myself. When I joined the order all the priests slept in the Temple. We have taken it in turns now that we have this house. Maybe we have grown soft."

His eyes bore into mine, he was starting to play games, to test me by dropping half answers which begged further questions. Why was he being so obstructive, what did he have to hide?

"This is a good house," I said appraising the room but my question obvious as his eyes lifted to the ceiling and then fell back on my own.

"A gift from a servant of Vulcan given freely in his will. You can check it at the Temple if you wish to do so."

I did and nodded to Graccus to make a note, as he was scribing. The records would be housed in the Temple of Saturn so it wasn't far to go to check them.

"Is it normal to take the statues from the Temple when you travel?" I sat back slightly, trying to relax but watching his reaction to my words closely as I changed tact again.

"Sometimes we do and sometimes we don't," he answered, his eyebrows meeting in a frown as he tried to guess what I would ask next. I could see his mind working behind his eyes.

"And who decided that this time you would take them? Was it you?"

"No," he said with a glint in his eye. "It was Titus. He'd dreamt that they should go to Ostia."

"Titus?" I pretended not to know his name.

"The man who died to defend our Temple and our ways," he said with a hint of triumph.

I knew the name, of course, but hadn't expected that answer, which surprised me and it clearly showed as he sat back on his seat and interlocked his fingers as he seemed to have gotten the upper hand. I'd also just heard something else that I needed to investigate. Why had the man dreamt that he needed to stay at the Temple? I noted this but moved on quickly as the Flamen curled his lip at my frowning face. But I was getting good at this and took a moment to look as puzzled as I possibly could, and to make a mental note that I would sacrifice a duck to Vulcan later this day if my next words led me to a very different conversation.

"Then why was Titus tied to the altar and murdered?"

IV

Graccus was full of praise as we arrived back at the Temple of Jupiter in the fading light of the day. "That was Masterful" he said. "How you choked him up and got that story out of him," he was shaking his head in wonder at my questioning.

"Well he didn't know that Titus had his throat cut, that's for sure. And as for being tied to the altar," I was shaking my head too now. The religious significance of that act could be important; the iron ring was where animals were tied before sacrifices were made. Had Titus been sacrificed? If he had been then this was not just a murder, but something more. But what?

I considered what we'd learned when we'd visited the body in the cellar at the Temple of Jupiter, the one where Brocchus had been branded, I knew instantly what had happened when I saw the corpse but I needed to confirm this with actual evidence.

'Why are his hands reaching up like that?' I'd asked. The body seemed to be stretching out, as if reaching for something above his head.

'He must have been reaching for one of his attackers as they stabbed him, or for his spear,' replied Novius quickly, making the assumption that he was defending the altar and had reached out after falling to the floor.

'Can you tell me,' I held my breath as I leant over the stinking corpse, a mixture of burnt and rotting flesh. 'Is there blood soaked into his collar and hair where he was lying?'

The answer was a clear yes and it was also on his robes at the left shoulder as Novius had indicated earlier.

'And on his chest and belly where he was stabbed, has it run through to the floor and on the reed mat?' Novius had given me a strange look and half turned the body with a questioning gaze before turning back to me and shaking his head in surprise. I looked at the charred mess. 'Is there evidence of blood where he was stabbed in the chest?'

Novius had given me that appraising look again and pushed open the clothes, where they weren't seared to the body. He'd cut them apart earlier in his investigation to check the wounds and the dark scraps were charred and burnt with small gold etchings at the neck and cuff where patterns were made to distinguish the priests. He'd said they were quite clean, as were the majority his robes which were not caught by the flames, and turned to Scavolo, who was now stern-faced as recognition of the fact that the body must have already been dead before he was stabbed in the chest several times showed in his facial expression.

'So they could have been done after he was dead?' Novius poked his dagger at the holes which he now saw were strictly between the ribs and too well placed to have been inflicted during a struggle. He said as much, his head shaking again at what he'd missed by presuming the man had died defending the Temple. He pointed to the cuts and said, his tone of voice showing that he understood what was being asked and explaining that he'd been hurried when checking the body as the smell was so bad and they had jumped to the obvious assumption that he had been defending himself. These words had been more to Scavolo than me and I felt that he was suddenly under scrutiny. I moved on quickly and suggested that this was cleverly done and it had taken a great deal of questions and answers to get to this point which he hadn't had time to do. I could see him glance to Scavolo as he nodded his thanks at my words. Scavolo was a hard bastard and I hoped what I'd said would soften what might be a strong rebuke. I bent over the corpse, a cloth over my mouth at the reeking stench, like rotten half-cooked pork, which made me want to gag. I placed my own dagger on his throat, which was seared with crusts of hair and burnt flesh so that it was not easy to see.

'Does it look like his throat was cut?' Scavolo was beside me, his bone handled knife picking at the hair to reveal a cut across his windpipe and deep into his neck along the line of what remained of his charred beard. He grunted, as did Novius, Graccus trying to peer from behind the three heads that were inspecting the rotting carcass.

'One last question,' I'd said next. 'Is there any evidence that he was tied with rope at the hands?'

This wasn't as clear but with some scraping and a little water Novius was able to find strands of a rope burned into the skin on the dead man's wrists.

'The bastard's tied him up and cut his throat,' Scavolo said, baring his teeth and giving Novius a hard-faced glare.

We all nodded at the words. I looked at the hands and could see the rope marks despite the burnt skin. The hands seemed clean and soft where water had been used to clean them and I let my eyes search up and down the body for any other signs of anything that might have been missed.

'Why would they tie him up like a sacrificial goat?' It was a question that none of us had an answer to.

'His death is central to this. I am sure. And why is he wearing a cloak if he was inside and defending the Temple?' I added to everyone's surprised looks as the question hit them like a thunderbolt from Jupiter. 'If we can find out why he was killed, we might also find Fusus' ingots.'

****

Back at the Vulcanal Graccus was clearly thinking about the dead body as well and wiped his nose as a line of snot was starting to drip. "So whoever killed him did it in cold blood. It wasn't a fight." He'd spoken quietly as a few people still milled around the site. I agreed, and then Graccus elbowed me on the arm and flicked his head towards the remains of the burned building. Coming from the rear of the altar, he must have been below in the strongroom, was Caelius with another priest.

I waved and his face fell but he walked across slowly. "Greetings Secundus Sulpicius," he said, bowing slowly and ignoring Graccus who was too far below his status to note his presence.

"Greetings Caelius, and?" I turned to the other man, his dark tunic still covered in dust but the gold band around his neck marked him as a priest of Vulcan.

"Regicius," he smiled, no warmth in his guarded features. He was taller than me, a high forehead and sallow skin with deep brown eyes that appraised everything with a steady, calculating, gaze. His hands were large and covered in small cuts from the work they had all being doing. He rubbed his smooth chin as he looked down his nose at me.

I nodded to him. "We are finishing our investigations for today and have been with the Flamen at your house," I said to their surprised glances to one another. "I understand that Titus wasn't liked by many of you?" It was a statement and a question, which they clearly didn't want to answer by the look it brought to their faces. "Athitatus has told us that he had visions of fire and he was keen to stay behind at the Temple when you made your trip to Ostia to ensure that the Temple was safe."

This comment gave them both a start and I noticed that they visibly tensed and shared a further glance. It was a level of information that only one of their own could give, as the Flamen had done just moments before and I saw the look of surprise which they shared.

"He had recently been having strange dreams and visions, yes," said Regicius coolly and in an off-hand manner. "But that is not uncommon in the order."

I considered this for a moment, wondering what he meant but Caelius spoke almost immediately and put the thought from my mind.

"The poor man was racked with concern regarding some of the changes that were being proposed for the Temple," he said. "He didn't like them, preferring to maintain the old ways. I am sure the Flamen has informed you of this."

"Athitatus said as much," I half-lied, picking up this morsel and putting it to the back of my mind to come back to it. "And it was Titus that suggested you take the statues and visit the site at Ostia to help you to make the decision on your future plans?"

It was what Athitatus had said, but it still concerned me that the silver was being moved into the Temple during this time and suddenly they had all decided to leave, with just one man as guard. It didn't make sense. I was shaking my head. "Poor man to have not foreseen the danger he put himself in through his visions." Graccus and I both shook our heads sadly, the priests didn't flinch but simply stood motionless and with blank faces.

"He had his reasons to suggest we went as I am sure the Flamen has told you," came the stone-faced response from Regicius to which Caelius tilted his head slightly with a glance to his fellow priest.

They were starting to close ranks again.

"Indeed. But it seems your time was wasted in Ostia as you have no clue as to the meanings of his dreams, except that you returned to find the Temple alight and Titus dead inside," I replied with a frown. "He tried valiantly to save the ingots from the murdering thieves," I said sharply, adding a strong tone of anger to my voice to see if they reacted. I was watching them closely as I spoke but they were like statues, unblinking and calm, reminding me of Scavolo.

It was about a half day's walk to Ostia for a fit man and seeing I was getting nowhere with this line of questions I tried another. "Who decided that you should go so urgently to Ostia at this busy time and with so much precious metal in your strongroom?" I was making a gamble by accusing them and it raised distrustful glares.

"You must speak to Athitatus about that. Only he has the power to make these decisions."

It was said with barely concealed anger and they both crossed their arms to show that they didn't want to answer any more questions as the slur against them all was evident.

They reminded me of Scavolo once more as I saw the anger building within them and so I turned as if Graccus and I were going to leave, before stopping and then returning my gaze to both men.

"Which other of the priests might not have liked the changes that were being proposed to the order and the Temple? Were there any fall-outs between you?" I asked with my warmest smile, bringing two cold stares from them both as they shook their heads without answering. In truth I didn't expect an answer but I knew they'd be warning their fellows that I'd be back asking questions the next day.

It was my father's idea to join him in the bath. He looked older and more tired than I'd ever seen him, his eyes red-rimmed from lack of sleep. My brother stared at the wall in shock as I finished the first part of the tale as we knew it. Scavolo stood and rubbed at his balls with a scraper, leering playfully at Ministria, a pretty female slave who had just brought us a jug of wine. The steam rose as more hot water was added to the Lavatrina and I pushed slightly to get a bit more space, three in the same tub was a little too much for me but I had no intentions of squeezing in next to my old boss and my father's bare arse was a better option than that of Scavolo right now. I'd just finished explaining what I knew of Titus' death, Scavolo adding his own thoughts as I did so. I was starting to expand on what Athitatus had told us as the wine was poured.

"The old man seemed reluctant to tell us about the priests and their relationships but when I explained that Titus had been murdered at his own altar he was almost in tears. It seemed to break his resolve."

Scavolo was waving the scraper to Sul who stepped out of the water and took it, wiping his arms and legs as Scavolo watched him. I moved into the gap my brother left behind.

"It seems that Titus had been having strange dreams for weeks and then started to have nightly visions of fire wrecking the Temple. He'd taken to sleeping at the foot of the altar every night, rarely coming back to the house on the Clivus Capitolinus. Athitatus told us that he'd chastised the younger men for sleeping at the new house, which they'd received in a will not long before. They'd argued about the old ways, poverty and simplicity without the trappings of modern life against the developments that some of the other local Temples had made, better standards of living and bigger festivals which would bring more devotees and gifts. Some of the priests, especially Hector, Nesta and Marcus had decided that if he was going to sleep at the Temple every night then he could do their guard shifts for them, suggesting to him that his frenzied dreams and nightly waking were enough to keep anyone away from the Temple." It made sense, nobody liked a mad man.

"We should drag in their house slave. Whip the bastard until he tells us all their secrets," said Scavolo with a glance to my father, whose eyebrows had raised and he was nodding.

"That wouldn't help," I replied. "He'd just tell us what he thought we wanted to hear to stop the flogging," I was shaking my head.

"I don't know," said Scavolo. "It's worked in the past and is a good method."

I looked to my father, who was appraising the suggestion by the look on his face.

"I can't see it adding any weight at this point. It would only close doors that have yet to be opened. There is much more to this than we can see so far. Let me explain the rest of what I know and then we can decide." This got a nod from my father, much to Scavolo's dismay. "The Flamen let it slip that he'd listened to all of the arguments and decided to make changes to the Temple and buildings, especially a new altar to

Vulcan, a much larger one which would bring more gifts and devotions. Titus had argued against this, saying that it was a betrayal of the god and the order of Vulcan. But the Flamen told them that the Temple of Saturn had made several changes recently and more people were attending ceremonies at the new sanctuary so the god must have been happy."

My father spoke at this. "Yes, a petition for funds for the Vulcanal came to us a few kalends ago did it not Gaius?"

"It did," said Scavolo, now sat back in his bath as my brother Sul stood next to him towelling his back and flapping his genitals around. It wasn't a pretty sight. "We turned it down, not a good use of public funds. If some rich man wants to stump up the funds then that's fine, but the people of Rome have too many temples to start giving funds to any one of them just because they want to make changes. Everyone agreed that it would start an avalanche of requests if we did so." Scavolo had glanced to my father and he nodded at the words.

It wasn't usual for public funds to be used for a Temple unless they were linked to the spoils of a recent conquest and Scavolo was right, there was too much at stake to start giving public funds to the many Temples around the city, most of which were old and archaic and needed major restoration.

"What significance do these dreams have?" It was my brother asking.

"From what I understand Titus was trying to retain the old ways of the order and maintain the simple life they had led for years. Nesta and Caelius wanted to embrace modern ways and introduce more dancing and singing to the festivals and Athitatus was in agreement with them. I didn't hear much about the others though, it seemed these two were the most vocal. Titus was out- voted but had then started to have dreams about the Temple burning down. It was becoming difficult for them to live together."

"Likely he wanted to get his own way and was pretending the god was with him and trying it on to make them change their minds, prick."

Scavolo's comment got grunts of agreement from everyone, me included. I understood what he was saying. My brother was rubbing at his cock as if it needed a thrashing, the movements caught everyone's eye. It took me a second to get my thoughts back to the mystery as I quickly looked away but couldn't help seeing his jostling actions with the rough towel.

"Well, whatever it was the others were starting to get fed up with him and his dreams every night. They shared a single room in their new house," I added to emphasise how hard it must be for them to be kept awake every night by someone screeching and wailing, although in truth I had no idea what form his nightly visions took. I remembered my own dreams of Lucilla quite clearly. "Regicius and Titus came to blows about it. And then Athitatus said that the decision had been made and they would look to the future but remember their past. It was at that point that Titus had moved to the Temple, blaming the impact he was having on the others. And it was a few days later that Titus started to suggest that they needed to visit Ostia and ask their Flamen for his views on changes. The Temple at Ostia is smaller than the one here in the Forum, but it has a greater standing in the community and brings in much more wealth as they have embraced more modern ways, including selling some of their land and giving up growing their own crops. Titus had argued that he had heard that the Ostian Temple was fraught with problems since they changed their ways and they needed to visit it and discuss this with their head priest before they made any decision. He stated that they needed to do this before the full moon and that they therefore needed to leave on the day of the last delivery from Fusus. Athitatus said that they'd argued about it for some time but finally accepted that the visions had been given under the godly ceremony with the berry juice of the Lotus tree and so should be followed."

Everyone nodded at this. The priests were fastidious regarding the visions and following their lead.

"How did he know about the Ostian Temple? Had he been?" It was my brother asking, now sat on the stone ledge at the side of the smaller pool, the one from which he'd told me I'd better not cock up his future only weeks before whilst searching for the man who killed Lucilla.

It was a good question and one I'd not asked. "I didn't ask, but I will do," I replied with a nod, he was smiling that he'd contributed something to the conversation.

It was a sorry tale of change, of the old ways versus the new. I splashed water on my face as a moment of silence spread into the room. "When did the plan for the silver get shared to the priests?" It was a line of questioning I'd not considered yet.

Eyes turned to Scavolo. "Two weeks ago. Fusus had his man sign documents with the Flamen and the details were agreed, the Temple was double checked for security and everything seemed on track from what we have found out from Fusus' men. They agreed the final dates for the transfer and Fusus had inspected the temple himself only the day before the first delivery. The signed agreement would have taken place in the temple and the ingots transported back to Ostia today," he raised his eyebrows at the importance. I nodded. All contracts had to be signed in a Temple and for Fusus to sign it here meant that the responsibility and cost of transporting the ingots to Ostia lay with the contractor. It made good business sense.

"Can he trust them, the boat builders?" I asked.

"A cousin of some renown in Ostia, has a flourishing business. They have several boats together and have worked together for three generations." It gave them credit and we all fell silent as it was highly unlikely that such links would have been broken. "We checked with them, asked about on the docks too. Nothings come back to even suggest that there was anything out of place with the arrangement."

"Who was moving the silver to the Temple?"

"Fusus' son and some of his own men and slaves. Small trips of a few ingots over three nights and plenty of muscle for extra security. No incidents reported."

"Does the son have hidden debts? A problem that he's hiding?"

Scavolo was enjoying the questions as it showed my father that he'd done his job properly. "Albinus Furius Fusus is the only living son and stands to lose everything if his father loses his fortune. I can't see it."

"I agree, the man is steadfast."

It was a statement of the highest regard from my father so I moved on. "Were the carts their own or hired?"

Scavolo's brows creased at this. "I'll check that out. Good question," he said, a small angle he'd not considered as few people owned carts and it was a loose end which could add further to the knowledge that the ingots were being moved.

"I assume the silver was signed for when they arrived?"

Scavolo nodded and said that everything was done by the agreed list, dated and documented and that copies of these were held with the Flamen and Fusus, they'd seen both copies and they seemed correct.

I was shaking my head as each question seemed to have been covered and no gaps could be found. "So the only window of time that the ingots could be removed is in the time between the priests leaving for Ostia and Titus being found dead. And that's assuming the dead priest wasn't in some way part of the theft."

The statement was to the room in general though I was still working through timelines and the different items we'd learned as I stated it. I felt I'd missed something important but the heat and wine was playing with my mind.

"There doesn't seem to be any way that the ingots could have been moved out of the temple between the close of the day and the fire being seen by the locals." I was rubbing my chin and my head was shaking.

"I agree," said Scavolo loudly, bringing me back to the room as I had been stuck with thoughts of the silver transport and what information could have been leaked. "We hadn't considered the role of Titus being part of the theft but after your revelation today that he was murdered it has been discussed," he looked to my father and I guessed they'd debated this whilst I was out searching for further clues. It made some sense that the man was part of the plot, but why would they ritually sacrifice him at the altar? That didn't make sense at all unless the thieves had a fall out and he was removed.

"And I am as confused by the fact that it is suggested that Titus made them take the statues to Ostia, almost as if he knew there was a possibility they would be stolen if the site was broken into. If he knew that the thieves were coming, it would make sense that he asked for the relics to be moved to protect them from being stolen in the raid," I said as faces seemed to agree with my words.

"This is complex," stated Sul.

Then my father turned to me and asked, "as much as this is interesting and the man had his throat cut rather than died a hero's death, how is it going to find Fusus' ingots and get us out of the shit-hole we're in?"

I didn't know and said as much.

"I don't care who killed the priest, I want to know who stole the silver," he remarked with a look to Scavolo, who turned his face to mine and I shrugged.

"We have no clues yet Marcus. It has only been a short time that the treasure has been missing," he said in reply as none of us had any ideas beyond those we'd discussed. "Nobody saw anything. Nobody knows anything."

My father was getting agitated and was about to speak but I spoke quickly to try to appease the tension that was building in the small room. "Have those who knew the treasures were being moved been spoken to, what about Fusus' own inner circle, does anyone have a grudge that might turn them to this act?"

There were too many questions to answer at once. Scavolo said that his men had been out today to speak to any-and-everyone involved from a list that Fusus had given them and he'd have more information in the morning. My father seemed at least quietened by this if not totally happy. "My guess, and I am sure that we all agree, is that someone in the Temple is linked to this. Therefore, if we focus on the priests we may get one of them to crack. There is more to the priests than they are letting us know. The act of sacrificing this man Titus at the altar has something to do with this mystery, and we will find out if we poke with our spears sharply enough. And what part does Maelius have in this?" It was a question to the room at large but my father picked up on it.

"Maelius?" he'd addressed this to Scavolo. He was rubbing his chin in thought.

"He was throwing his weight around at the Temple, telling the priests they had nothing to answer to as they were away from the Temple at the time." My father raised his brows at this, it was a detail that Scavolo clearly hadn't shared.

"How did he know that?" asked my brother, another contribution. He was warming to this.

"He lives up the Hill from the Temple, he must have been called when the fire started," answered Scavolo. "You know what it's like?" he was addressing my father. "The locals always run to the nearest patrician for help when something goes wrong."

He received a grunt of agreement from all three of us.

"Athitatus told us that a few locals were trying to put the fire out with water when they arrived home," I said remembering his words. "He never mentioned Maelius, although he had no reason to do so as I didn't ask who or how many locals were there nor did I ask how long the fire had been ablaze."

"I have the name of the pleb who raised the alarm."

"I think we may need to visit him in the morning" I said quietly.

"One more thing," it was my father, a strange look on his face. "If you didn't know it," he was looking to me. "Maelius' main business dealings are in the transport and sale of grain."

The significance of that fact fell on us like a boulder rolled over a cliff top.

V

I hadn't dreamt of the fuller's daughter or of Perdita and I awoke with a clear head. I thanked Somnus for a peaceful night and considered what we'd discussed and what had been in my thoughts as I drifted to sleep. Maelius' business was grain and Scavolo suggested this could easily be a ploy to stop Fusus undercutting his prices and muscling in on his business, although it did seem an extreme way to do so. I needed to know more. I'd send Graccus to find out more about the patrician and his businesses. I made a note on a wax tablet, something I'd started to do recently as I found my mornings were often alive with thoughts which then disappeared as quickly as my coins when I visited Milo's. And I also needed to visit the local houses to check out their stories, when had the fire started, who had seen anything strange before or after the blaze? I made that note too.

What other information had I missed? What was the feud between the priests and Titus and how had it played a part in this story? It seemed important, or was it just Vulcan playing with my mind?

I needed to sacrifice a duck this morning as I had not done so the previous day. I wrote 'duck'. I sat up with another realisation now dawning like the sun outside slowly moving across the landscape. Vulcan was the god that averted harmful fires, he didn't start them. It seemed strange but it didn't fit with the half-story of Titus and his madness. I needed more information about his dreams and what they were, and to do that I needed to get each of the priests alone and question them. My brain was filled with possibilities as I dressed, pissing in the pot in the corner and remembering Fucilla and her family as I did so. I wondered how they had been since I last saw them. I had heard that Larce and his family had been banished to the north and that Hastius had paid a large fee in compensation to Ducus. I hadn't been at the trial, which was a shame as I would have liked to have seen their reactions. Graccus had given me the news. Another thing hit me as I opened the door. Scavolo still had the silver ring. I made a note of this too.

Micus accompanied me to the Temple, the boy chatting and singing as we walked, his new sandals were very clean as he evidently took pride in them and covered them in fat each night to keep them soft. As we rounded the edge of the Forum and passed the stone of Lapis Niger the long slope of the Clivus up to the Capitol awaited us. I stopped and looked to my left towards the burned shell of the Temple. I remembered my notes and then had a thought.

"Micus, how do you fancy doing a little job for me?" I asked lifting a copper coin.

"Anything Master."

"Go along the road here and ask about what happened to the Temple. See if you can find out anything or anyone who saw anything out of the ordinary or might have seen anyone hanging around in the days before the fire. Make sure you ask about the days before."

He nodded apprehensively, the whites of his eyes showing as his eyebrows rose. "What if I forget to ask something, Master, or forget what they say," he was looking fearful.

"See that food shop," I was pointing to Milo's near the top of the rise. He nodded. "If you get some good information run up there and tell him I sent you. If you tell him what you heard he'll remember it and pass it on to me. Then you can go back and ask around some more. Is that a deal?"

"Yes, Master," he said with a broad beaming grin.

"And Micus," he had half turned to walk away in the direction of the Vulcanal. "Tell Milo that I said you can have as much soup as you can eat when you've finished."

His little face lit up and he bent to his knees to thank me. I patted his head, he was a good lad.

I walked up the hill with renewed energy, looking left and right to see if I could tell which house belonged to Maelius but there were too many high walls and narrow streets which backed to the rock of the Capitol to see beyond into the town-houses so I soon gave up looking.

Graccus was at the door of the Temple with Philus, who I remembered had told him I was never coming back, the little gossip. I took a moment to look down my nose at him, putting him out of sorts, before striding in as he bowed and followed asking if we wanted anything bringing to our room. I ignored him, Graccus asked for hot bread and cold water with lemons.

Moments later we were going through the plan I had for Graccus' day when Novius and Pemptor arrived at the door. "Secundus, just to let you know that Scavolo is sick, he's at home. If you need us you know where we are."

"What's up with him?" I was worried, he'd been at my house in the bath with us until late.

"Shits!" came the reply.

I grinned.

Graccus grinned.

The two men left smiling. It was always funny when someone else had the shits, but I didn't think Scavolo had ever been ill. He *was* human after all.

"So you know what to do?"

"I'll be back at Milo's for a late lunch, see you there."

Graccus took one of the bread rolls and left, drawing his sleeve across his face as he did so.

I picked up a stylus and wrote the names of the priests from the Temple. Athitatus, Caelius, Nesta, Regicius, Marcus and Hector. I hadn't formally met three of the six although I had seen them in the rubble the day before. I needed to get the Flamen to agree to me speaking to each man alone, which could be difficult. I also had the question of the dreams to pose to the Temple of Vulcan's head priest too. I had my work cut out today for sure. I looked at the wine cupboard and realised Graccus had taken the key, bastard. I downed the lemon-water and set off.

The Temple was silent as I arrived to see the blackened piles of wood and brighter terracotta roof tiles that had been saved piled into neat rows which stretched across the rear of the site. I'd bought a duck at the Forum, a scrawny cheap looking thing as the prices were high at this time of the year and I was short of coin. I approached the site, with the larger Temple of Saturn behind, to find two men standing and looking at the ruins. There were three boys kicking a stone around and a woman dressed in mourning clothes away to the right who looked like she'd stopped momentarily to look at the ruins before she carried on towards the Forum, probably to get her daily supplies.

Her eyes lifted to the scene, a flash of red hair under her hood as she turned to walk away. One of the boys, his dark hair and brown tunic suggesting he was a slave was called from the doorway of a house along the street and he raced away to leave the others continuing their game. He reminded me of Micus. Life went on as normal. The two men saw me approaching and stepped back out of the way.

"Good morning gentlemen," I said. "What a sorry sight this is on such a bright morning. I brought a duck to sacrifice to Vulcan for good luck in finding the men who did this." I lifted the sorry creature which had the good sense to make a honking squeak which caught their attention. They made noises which suggested agreement but did not answer. "Are you local?" I asked.

"What's it to you?" replied one of them, a hard-faced man, hands at his side and a suspicious glance in my direction.

"Just asking," I replied, shrugging and walking towards the sacred Lotus Tree where I saw flowers and garlands had been placed. "I wasn't here when it happened so I have no idea what caused it." I'd spoken casually, but I was dressed in a light tunic of high quality wool so was obviously more than just a passing stranger.

"Speak to the priests, they probably know," came the reply. I accepted it with a smile as they wandered off towards the Forum, miserable buggers. I hoped that my gamble of Micus, a slave boy, asking questions would receive a better response than I had received. It was a good idea to send him, everyone knew that slaves loved nothing more than a good gossip.

Standing at the sacred tree I felt a sudden sadness pass over me and I wasn't sure whether to let the duck go. Its wings were tied back so it couldn't fly but it would be easy for me to cut the ties and set it free. It turned its head to me with a pathetic look which suggested it was reading my thoughts. I was about to do just that when a man appeared from behind me wearing the dark robes with gold collar of the order. His clothes seemed damp, as if they hadn't yet dried after being washed overnight. It was Caelius.

"Secundus Sulpicius," his smile was warmer now that he knew me. "Is that for the Temple?" The duck's reprieve had failed.

I said that it was and he took the duck from me, the creature seemed to sag in resignation as he did so. Caelius asked me to wait whilst he placed it in a cage, saying Hector was performing the morning sacrifices and would arrive soon. He returned almost immediately and turned with a sad look to the ruins of the Temple.

"Are you planning to raise funds to rebuild?" I asked.

He nodded. "We have a benefactor who has offered some support but we need more."

I hoped he wasn't going to ask me for any and rued my question for a second before he continued and spared me a blustering answer about lack of personal funds. "The Flamen has suggested that we honour Titus' deed and retain the look and feel of the old Temple, keep to the old ways as much as we can whilst embracing as much of the new as we can. A new altar, a new set of windows which look out towards the temple of Jupiter Optimus Maximus and a small wall around the site." He was waving in general directions as he spoke, clearly excited by the news. "We'll have a new festival to mark the rebirth. Dancing, candles," he was smiling now.

Vulcan must be smiling on me and my offer of the scrawny duck, I thought, as the priest had led me directly to the path I wanted to take without my having to spend long minutes on small talk. I decided another, better duck would be sent along later regardless of the cost.

"What did Titus see in the old ways, surely it is right that you move with the changing times." I turned to the Temple of Saturn which had recently had several new steps built at the side of the old altar and which dominated the roadway from the Sacra Via. "As the priests of Saturn have done." It was a gamble but one that I hoped would work as the competition between the priests might help to bring out his true feelings.

He glanced up the road and pulled a sour face. "They always seem to have money for rebuilding projects," he said glumly.

"Is that what Titus said?" I was sure I was trying too hard now, the question was clearly designed to get him back on my path, but he simply turned down his mouth before answering.

"No, his dreams were more prophetic, or so he thought. He dreamt of cleansing fires turning the Temple to waste ground and said that it was a portent that we should return to the old ways, keep the Temple simple, maintain the old rules and all move back to live within the walls or the site would be raised to the ground by Vulcan." It appeared to have come true, but I kept my thoughts to myself on that front. "Poor Titus," he said. I was pleased at this as it suggested Athitatus had not yet let the fact that their fellow priest had been killed become common knowledge, just as I'd told him he must do.

"Yes, poor man," I replied. This was just as Athitatus had told us so I had no reason to ask further questions on that front. "Did he spend many nights here alone?" I asked out of curiosity.

"No, maybe five or six days before this happened."

It was almost in line with the signing of the agreement between Fusus and the Flamen and suggested a link. "And when did the ingots arrive, from Fusus," I said.

He looked to me for a second. "Of course you know about that," he said, as if he hadn't thought about it before, which surprised me. "I assume you are here to find them?" I nodded that I was. "The ingots came in three runs over three days, Fusus didn't want them to travel at once."

It was as Scavolo had told me.

"Makes sense with so many thieves around," I replied.

"Yes, the Flamen was very worried. He asked for additional guards but Fusus said it wasn't needed."

I hadn't heard this before and it didn't sound like the cautious patron I knew from his discussions with my father. I needed more answers so continued with my questions as the man seemed relaxed in my presence. "Did nobody else worry about the ingots? Did you post any more guards?"

His gesture suggested not. "Why would we? The key was kept up at the house and you can see it from the window there," he flicked his head towards the slope where I could make out the house now that I knew it was there. "And there has never been a break-in or theft in all the years of the Temple." He was looking glum now, his face turning back to the scorched ruins. "We've held more ingots when the blacksmiths have melted the spoils of war on several occasions since I have been a priest of the Temple. More iron than silver, granted," he said. "But we have had the vault filled to the roof and never lost a single one."

It seemed plausible and it made it even more probable that the theft had been pre-determined. I remembered one of my notes from earlier this morning and that the final delivery from Fusus' son had arrived on the very night of the fire. Two other priests appeared and gave dark looks towards us as I asked another question of Caelius. One was Regicius but the other I didn't know though their robes signalled them as priests of the Temple. Again their garments seemed darker than I had remembered and possibly damp.

It perplexed me for a second before I asked, "Titus seemed to dream of harmful fires, visions of terror and destruction," the priest's eyes widened. "But the Temple of Vulcan signifies the aversion of harmful fires. I am confused by this. What do you think his dreams meant?"

His lips tightened and he glanced to the two approaching men. "He was mad. He'd sucked too many Lotus berries," he said sharply. "His ramblings and visions were nothing to do with the god, something else was plaguing him. I don't know what it was Secundus, but he had lost his mind in those last days and his anger at Athitatus' decisions to move forward with our plans enraged him. He was possessed!"

It was a sharp claim and one that the Twelve Tables had laws against. Nobody had made that statement previously as they all probably knew the implications.

"Is that why you agreed to go to Ostia to visit the other Temple?"

He looked to me and then toward the others who were now only a few strides away. "I played no part in that decision. I did not want to go but Athitatus was very concerned by it."

"Had Titus been recently? To Ostia."

He frowned at me. "He had not left Rome for thirty years. None of us are allowed to go out of the city unless the Flamen agrees to it."

More questions were clashing in my mind like spears on a phalanx shield-wall but I didn't ask them as Regicius and the other man arrived and stared at me. "Gentlemen," I bowed.

"This is Nesta," said the taller of the two. I noted that he had tied his hair in a long braid as I bowed to the newcomer.

Nesta was short and stocky and gazed at me down a long Sabine nose. His eyes were bright and his chin held a scar below his lower lip which must have been from years before as it didn't look new, unlike a small scratch below his nose from the mornings ritual of shaving. His arms hung free from the blue tunic with the gold band, which had patches of damp as did the other priests.

"I am pleased to meet you and sorry that it is at such a difficult time."

I thought it was well said but he simply shrugged. "Vulcan will dictate what happens in this world, we are his servants. If it is difficult, it is his will and we must follow his designs. We have work to do."

This last comment was to Caelius, a flash of anger in his eyes as the two men turned faces to one another.

"We must go, Secundus Sulpicius," it was formal names now that his fellow priests were with us. "Athitatus will be along soon with the others, they are buying new robes, as you can see we only have the clothes we are standing in."

That seemed odd but then I remembered Scavolo's comment regarding the oil and cloth and considered that their spare robes were used to start the blaze and they likely had to wash them each night and hence they were still damp. They turned to leave. "Do you only keep one set of robes?" I asked in surprise.

It was Regicius who answered, though he didn't turn to look at me as he did so. "All of our spare tunics, robes and clothes were kept in the Temple," his hand was waving at the ruins. "They, and all of our shoes, were burned."

I looked to their feet and realised none of them wore sandals.

****

Athitatus had said that I must come back later as they had too much work to do for them to stop and talk to me this morning. I was dismissed quickly, having been introduced to the remaining priests I had not been introduced to so far in my visits.

Marcus was an unremarkable man with a shrew-like face, narrow with a thin nose and eyes that were impossibly close together so that he looked like he had a permanent squint. Hector was as tall as Regicius and held brooding eyes under heavy lids. His right arm had clearly been broken in past years as he has a fixed lump just above the wrist which seemed to hamper his movements, though not so much that he couldn't carry large stones from the site. I'd acknowledged them all and accepted the Flamens decision, it would be impolite not to do so. For a while I stood by the Lotus Tree and looked at the vegetable plot, neat rows of greenery. I turned back to the Temple, considering what it was like before the fire and how Titus might have seen it with his desire to return to the old, simple, ways. A thought came to me and I walked along to the Temple of Saturn, only a few moments along the wide road with the Via Sacra on my left. Straight ahead the Vicus Jugarius, one of the oldest roads in the city continued towards the Tiber.

I was thinking through how I would have planned to remove the treasures from the Temple. If the ingots had been carried by hand, not by cart as nobody seemed to have seen nor heard anything, how could they have been transported and to where? If they had been deposited locally to collect at a later date, maybe someone had seen something in the days before or on the night of the fire from further along the road as the priests had returned this way and said they had seen nothing. I then realised that they must have walked through the night on their return from Ostia.

Why was this?

Not only was it dangerous to do so under normal circumstances but they carried their sacred statues too, which would likely have attracted unwanted attention. As I considered this I had a vision of the thieves taking armfuls of ingots and dropping them into a pit or over the wall of a disused villa along the road. They'd need to be strong men as I knew from moving some of my father's bronze ingots that I could probably carry two or three at a push, although we didn't have as large a sum as Fusus had deposited at the Temple and I knew that carrying three was hard work. Each ingot was as long as my forearm and probably just as thick. Silver was slightly lighter but not by much. So ten men could move thirty ingots. Five could move ten or fifteen at the most. I was still walking as I ran the system through my mind. A man would probably walk ten or fifteen minutes before starting to struggle with the weight, less if they were concealing the ingots or moving them in the dark. It didn't make sense. I was basing this on my own weak frame and so added five minutes to my calculations. If that were the case, then to move Fusus' ingots would have taken ten men almost an hour alone, on the basis that they would have to return several times to remove the lot. I just could not see how it was done. It was improbable that five men, or ten for that matter, would not have been seen either on the night of the fire as I knew that the last of the ingots were delivered on the day that the fire started. My simple logic told me that the ingots weren't far away and were very likely hidden to collect at a later date. My mind went back to Maelius. I hoped that Graccus had some answers for me on that front.

At the far end of the Capitol, the Hill stretching far above my right shoulder, I turned to look around. Low houses of one or two-storeys were situated along the road. It was a more prosperous area and so the houses weren't crammed on top of each other as they were in other parts of the city. Most were built of timber, though some were stone-based with thatched or tiled roofs if the householder had the funds or skills to improve their premises. The road was wide enough for two carts to pass and a number of locals were out tending their gardens and vegetables. On my right I counted twelve houses as far as I could see and only nine on the left as two or three were larger than their neighbours. Two of these larger dwellings fronted the road and had shops built into the walls, one a cloth merchant and another a food store not dissimilar to Milo's, the three holes in the counter filled with something hot that gave off a brothy aroma. The cloth merchant seemed busy and he gave me an appraising glance as I came by, his keen eyes looking me up and down as if he was sizing me for a garment. I smiled but kept walking. If I carried straight on, over the rise and down the other side I would reach the Forum Halitorium and the Tiber beyond that. One of the houses on my right was shuttered, the owners must be away for the hot months as many of the richer family did these days, as much to avoid the flies and plagues as to avoid the heat.

This area of the city used to be part of the old marshlands which were partly drained as the city expanded and the Cloaca Maxima was built to take the rainwater away to the Tiber. *That* marvel of engineering lay behind the houses to my left, and some distance beyond the large houses I could see high walls which suggested that these backed onto the poorer parts of the city which continued through the Velabrum across the Vicus Tuscus and to the lower slopes of the Palatine. Lucius and Fucilla lived someone in that general direction as did many of the Etruscans who had earned their rights as citizens of our great Republic. I remembered Lucius telling me that he had a direct link to the Cloaca as it flowed under his house so that he could drain the used piss pots without the cost of transporting them to the river. Location was important he'd said, imparting his wisdom. I wondered why it struck me at that precise moment.

People looked at me with suspicion at my stopping in the road and searching looks to the houses on my left and right, looking up at windows and down at the small gardens, vegetables in tidy rows and high walls. I took in the surroundings and felt like this was a good place to live. I took a moment to retrace my steps, moving slowly until I saw an old greybeard, his eyes half-closed as he sat basking in the sun on a bench at the gate to one of the smaller houses on the street but with ample grounds stretching around the domus. It was neat and tidy with several olive trees visible behind the half-sleeping form of the aged man. I noticed that the trees were kept short so that the fruit could easily be picked when it was ripe and I noted he had a couple of small apples in a clay bowl at his feet.

"Fine day," he said as I covered the sun and cast a shadow over him. He looked pissed at this intrusion into his daily ritual.

"Indeed it is," I said jovially, moving to the left and allowing the warmth to strike him again. His skin was leathery and his arms and legs, which stuck out like some of my mother's long thin hairpins, were covered in fine white hairs such that his brown skin was exemplified and made him look like a hairy nut. He smelled slightly of piss, reminding me of the fuller's yard, maybe that was what had brought Lucius to my mind.

"You have fine trees" I said with a look to his garden.

"What are you after?"

He was clearly bright enough to see that I was after something.

"I'm working for the Temple," I lifted my chin back up towards the Forum. He cracked open a lid and gave me a stare which suggested that he didn't believe a word. "The Flamen has asked me to see if anyone saw anything on the night of the fire."

"No!"

It was said with the usual *I wouldn't tell you if I did* tone that I'd come to expect from this new line of work that Minerva had forced me into. I stood and held my place, looking to the neighbour's house and seeing that next doors garden was almost completely composed of apple trees, they obviously traded olives for apples as a small clay bowl of the same size, colour and shape as the one at his feet, sat just beside the gate.

"No problem," I replied.

"Is there a reward?" he asked after I'd taken a few steps.

Glancing back I saw both eyes now cracked open but he'd tensed in the shoulders, suggesting he was keen to gossip if I paid for it.

Pay the plebs and the plebs will pay you back.

It was strange that the words of my father popped into my thoughts at that moment. I cursed that I had few coins and had given my best to Micus.

"Only if it's useful," I shrugged, now leaning against a waist high fence post which bordered his land and looking into the trees beyond as if I was just passing the time of day.

The house next to his was the shuttered one but the lands were tidy. I saw vegetables in neat rows which must have been tended recently so they clearly left others to keep on top of the produce. A red flag was positioned by the door, flapping slightly in the light wind and I remembered that meant the place might be for sale. This caught my attention. I nodded at the lay-out and position and thoughts of Fabia and a house in Rome flew into my mind and brought a smile to my lips.

He breathed a croaky breath and coughed lightly at my change in expression.

"What sort of information you after?" He saw me looking at the place next door. "She's lost her husband this last year," he said. "He had no family left and she was his..." his eyes narrowed before he finished by changing whatever he was going to add. "She's below his status and got no family as such. You'd get a good price if you bartered hard enough but the priests and lawyers are hard bastards so you'd have to bribe them. Though I don't know who is the lasses priest now."

It was well known that bribing those at the heart of the deal-making system worked. I put the thought to the back of my mind, but I glanced back at the building. It might be worth pursuing but I'd need to solve this case first. Was this Vulcans way of pushing me to get to the solution, giving me something to work for. I realised I'd not sorted that bigger duck for sacrificing and shook my head at the thought. I needed to pay closer attention to the will of the gods and the signs they gave me.

"No, not for you then?" He misinterpreted my head movement. "She's in there, just keeps the place locked up tight, you know what it's like, a woman on her own is too much of an opportunity for some of the low life around here. They'd ransack the place like a force of Volscans if they had a chance. She has a couple of slaves, the head man's a tough bastard so you want to watch out for him, and a few others come in and keep the place tidy though, do the gardens and stuff, you know."

I nodded to his words, it was true that people saw an opportunity in the disasters of others.

"I might be, but I have work to do before then," I replied. "I'm after information about the fire at the Vulcanal. Did you see any carts or horses going past on the night of the fire or late on the nights before?"

His mouth and eyes tightened as his brows furrowed. "No. Not slept well for ten years. I'd have heard something."

It wasn't reliable but it was a start. I looked at his eager face and started to fumble in my pocket. He followed my hand, the whites of his eyes showing in anticipation of payment.

"Any men walking past carrying bundles or sacks, anyone out on the road at all in the days before or after?"

"Nothing unusual on the night the Temple burnt down. Not until the alarm was raised by Fabius over there," his chin suggested a house somewhere over the road but not a specific domus. "Then the priests came past in a hurry as someone saw them and ran down the road to tell them their Temple was ruined."

"Did you go up and have a look?"

"Of course I did, dimwit," he said shaking his head. I grinned at him and he actually grinned back at me, three of his teeth missing in his mouth.

"Did you see anyone acting suspiciously or maybe carrying heavy loads out of the fire? Anything at all?"

He was shaking his head as he looked back up the road searching his memories. "There were a lot of people around, lots of noise. I can't say that anyone was carrying anything much. What sorts of things are you talking about?"

"I don't know? Large sacks or heavy bundles. Horses or carts? Did you see anyone take a spear from within the ruins of the temple?"

"No. Not that I recall." His hair was swaying with his moving head and he rubbed at his chin through the straggly beard. "Didn't see any carts or horses. Most people were carrying water from their own barrels to save the Lotus Tree as sparks were flying everywhere. It's a good job the Temple is a distance from the houses. We all," at which his hand lifted to suggest some of the local houses, "Went up there and carried water to put out the fire. Didn't want it coming down here."

He was giving me the look of a man who knew the damage fire could do if it spread to the streets where most of the houses were built of dry timber.

I agreed with this and pulled out a small bronze coin, which lit up his face. I was disappointed that the slight information he'd given me had come at the cost. I knew he could get half a dozen apples or even a small hen for this much bronze. I clung to it before I handed it over as something he'd said fell into my brain like one of those apples falling from a tree.

"When you said *not on the night of the fire* what did you mean?"

VI

Milo was delighted to see me, Micus had obviously been to see him and given him plenty to talk about. "You're investigating the fire then." It was a statement rather than a question, I guessed, as he answered it himself. "Makes sense considering how you solved that fuller's daughter's murder. Poor girl." He appraised me with a long look. "Never had you as the clever type," he added this small insult to the even smaller praise he'd given me. I wondered if he was related to Scavolo.

"I'd prefer that fact to remain as much a secret as possible," I replied to his comment. "I take it my boy has been up," I was inclining my head towards the city below and the fact that Micus would have to have come up the Hill to impart Milo with any information he'd gleaned.

"Oh yes, two or three times. Got it here if you need anything," he tapped his head. At least it seemed encouraging that the young boy had been up to see Milo.

"Fish stew with dark olives today," he waved a hand at the large metal urn which sat bubbling in the cement top of his main counter. "It's bloody good today even if I do say so myself." He'd spoken loudly as two men were seen staring across at the counter and wondering if they should approach.

I fumbled in my pocket. "I might have to pay you tomorrow." I replied quietly as the men came over to inspect what was on offer. I didn't want to look like I didn't have the means to pay.

"For a loyal customer like you, a man going up in the world," he gave me a broad smile "credit is fine. I'll get a tab for you."

He'd returned in a minute with a full steaming bowl and a small slate with *two soup, one bread* written in well scripted Latin next to the date Dies Lunae. I scribbled my mark with the hard-tipped stylus he handed across and wondered why he'd never offered me credit before.

"Micus had soup *and bread*?" I asked before he could leave and inclining my head to my new slate.

"Soup," he said. "Only got one pair of hands," he held the slate up as proof. "Just getting your bread, nice and hot, fresh for good customers with an account. Thank you Secundus Sulpicius Merenda," he was speaking overly-loudly again as the two men were looking in our direction. "It's always good to have the *son of the Quaestores* eating here each day."

I was shaking my head at him. In the month or so that I'd eaten here with Graccus I'd never seen more than about three people eating at his tables and now he was milking my family status as if we were best friends. It worked, the men came across and ordered two bowls. I made a mental note to see if I could barter a discount onto my account but my thoughts were interrupted as Micus appeared, his face lighting up as he saw me.

"Master," he sat as I bid him to join me, panting as if he'd raced up the Clivus. I waved to Milo and asked for some cool water, which he brought across as soon as he'd served the two men.

"Alright Micus," he ruffled the lads hair, which I frowned at as the lad wasn't his property.

"Thanks Milo," said the boy in a tone which suggested they were bosom buddies, gulping at the water as if he hadn't had a drink for a week.

"Slow down, you'll get gut ache," I said it without thinking and realised I was turning into my mother. It was exactly what she used to say to me and Sul when we came in from chasing around the garden.

He apologised, I waved it away and told him to take his time. I started on the fish and olives which was, just as Milo had proclaimed, very good. I looked over to see him ladling a further two bowls to a man and woman, likely merchants by the look of their clothes, the man wearing a wide-brimmed hat and what I assumed was his wife, heavily pregnant at his side. He was pointing them to a seat across from where I sat with Micus. I realised that I'd never seen more than three or four people at Milo's as he only had three or four tables. He had three stools along the counter for passing trade, but if you wanted to sit and take a rest it was, in reality, quite a small place.

I waited till my father's slave boy had drunk most of the cup and then asked, "So, what have you learned Micus? Tell me slowly and quietly. I don't want others hearing our business."

I winked and his eager face picked up my movement.

He glanced to Milo but I waved him on and pointed to the warm bread, which he helped himself to with a happy smile. "At the fifth house, the one with a green door and a boot-scraper, Lavia," a common name for a female bath slave "said that her Master had been one of the first to see the fire and raise the alarm."

I nodded at this as it reminded me that Scavolo had mentioned the house.

"He had all the slaves and his own two sons out on the street. She says that the Flamen was whipping the priests, shouting at them for being too slow in returning to the Temple."

That seemed interesting.

"He had that statue, the one of Romulus and was waving it around like a club." It did seem like odd behaviour.

"Did she see anything else? Anything at all, however small or what you might think is not of interest. Anything?"

His concentration screwed his face into a tight ball. "When the patrician from up the Hill came they were all sent back, their Master doesn't like him."

"Oh, why's that?"

He shrugged and looked down at the table, picking at the bread with his fingernails. "I need to know Micus, you are my spy," I whispered as I leant closer to him.

Glancing to the sides he carried on quickly. "He's a bad Master. He whips his slaves for the slightest thing."

I nodded. Not the gossip I wanted and common practice, but obviously something that he felt was important. It was strange how people's minds worked.

"What else did you find out?"

He pushed out his lips, extending them with puffed cheeks before saying, "A man named Briatus had let his dogs out in the street to shit earlier in the evening and they'd been barking loudly, but nobody could see anything except the priest doing his rounds, watering the vegetables and walking around the temple praying." I picked my ears up at this as it linked to something the old man had said about Titus' evidently increasing nocturnal habits. I gestured for him to continue. "Marcurius," another slave name "said that the mad priest had taken to walking around a lot, mumbling about fires and returning to the old ways of Vulcan."

It made further sense and I was pleased that my bronze coin had been well placed with the grey beard who had given plenty of interesting pieces of information which had also set my mind running. This slave had just added to that line of reasoning.

"Did Marcurius have anything else to say?"

"No," he said and then frowned. "Except that the priest was often drunk and staggered around at night making a lot of noise and annoying the dogs. His Master had been to the Flamen to complain. He said that the priest was stupid and deserved what he got. Sorry Master," he'd spoken ill of the dead, which he knew should not be done.

"They were his words, not yours Micus," I reassured him.

"I came up here, Master," at which he pointed towards the slope of the Clivus Capitolinus "because I thought that those first two houses had a good view of the Temple."

I turned to look. He was right, they did. I was impressed.

"The large house wouldn't answer the door, the one next to it I waited for two of the boys to come out to go to the Forum and followed them."

I was starting to think that Micus was doing a better job than Graccus.

"But I lost them in the crowds."

Maybe not.

"And then I came back and waited as I knew they'd have to return."

He was back in my good books.

"The bigger boy wasn't friendly but I said I was new to the street and looking for news of what happened as I was scared of fires as I lost my mother in a fire."

A very good story as there were a lot of fires across the city and many died each year.

Micus was obviously good at this. "He said that his Master had been talking about the Temple being full of silver ingots two nights before the fire."

My jaw dropped at this news. How did he know that the temple was full of Fusus' ingots? It was another lead that I thought I'd leave to Scavolo and his men to follow as they had more resources than I when he got off his sick bed but it was an interesting development. How did a local house know that there was additional silver in the temple?

It needed further investigations for sure.

That was all Micus could tell me, but it was a treasure trove of good information that I knew I would never have gained if I'd tried to ask at the doors he'd navigated due to his status as one of them, a slave. I handed him my last coin and told him that he had done well. Milo appeared with a glance to the boy and my nearly empty bowl and soon a small bowl of soup was given to the lad, I'd eaten enough. I scribbled my sign on my new slate, noting that it was filling up quickly as a piss pot on the street outside a tavern.

I sat back, armed with all of the information from the morning, wondering if I should go and see Novius and ask him to speak to the owner of the second house on the road below who had been talking about the silver. We needed to know how the man knew that fact and who he'd told about it. It was a very good lead. And I also needed to go and speak to Athitatus about the drunken wonderings of Titus that was now playing on my mind more than anything else I'd heard, especially from what the leathery old man from the Jugarius had said. I was still convinced that the death of the priest was central to this case. I sat in silence for a while as Micus ate his hot broth, my thoughts running over and over what I'd heard. After a while I decided that I couldn't stay any longer at the food shop and sent Micus to give Novius the task of speaking to the house owner as I couldn't wait for that soft-arse Scavolo to return to work, time was running out. I then decided to head back to the Vulcanal and I meandered down the hill and turned towards the Temple.

I arrived to find two men arguing on the road just before the Temple, so stood watching along with the small crowd of on-lookers. One of the men, the more aggressive was waving his arms around and shouting. The other was standing his ground with his chest puffed out like a cock defending his hens.

"What's happening?" I asked a younger man, wispy beads of hair on his chin who was stood with an older woman. He wore a deep green tunic with a red stripe across the shoulders, an expensive item. His mother, if that's what she was, she may have been his grandmother by the sagging eyelids just visible under her head cover, wore an olive stola and a white shawl over her head and shoulders, very much the modern matron of a household. She was straight-backed and looked as miserable as a man with the pox. They exuded some wealth though they were clearly plebs. I maintained a respectable distance.

"The shouter is accusing the other of sleeping with his wife," he said with a long sigh. "Idiot."

I nodded my appreciation of the man's stupidity. "What a prick," I said, shaking my head. I'd spent a few days with Festus recently calling out to those accused of wrong-doing under the Twelve Tables and it still surprised me that people didn't have a basic grasp of the law. "We're all witnesses to it as well."

The boy could see that I understood the law too. "Dick!" said the boy, getting a reproachful glance from his elderly relative.

"You seem to know the law," I smiled to the boy as aggressor took a swinging punch at the cock, who stepped back to allow the punch to sail wide. The majority of the crowd *oohed* in unison. It was turning into a good show and more people were stopping to watch, everyone loves a good fight.

"Been scribing at the Temple of Diana these past weeks," he said, "and I have an interview this afternoon for a job in one of the offices of the Temple of Jupiter."

The Temple of Diana on the Aventine was a busy place and I Knew some of the scribes as they often met with Graccus on the streets, my friend having worked his way to the temple of Jupiter Optimus Maximus as it was Rome's most glorious and had a reputation for the best record keeping in Rome. How Graccus had gotten there I'd never know. I hadn't seen this boy before, but that didn't surprise me.

"Oh, good fortune with that" I said as aggressor now launched a second punch and a third, all of which were avoided with very neat footwork. *Aaaah* cooed the crowd of onlookers, the boy's mother clapping lightly with a gleeful expression. She clearly enjoyed a street fight as much as everyone else did despite her austere appearance. The crowd surged left and right, bunching closer to the action as the two men circled each other making aggressive steps forward and then retreating as a wayward punch or kick was thrown. In truth it was a poor show with little action.

"What's your name?" I asked to his guarded glance at me.

"Maximus," he replied. "Maximus Fastius Tattinus," his chin jutted out as he spoke, proud of his heritage. I knew the family name but it was unremarkable so simply smiled at him.

The cock turned and grabbed the flailing arm that was heading for his face and twisted the body of the assailant to throw him to the floor. It was a good move, named *the goose* if I remembered from my wrestling training as it mimicked the goose raising its wing to turn in a circle and lead the opponent to fall forwards as it span. A few people clapped, including myself. I was impressed, but the attacker seemed like a drunken idiot, he kept missing his punches and tripping over his own feet. Fool. He fell into the crowd and was lifted and pushed back by two men who laughed loudly at his idiocy.

"Tattinus?" I said quietly. I knew from my brother that a Gaius Tattinus had served well in the previous year's skirmishes in the war with the Veintes and had won a bronze heart-saver in hand-to-hand fighting with a local tribal leader. It had been a big deal at the time and he'd told us all the tale when he returned with his own spoils of war and a scar on his right thigh. "Are you related to Gaius Tattinus?" I asked, quite interested now.

His grandmother, or whatever relation she was, turned a prune-faced look to me.

"And who are you young man to be asking such questions in the street?"

The boy dropped his head, obviously used to the old crone's snooty approach.

I shrugged. "Nobody," I replied as the cock aimed a kick at aggressor which landed in his guts with a loud *oof*. He, the aggressor, then turned and ran off up the Sacra Via to hoots from the crowd as cock waved his arms and then ran after him. It all seemed somewhat staged to me but I shrugged it off as I turned to the woman and replied, "I've heard the name that's all."

"It's none of your business," she said curtly. "Come Maximus."

He responded to the order by trudging along at her side with a baleful glance to me.

I watched them go and then headed over to the Lotus Tree, thinking that the lad might end up in the office where Graccus and I sat until recently. It made me smile and I wondered if he were a farter or a nose-wiper, or both.

I was going to check a theory I had gained whilst sitting listening to Micus and as I reached the Temple I was greeted by the old guard I'd seen the day before. He smiled and waved to me. "Did you see that?" he said with a shake of the head.

"I did, what a prick," I replied. "He's sure to get a summons now for attacking..."

"No, not that," he cut me off. "The pickpockets."

"What?" I had turned to see a few of the crowd now starting to realise that their purses had been taken. "Did you see them?"

"I shouted but the noise was too loud and I can't leave this station." He gave a heavy shouldered motion to show he couldn't have done any more than he had done.

"Is Athitatus here?" I asked, ignoring the idiots who'd fallen victim to the thieves and instinctively patting my empty purse even though I knew that it held nothing but fluff.

"By the gate at the back, go around the left there," he was pointing. I thanked him and approached the Flamen, who was with Hector, the man scowling at whatever he was being told. I kept back a little to eavesdrop but they saw my approach and seemed to bristle before both turning to me in one movement. I got the impression I wasn't welcome.

I bowed, they responded with the same. "A bad time?" I asked to their unsmiling faces.

"Look at the state of the place, of course it's a bad time," the Flamen responded acerbically. He seemed in a bad mood so I let my head incline and stepped back a little. "I will return later, my apologies" I answered to his puce face and dismissive glare.

"No, you're here now, you can ask Hector anything you want, the man's useless anyway," snapped the old priest, his bent back straightening a little as his mouth turned down. He stomped off, slapping a stick on his thigh as he walked.

My brows rose as I turned to Hector and tilted my head as much to show him some support as to express that I didn't wish to ask anything about the reason for the Flamen's mood, though I clearly did.

"He's a good man really" came the reply to my expressive face. "He just wants it all to be sorted as soon as possible. It is a terrible thing to have this happen whist you are the Flamen, it doesn't augur well for him, very unlucky," he said.

I suddenly realised what he was saying. If the Temple burned down on his watch, then the god Vulcan must be unhappy with his leadership. It made sense now why he was so angry and frustrated. I wondered if he had let it slip about Titus being murdered so I chanced a question.

"Did Titus think the same, that the visions were a sign from Vulcan of poor leadership?" It brought a sharp glance at me. I'd found something, but the man held back so gaining nothing more than narrowed eyes in response I continued. "It would make sense I guess. Anyway, can I ask you a question about the vegetable patch?" He looked confused but nodded. I motioned him to follow, which he did. "Can you tell me if any areas have been dug recently or changed? This fallow area for example." I pointed to small area which looked recently turned.

His mouth turned down for a second before he answered, obviously thinking I'd lost my wits but giving me the benefit of the doubt. "We turn each area every few weeks and plant in a cycle each six kalends to keep the ground fresh."

It was good farming protocol and I understood it.

"So only this area has been turned recently?"

He nodded.

"May I have a spade and turn it over a few times?" I watched his reaction and saw no understanding and he rolled his eyes as he wandered off to get me something with which to dig. It was a wild gamble but I had considered that if the treasure hadn't been moved, by my calculations it might take hours and many men to do so, it could be here still, hidden close at hand. The old greybeard down the road had told me that Titus had taken to wandering the roads at night drunk, sometimes singing and shouting but mostly chanting prayers to Vulcan. It seemed the lout often pissed on the gate post by his house or those of his neighbours and that the Flamen had been informed but nothing had changed. The opportunity to wander the streets and drop off silver in a local hideaway had run through my mind as I'd considered what may have happened. In a similar way he could have buried them closer to home. People had gotten used to his nightly rambling and soon he was given no credence and left to his own devices. If this was a ruse, and he was part of a plot to steal the ingots he could have easily buried the ingots here in the vegetable plot or somewhere close and his accomplices would collect it once the noise died down. Maybe they'd backed out on the deal at the last moment and gotten rid of him as he was becoming a liability. It was worth a bit of time with the spade to see if I could, literally, dig up any clues.

As I started to dig Hector stood and watched.

"How did Titus know about the Temple at Ostia?" I asked as I pushed the spade in with my foot. "He suggested you went to seek answers to your problems here didn't he?" I said with a glance as he didn't answer immediately. "I hear he'd not left Rome for years."

"He said he'd written to them for advice on the problems faced with modernising the Temple," came the reply.

I acknowledged the response. It made sense and I hadn't considered it.

"Tell me," I said as the soft soil gave way easily. "How do you think the ingots were removed?"

He looked at me long and hard before nodding at the ground. "You think they're here?" he thrust out a lip. "That's a good idea."

I stopped and looked at him.

"I was talking to the others about it earlier. None of us have any idea how that much metal was moved so quickly. Athitatus has been pushing us to search everywhere. We've been through all the piles of rubbish, tapped the floor of the strongroom for a secret hole," that was going to be my next place to look even though I'd tested it quickly when I first arrived "and even dug around the Lotus Tree," he added with a flick towards the sacred object. "Nothing" he said. "We never thought of here," he was smiling as I continued.

"Want to help?"

"Not really, I'm supposed to be moving those tiles. We've got a man coming later to give us a price to rebuild the roof and start the changes to the temple while the weather's good and the Flamen wants all the best tiles on show so that he can't over-charge us for more stock."

Another thing came to me. "Athitatus said that a store of weapons were taken in the raid. What were they?"

"Broken Gallic swords, an old Etruscan helmet, a few bent spearheads," he said dismissively. "I wouldn't say they were weapons as such, there were only an armful at most and mostly worthless. They'd been there for years."

I nodded, It still seemed odd that they had been taken. "Are all the priests' skilled blacksmiths before they join the order?" It was something I had remembered from somewhere.

"Not anymore. Only Titus and Athitatus had any real skill in that area. Caelius is learning, he still thinks we should do more with the old ways but he's happy to embrace the new as well."

He looked up as if he'd said too much.

I turned and pointed towards the Capitol. "Do you know who owns that house, second on the Clivus Capitolinus?"

He turned his face towards the hill and answered, "Yes, it's Titus' fathers' house."

"Shit, really?"

I'd said it out loud without thought and apologised before thanking him, shovelling over the hole as quickly as possible. I couldn't believe what I'd heard and dropped the spade, it didn't seem likely from the three holes I'd dug that the silver was there anyway and I headed straight to the roadway apologising to the priest for my sudden change of heart. If Novius was knocking down that door I needed to be there. I bit my lip in anger. I'd forgotten the bigger duck offering and Vulcan was sending me confusing messages now in anger, playing with me for my lack of devotion and sacrifices. I'd better sort that as soon as possible.

By fortune I turned the corner of the Hill just as I saw Graccus and Novius, with Manius, about to knock on the door to the second domus. Maybe I was wrong and Vulcan was truly on my side and I was simply misreading the signs? I called out and they turned to me, lifting a hand in acknowledgment and waiting for my arrival. I'd only walked a short part of the Clivus but was already out of breath as I reached them.

"Wait," I said, deep breaths coming sharply. "I've just been told that the man who owns this house is the father of Titus, the dead priest."

Novius and Manius shared a look. "That changes things a bit."

"It certainly does. Let me handle the questions."

VII

We returned to the Temple less than ten minutes after knocking on Titus' father's door; dejected and lost for words. As I reached the entranceway there was a small queue of people waiting to get in and I bypassed the waiting crowd with Novius leading the way by helpfully shoving people aside.

Inside the vast altar room the light was fading but I saw Philus walking towards me with two people I had met previously. "Just a moment," I said as I turned toward the Temple slave, Graccus following me.

The woman with Philus was complaining as we approached, telling the slave that she had friends in the college of priests and would be protesting to them about *this delay*. I got the feeling she did nothing but moan and nothing was ever good enough for her. As I approached Philus stopped and bowed and then looked up at me as I came to stand beside him. Graccus nodded to the boy, a flicker of recognition. The elder lady had been complaining to Philus about how long it had taken to interview the lad as he was clearly competent at writing notes and then asked why there would be no news for a few days. In her terms it was easy to see that the boy was good enough to work as an assistant to a jumped up slave and that complaining loudly would get her what she wanted. Maximus gave me a pained look and then came and stood next to Graccus.

"Hi Graccus. I heard you were working here, I hoped I'd bump into you earlier," he said with a frown. "I was hoping for interview tips."

He looked at Philus with a resigned face.

His words were drowned by the austere voice of his grandmother, for that was what she surely was now that she had removed her shawl and I could see her more clearly. Her thin face was framed by darkened hair which was braided tight to her head. Her eyes were framed in some sort of coloured lotion and her face in some leaden-paste which was deathly white and gave her the appearance of a ghost. It was scary. Her critical gaze fell on me and she looked me up and down with a glower of recognition.

"Get out of my way young man," she said as if I was a turd she'd come across in the street.

Philus nearly died.

He spluttered and whirled to the woman, his voice rising enough to be heard across the large space that fronted the centre of the Temple where we stood.

"Madam!"

He'd saved his most affronted voice for this moment. I was impressed.

"Do you know to whom you speak?" His eyebrows were so high that his forehead seemed to disappear into his hairline.

She was startled by the words and was turning a frowning glance to me with a modicum of concern etched behind her haughty eyes as she looked me up and down.

I saw Graccus nudge the boy as I placed my features into the best statue-like expression that I could produce as I tried to hold back laughter.

"Well..." she was instantly on her guard, her gaze now trying to understand who I was.

She looked at Novius, a burly ex-soldier who had turned his face to one of anger and distaste as he crossed his large arms over his expansive chest, then to Graccus, who was half-smiling but trying to fix his face. It wasn't working. And then back to myself. She was flapping now, mouth opening and closing with no noise coming from her throat.

I bowed. She gaped. I turned to her grandson and bowed to him.

"Secundus Sulpicius Merenda," I said as I put my hand out to the boy. "How was your interview?"

I heard a gasp and saw that the old lady had realised just whose son I was and in her startled state had almost fainted, Philus gripping her as she became unsteady on her feet. As he did so he got a handful of her breast, which caused her to stifle a further gasp and stare at him as if he was attacking her like Sextus Tarquinius in his rape of Lucretia. She shrugged him off with more strength than I'd give her credit and her head shook violently as she tried to recover her wits, her eyes wide and staring as she sucked in great gasps of air.

"Answer your betters. Don't stand there like a wet fish," she said urgently to Maximus who was doing his best not to laugh.

He glanced to Philus before he answered my question. "I will know within the week," he said. Philus turning a downcast mouth to the older lady and then back to me.

I felt I needed to defend him, although the bastard had sold me out to Graccus only a day earlier when he'd suggested I'd never be returning. "Philus is correct Maximus, there are always more people to see and review and these things take time. But why not come in tomorrow and spend the day here with Graccus," I turned to my friend who was eagerly nodding. "See if you like it here and if you feel you will fit in."

I turned back to Philus and asked him "If that is acceptable to our head man," I said, giving him a status far above his standing.

The grandmother stared at him with a shocked expression. In her view now she had not only insulted the Quaestores son, but she had misunderstood Philus' status in the Temple and been dismissive toward him as well. She brushed at her clothes and her eyes showed how difficult she was suddenly finding the situation.

"It will do." Philus played it well as he spoke the words slowly and lifted his chin. "If you wish it to be so, Master."

"Then it is done." I turned to Maximus. "We get here early. Don't be late."

I thanked his grandmother with a curt nod and strode off, my small retinue following.

I heard her whisper to Maximus. "You know he was chosen by Minerva. The ladies at the shrine told me so, wait till I tell them we met him and he's offered to see you tomorrow."

****

We reached my room to see the door open wide. Inside a dirt-covered lout was drinking my best wine, the lock picked and the straggle-haired man standing looking out of the window. He wore a tunic ripped in several places and he looked like he'd been through the Cloaca Maximus headfirst, and he smelled as if he had too.

"Who the fuck..." I said as he turned to face us. My brows rose and I uttered his name in shock, "Scavolo, what are you doing here, they said you had the shits?"

The ex-centurion turned and sat in my chair, sighing heavily.

"Did you really think I had the shits?" His gesture suggested we were all dim-witted fools as we exclaimed that we had all accepted he was ill. "This case needs brains" he tapped his head to show that he had them locked in his skull and was using them whilst we were all lacking in this area as if Coalemus had taken our wits.

It was my turn to sigh, which made his lip curl, but it did ring a bell in my mind. I'd just thought of something and needed to see the family of Brocchus, the lad who had been freed from almost certain death by my actions and the fortune of Minerva and Janus.

"Whilst you've been strutting around that Temple like you own the place I've been looking for signs of the missing silver" continued Scavolo. My ears pricked up at this. "Your father had a tip-off that someone in the Subura had a lot of silver to sell. He asked me to check it out. It was better everyone thought I was sick so nobody would ask where I was."

I gaped angrily.

Yet again my father had no faith in my abilities and preferred to keep me out of the loop on important matters related to the case. It also appeared that he had spies in the Subura too, or at least people who would happily sell their tales for a few coins or a sack of grain. His phrase about paying the plebs hit me once again. He was clearly smarter than I gave him credit for all these years. Scavolo ignored my indignant glare and continued to tell his story as Novius dropped a cup on the table and his boss poured him a drink from my amphora, which he was holding as if it was a new-born babe. I was fuming and looked to Graccus, who completely misread my movements and ran to get me a cup. On his return he almost wrestled the amphora from Scavolo, who had re-filled his own before relinquishing it.

"I disguised myself and went off with a handful of copper and silver coins to see what I could find. After two or three useless taverns I found someone who thought he knew about a consignment of silver that was for sale. He was being shifty and kept his head down. I didn't know him, but he seemed legitimate as he seemed to have some idea of the volume of silver that was stolen." I glanced to Graccus who pointedly kept his face on Scavolo. "I said I might know a buyer if it was not marked and could easily be transported. He was suspicious because of my looks so I flashed a handful of silver which seemed to win him over. It took me a jug of wine to convince him that I was in the pay of a landowner from Veii who had the funds."

He looked to Novius who was nodding as the nearest Etruscan town was a continued threat to the Roman state and had supported the kings at the time of the creation of the Republic, both men having fought them several times. To emphasise this Scavolo took a heavy bronze ring with a Rearing Bull adorned at its centre from his finger, a symbol of Veii, and placed it on the table. I hadn't looked at him closely due to the smell and general appearance, but I now realised that he had a silver necklace with the goddess Juno Regina pressed into its heart.

I was impressed, he had certainly gone to some effort to prepare and I felt abashed for not giving him any credit either. I also wondered if the glance to Novius showed that they shared some recollection of how he came about these precious objects. Were they conquests from a fight against the Veintes? He was still talking so I paid closer attention.

"He suggested he was going to speak to his boss and see what price could be agreed and I said I'd come back tomorrow at the same hour. He seemed happy with that so I left and then followed him because the prick came straight out and headed up the Esquiline without even looking over his shoulder and without a guard."

Novius and Scavolo were both rolling their eyes at this behaviour. I made a note as I had not considered that I was now known as investigating this case and someone with something to hide could easily be following me.

"I tracked him for a while and it was clear he had no idea he was being followed. I know the roads and so managed to get ahead at a few turns and then let him pass, just in case he was smarter than I thought, but it didn't seem so. He didn't see me."

Graccus poured me a drink and I lifted my head to tell him to fill my cup to the top, Novius quickly downing the remains in his own vessel and holding it out again. I glared at Graccus who slopped out the smallest amount he could manage as the larger man kept flicking his chin to suggest he keep pouring.

"I know those gangs up there" he said with a glance to his man, who was now sipping at his own refreshed cup. "So I guessed where he was heading. I ran ahead and managed to find my way into the garden of that bastard Marcus Curtius." He was looking to Novius again, this time shaking his head and letting out a long breath. I'd never heard of him but guessed that if these two man-mountains thought he was a tough bastard, then he was. "Anyway, it took a bit of doing to get close enough to hear what was being said, one of his dogs got my dagger, and I thanked the gods that I hadn't been found."

It was a statement made quickly but I gaped that he'd had to fight a guard dog and had won.

"I was lying in a shithole, the water of the latrine running beside me."

It smelled like he wasn't lying that was for sure and I wrinkled my nose. "The man I met in the tavern was talking about the silver and I struggled to hear as they were on the other side of the wall so I crept closer. I overheard them say that they'd bring one ingot of silver and then arrange to meet at the old burial grounds on the road out of the Viminal to Praeneste. But then I heard them say that they needed to get someone to follow me so that they could set a trap and ambush me on the way from Veii with the funds, they wanted gold. The bastards were trying to set up a trap. They don't have the ingots but they were trying to get someone to stump up gold and then ambush them."

He was shaking his head.

"Wasted my fucking time."

That was his final comment as he slurped at my wine and then held it out for another re-fill which Graccus did far too quickly for my liking.

"There is one thing that is troubling about your tale though," I said with a glum expression. He raised his eyes at this and held me with a questioning look. "Someone knows that a lot of silver was taken. That surely means that it won't be long before Fusus is implicated."

"Fuck!" said Scavolo.

I'd become more and more tense as he'd spoken. So the thieves had not been found after all and his brains were not as clever as he had thought. "Well, you're not going to believe this," I said as I lifted my cup and spilled a good portion from my over-filled vessel on my lap. "We had a story that one of the slaves at a house on the Clivus Capitolinus has been spreading a tale for a few days that his Master knew about the silver being in the Temple." I tried to sip the wine dramatically without spilling it and failed as it dripped down my chin. "Novius, Graccus, Manius and I visited the house just now and it turns out the house is owned by the father of the dead priest."

This brought raised eyebrows.

"Really?" the question was to Novius who was confirming with a gesture and then held his cup out once more. The amphora was almost empty now for sure based on the rate these bastards were downing my wine.

"And" I added. "The slaves told us that their Master is missing and they've not seen him since the night of the fire at the Temple."

****

Fusus was angry, the type of anger which churns and brews quietly. You couldn't see it but there were signs that it was waiting to erupt like a volcano smoking with the fire of Vulcan within. He'd called this meeting with us at his home on the lower slopes of the Oppian Hill in the Carinae district as soon as he'd been informed of the disappearance of Titus' father. I'd pulled Graccus aside as we left the Temple and explained what I needed him to do, asking him to visit the Brocchus family and ask for their assistance. His eyes widened at what I asked and he'd set off to complete his task quickly.

The home of Fusus was a grand affair sat within large rectangular walls. It was growing dark as we arrived, with a full retinue of Temple guards slogging down one hill and back up the next, in tow, with my father being carried and Scavolo and I marching at his rear. Several large dogs on chains were man-handled away as we were allowed in and I saw, in the half-light, a series of well-designed gardens, flowers and shrubs which were interspersed with painted statues that stretched as far as the eye could see. One such figure, of a nymph, was peeking from a bush next to a pool and it caught my eye with its playful look. I smiled in return before realising I was responding to a stone object and turned my face back to that which I'd been told I must maintain as Fusus was a stickler for the traditional ways.

The room we entered was magnificent. There was a high ceiling with several doorways along the back wall where tapestries of hunting scenes and images of the Trojan War fell from iron bars which were fixed above the windows and doorways. It was a show of wealth, and the fact that he could lose the lot was not lost on any of us. The retinue were shown to a private kitchen to await the close of our meeting, only myself, my father and Scavolo had been admitted to this inner sanctum.

Fusus sat on an ebony wood Stella, large and red-cushioned. The legs were carved like those of a gryphon or a lion and the feet were edged in gold leaf. It was as magnificent as his room and he reminded me of a king on his throne. I turned this thought away quickly as such things could easily get me and my family into trouble if I mentioned it. Inlaid tables of multi-coloured marble were laid at the sides as four chairs were placed into a square, large iron braziers filled with hot stones and wood blazed to keep the room warm as the night air was now beginning to send a chill into the room from the door through which we had entered. A Nubian slave, I'd not seen many in Rome, pulled a tapestry across the doorway as we sat, my father to the *king's* right hand side, Scavolo to his left and I was left with a hard wooden chair with a thin cushion on which I sat once my elders had seated. I noted that Scavolo sat before me and Fusus didn't comment, so much for traditions. Wine was offered, watered and handed out by the Nubian as well as a pale Gallic female slave with bright red hair. She was very pretty but I tried not to stare.

"Tell me what this means?" Fusus had asked once my father had explained the bare bones of our investigations to date and Scavolo had expanded on what we knew so far. He'd reached the part where the father of the dead priest had entered the story and that his men had searched the house to find it almost empty of all furniture and no sign of any piles of stolen metal. The slave at the house seemed to know nothing but Scavolo had taken him, and one other, from the house and detained them in the cellar at the temple of Jupiter in case a night on a cold floor would help to jog their memories.

"We still have some investigating to do to understand..." Scavolo continued the story as I watched the power play between the men in the room. My father had started, as usual, and Scavolo was taking control of the detail. Also as usual. But Fusus was a man in a hurry and interrupted frequently, wanting to cut to the chase and dismissing Scavolo's words by talking over him. It was irritating but I'd been given clear instructions to keep my opinions to myself and keep my face fixed and my emotions in check.

"Surely the fact that the man is missing suggests the bastard was involved in stealing my ingots." His face told us that he was convinced of this fact and we would be hard pushed to have his mind changed.

"It may be true Agrippa Furius Fusus," Scavolo was keeping it formal "but we have no evidence to this fact at the moment. It could be simple coincidence that..."

"The bastards run!" he exclaimed in exasperation. "That's evidence enough."

It was Brocchus' trial all over again.

"Not necessarily," said my father's man remaining calm under the pressure of our patron. I was impressed. "Why would he leave the house intact? Why not sell it?"

"He doesn't need to sell that pile of shit now he's got my ingots."

I was enjoying this as Scavolo tried his best to maintain his poise but was struggling under the incessant interruptions. It was a close run thing and I could detect his eyebrows twitching constantly as he braved the tirade.

"That may be the case but my experience tells me that we can't put all of our eggs into one basket lest we drop it and smash the lot."

It was well said, a phrase I'd not heard before but thought I'd use myself as it sounded very philosophical, very Greek, which was all the rage.

"I have men out asking for news of his leaving the city, or anyone who may have spotted him in recent days, to see what he was doing, who he met, where he went." Fusus was nodding slowly at this news but his deep furrowed brows suggested he still wasn't too happy.

"He could have left the city by now," he said as the anger started to bubble to the surface once again.

"No large groups of carts or horses have been seen leaving since the fire."

Fusus still didn't seem appeased. "So you have no news. Nothing of any value at least."

His assassination of our two days of efforts was complete and Scavolo sat and looked to my father for help.

"These things take time Agrippa." He was the only man in the room to have the relationship to be on first name terms. "We have moved forward and found so many things. The fact that the man was murdered and didn't die defending the Temple." A glance from Fusus was thrown to me. "The stories from the Temple priests that the dead man had visions of fires and was the only man sleeping at the Temple on the night of the fire whilst they were away."

"They should be hung for that neglect of their god-given duty, bastards. Athitatus needs stripping from his role," came the cold-hearted reply. Again the elder statesman's eyes found their way to mine.

"They could still hold the key to this as one of them was surely in collusion with the thieves. It could be any one of them."

"Flog the lot of them!" Fusus exclaimed with a hard stare at Scavolo who was his statue-like best. "Whip the answer from them, the bastards!"

"If only I could," said Scavolo in response. Fusus grunted at this, knowing that such an act was never going to be allowed but certain that Scavolo would do it in a heartbeat if it were in his power to do so.

My father continued. "And Maelius," he was shaking his head and I saw Fusus scowl at the mention of his name. "We still don't know what part he played in this, if any. But his hanging around and speaking on behalf of the priests doesn't sit right with me. You know as well as I that he is trying to build a political campaign for next year's elections."

"He'll be Consul over my dead body," snapped Fusus.

My father agreed vociferously and said, "Barbatus will never let it happen." I didn't know what they meant but I did know that Titus Quinctius Capitolinus Barbatus, a six times Consul and a man who favoured patrician rule without any input from the plebs was one of Fusus' patrons and a very senior man in Rome. My father continued. "And Scavolo's man told us that there is no bad word against Maelius from anyone at the Temple or the local roads. He continues to import grain from Etruria."

"Can we search Maelius' house?"

My father shook his head. "We would need evidence, as it says in the Twelve Tables. It could be as costly to accuse him now as losing all of the ingots over again. The news from Ostia is just as confusing, nobody has any information about any large deliveries in the past week beyond the usual supplies, most of which remain in the port. Gaius' men have checked all the documents and they are all in order."

This comment was followed by a deep glare from Fusus.

The information from Ostia was something I'd heard for the first time only minutes before as Scavolo had rattled through the updates, mentioning that his men had crawled across the port searching for any sign of high value metals or additional grain purchases, as well as checking with the contractors to see if he had heard anything whatsoever of the theft. It was a closed slate, there seemed to be nothing which gave a clear direction to this mystery.

Fusus turned to me. "You have very little to say." It was almost an accusation, as if I'd done nothing at all to help this investigation. "Has the goddess given up her patronage?"

It was out of his mouth before I could reply and my mouth opened and dropped for a second before I snapped it shut, but it was too late, he'd seen my reaction to his words.

My father closed his eyes for a briefest heartbeat and I saw his jaw tense.

Scavolo stared so hard at the wall that I thought the power of his mind might push it over.

I rallied. "The gods move in ways that I don't understand Agrippa Furius Fusus," I said as I fixed him with my best patrician smile. I wasn't going to let this pompous bastard look down his nose at me regardless of the social standing and power he held over all of us, although I knew in that moment just how fickle the patron-client system was. A whiff of success and everyone was your friend, a hint of disaster and you were left to swing like a thief at the end of a rope.

"When the ingots were taken everyone believed the priest had died trying to defend the Temple and its contents. I've disproved that theory." I'd seen those glances to me as Scavolo had explained all the searching and answers we'd found and I was going to play on them as much as I could. "We know that the priests' stories don't add up. Someone is lying or maybe two or three of them are working together for some reason. Breaking the shell of this nut is going to be tougher than it seems."

I lifted my hand as I could see he was about to retort.

"We all know that time is critical, sir," I replied to what I expected him to say and his lip curled into a scowl as I cut him off. "The priest, Titus, was seen staggering up and down the road each night, chanting and praying into the dark hours." Scavolo turned to me at this, I hadn't told him yet as I hadn't had time to do so. I was pleased he looked surprised, he wasn't the only one to be using his brain to solve this case. "What if he was staggering under the weight of an ingot or two?" this raised eyebrows around the room. "I've walked the Vicus Jugarius to search for places that a man could hide a pile of stolen silver if he moved them one or two at a time, but I only started on this line of investigation late this afternoon and then we learned that Titus' father had disappeared so I had to stop searching, but I will be back at it before dawn for certain."

Fusus sat forward at this and I cut him off again with another raised hand. My father's face twisted at the nature of my hand gesture, stopping the great man Fusus from interrupting could be seen at the least as rude and at the worst as disrespectful. I carried on, intent on trying to get us out of the room with at least a hint of respectability and support for future actions from the great man.

"Further to this."

Scavolo was truly engaged now and his brows creased, Fusus was captured too, I could tell by his shrewd eyes as he lifted his chin and looked down his nose at me.

"The Flamen has clearly lied to us. He told us that Titus had requested the visit to Ostia, but Caelius and Regicius, two of the priests, told me that it was the Flamen who said they should go as only he had the power to agree to the trip. And then it was suggested that Titus had written to the priests at Ostia for advice. That is unlikely as only the Flamen can request such information, so why would he lie to us? What purpose does it serve?" I rubbed my lower lip as I then added, "I have not had a chance to speak to the Flamen today to ask these questions and I also want to ask why they walked through the night to return to the temple. It seems a strange decision to do so even if they did wish to complete their morning ceremony. Titus could have done this on his own, or more of them could have stayed behind to guard your silver. There are too many parts to this mystery that are either basic errors or calculated plans."

Fusus narrowed his eyes and glanced to my father as my points were well made.

"And one more thing has been worrying me." It had just dropped into my thoughts and I spoke slowly as I asked. "Who signed for the silver on the last day? Athitatus was away if all of the stories we have heard are correct. Did Titus sign for the delivery?"

"It should have been the Flamen," said the *great man* with a glare at Scavolo as if he had some knowledge of this when we knew nothing of the secret movements of precious ingots until after they had been taken. Then he started to curl his lip and his eyes narrowed as he caught a hint of what I had suggested. "He has broken the contract," he beamed with an appraising look to me. My father's face started to brighten and Scavolo seemed happy for the briefest moment.

"If the sign is of the Flamen then yes, if not then the person who allowed another to sign the contract is at fault," it brought stern faces back to them all. "It is written in the Twelve Tables..." I started to explain.

"I know what the fucking law says," he was on his feet and calling for his son as he replied, his words said without malice but spoken, nonetheless.

His outburst gave me another brief moment of understanding of what it was like to be beholden to a man like Fusus, who would praise you one moment and spit at you the next. I looked briefly to my father who had remained as calm as possible through the audience with his patron and who still had the haunted look of a man awaiting a sentence to be passed on him.

After a moment the Nubian slave returned with Fusus' son. The Gallic slave girl topped up my cup, Scavolo leering at her as she filled his. The son, Albinus, had a hard face which gave me the impression he'd learned to treat those of lower status with the same disdain as his father. He carried the wax tablet in his hand as he approached, it was the family copy of the delivery contract. He was a big lad of a few years my senior. His face was the same as his fathers but his build was much larger, with thighs that suggested he rode daily and arms which evidenced many hours of training. I'd seen him before some years ago and he had put on muscle and size since that time. He gave me a cold look as he entered and then stood watching quietly and calmly as he handed the tablet to his father. I noted how good he was with creating a stoic persona, standing motionless but alert as Fusus read through the details he'd been given. I cursed my pathetic training and teacher.

"Here," Fusus handed the document to my father who inspected it with an intense expression. The Nubian and the girl handed out nibbles once more, which I took quickly, my belly suddenly feeling very empty. My father then handed me the contract, Scavolo stretching his neck to see over my shoulder.

I looked at the mark in the wax and the impression of the Flamen's ring beside it. "They are the same mark," I said slowly. "So the temple is at fault and Athitatus must have left his ring with Titus when the priests went to Ostia." This seemed to relax the tension in the room slightly as Fusus sat back and gulped down his wine, nodding to his son who smiled in response. "Although the temple is in ruins so they hold nothing of any value except the iron ingots that were removed after the fire," I added to dampen their spirits. Fusus was glaring at Scavolo now, thoughts of whipping the head priest plainly at the front of his mind.

"They have that house on the Clivus Capitolinus," said the son with evident glee at the thought of owning such a prestigious home. "That has to be worth something."

The statement of intent was clear and Fusus turned a shrewd eye to me before rotating his gaze slowly to my father.

"You are right, and it can be held as surety. But we must proceed with caution, sir." I said quietly but firmly. "We haven't had a chance to find any link between the Flamen and Titus' father yet. That could be vital to this case. What if they were plotting this between them? It would take several men some time to move those ingots or one or two men a few days, or nights," I added quickly.

The group inclined their heads in understanding.

"Remember Scavolo, you told me that a petition for funds to rebuild the Temple was requested and turned down." Scavolo grunted agreement. "Well I heard today from the priests that a *secret benefactor* has offered the funds to replace the roof. What if this is an elaborate plan to rebuild the Temple which went wrong?" I turned to Fusus and his son. "If we can find a link between the Flamen, this benefactor and the father of the dead man you would have a claim against the benefactor as well as the Flamen. But" my voice rose as I spoke and I could see Fusus and his son share a glance, "We cannot let anyone know this information yet, as to do so could close the door and see them go to ground and we'll never find a link." I nodded to the document, which was now back in the hands of Albinus and I asked him, "Did you see the man who signed it on the last delivery? Were all the ingots in the vault?"

The son nodded. "It was the Flamen. Well I assumed it was him, they all wear those cloaks and we arrived at dusk as we had agreed. It was dark by the time we left. As soon as I saw the ring I was happy to accept it was him and he pressed it into the contract and made his mark. It was clearly a ruse set up to trick us." He was shaking his head. "And yes, the ingots were there, piled up where we left them. It took three of the men about half an hour to get the last lot inside so I had plenty of time to see it, even though it was dark it was definitely there."

He was looking to his father who was nodding. I nodded too, thinking that my calculations of how long it would take five men to move the ingots wasn't far from the truth.

"Did you pile them on top of each other or in a new stack?"

He looked at me with a surprised face. "We kept them in three separate stacks so I could check them all. That is what I was told was agreed?" His father gave a deep frown which suggested that no such agreement was made.

"It was what I was told when we arrived at the Temple on the first night, to keep them in separate stacks so we could see the full delivery had been made and nothing moved."

"Makes sense," I said, although in truth it should have been included in the agreement. "In doing so you can see they are there and nothings been moved."

He nodded but I knew as did everyone in the room that the ingots from the centre could easily have been moved out and the shape maintained. Fusus turned a scowl to his son. I remembered that the body of Titus had been wearing a thick cloak and it had seemed odd when I had seen it but now I saw that any priest wearing a hood in the dark looked the same. Another memory flashed in my mind about the ring.

"Wait," I said looking up suddenly. "The Flamen was wearing his ring when I visited the Temple two days later. I saw it clearly. Did he recover it from the body of Titus? Was Titus wearing the ring when you recovered his body? Athitatus told us that the body was too hot to approach when they returned to the Temple." I had turned to Scavolo.

"Not that I know of, but I will check with Novius."

"Then there is something here." I was rubbing my chin again and looking to my father as I spoke. "How did he have the ring if it was Titus that signed for the delivery and the Flamen was away until after the fire, by which time Titus was dead?"

My question flew to raised eyebrows. "Bastard!" It was Fusus, anger flaring once again. "I'll have his balls."

He was on his feet.

"No," I said, a little too loudly and bringing his face to mine. "We cannot push too hard without proof. He might have gotten it from the body." Scavolo grunted agreement as I looked to him. "We need to be sure. If he knows we know about the ring, then he and his accomplices could move the ingots and we'll never see them again. We need to know how he and Titus' father are linked to this mystery." We were jumping to the conclusion that they are working together, which worried me. "It would be too easy for them to bury the ingots and leave them for years if they needed to."

My argument made sense and Fusus turned creased brows from me to my father, evidently considering everything despite his emotional outbursts.

"Secundus is correct. In legal terms if we accuse him too soon he could appeal against it and without iron-clad proof he could get away. The law says that in any dispute without complete agreement the negative view will prevail. We must find a link between him and this man, the priest Titus' father, although we must also not make the assumption that they are working together. It could as easily have been the Flamen working with Titus and then killing him or them both to keep the ingots for himself."

"We need to put a watch on the Temple day and night," I said to Scavolo. He agreed, Fusus nodding too, though his face was a picture of frustration and anger. His son stared at me with a cold, calculating, gaze.

The room turned sombre for a moment before Scavolo spoke to ease the silence.

"His father is called Flavius Aetius. I had it checked before we came. He has that house on the Clivus from his wife, who died of the plague a few years ago. He was a tenant farmer until recently when he sold his farm and now he lives a quiet life overlooking the Temple. Nobody seems to know much about him. Softly spoken, very quiet. He is a private citizen of no repute." Scavolo's words emphasised that we knew nothing of the man and the news brought glum expressions.

Fusus scowled at this. "So Merenda," it was back to formal names which held no suggestion of friendship. "What do we do next?"

His question was directed to my father, whose stoic face at the barb was magnificently passive. I made a note to myself that I really must spend time in front of my mother's bronze mirror perfecting this look.

"Secundus is leading the investigation. He seems to have a good handle on what is required, and with Gaius at his side I am sure we will resolve this situation favourably." He was turning his head to me.

I tried to look non-plussed, as if solving incredibly complex mysteries which would return wealth to everyone in the room were an everyday occurrence. Then I realised they all expected me to explain what I was going to do next and my jaw slackened.

Scavolo let out a slow breath as his lips tensed.

My father looked over my shoulder but his brows creased in exasperation for a second and Fusus' son sneered at my slack-jawed appearance, prick.

I gathered my thoughts. "We must not put all our eggs in one basket," I started. I was impressed with myself and glanced to Scavolo, who ignored my use of his phrase. "We must check out who the silent benefactor is. If it is Maelius then we must explore any links between him, this man Flavius Aetius and the Flamen. If he is linked and using your stolen silver to give him credibility for a political campaign as I believe you are thinking," at which I looked to my father. "Then we must tread carefully so that we trap all of them at the same time. I will continue to look for places where these men could have taken the ingots in the days before the fire and on the night of the fire. It cannot be far by my calculations if that is what they have done. We will close the net around our fish and haul them in once we have more clarity of the links between them."

Fusus turned to me, then to my father as we awaited his judgement of my words.

"The boy clearly has a gift." It was high praise.

"Make sure he doesn't fuck it up."

I turned to Scavolo, he grinned.

VIII

I'd brooded all night and woken with a heavy feeling that the case was running away from me. Fusus' words rang in my ears like the hammer of Vulcan smashing against his anvil. Thoughts were racing through my mind and I couldn't shake them away. The link between the silent benefactor and the Temple, in truth we hadn't asked so didn't know who it was, troubled me. I wrote that down. It was as convenient as Athitatus being in Ostia when the fire destroyed the Vulcanal. I remembered that I needed to ask him why he was travelling in the dark, and hurrying back to the Temple, what did he know that made him so angry he was whipping the priests? I wrote that too. I was worried that just as I believed I was making good headway a fog had descended to turn me off the path I was following. Part of me wanted to set Graccus onto one path and then I could pursue another, but I realised I didn't trust him enough to let him loose as Scavolo's dismissive words still hung over him like a dark raincloud. The gossiping to Milo was also playing on my mind. Had it set rumours galloping like a herd of mad horses which would, ultimately, cause the thieves to go to ground until the searching calmed down. They'd certainly planned it well so far if the lack of evidence was anything to go by. It was a dilemma and I saw Fusus telling me I'd fucked it up as I closed my eyes momentarily. Had I upset Vulcan again in some way? The twists and changes were starting to become too difficult to understand and put into a logical order. I didn't like it, something wasn't right but the gods were choosing to throw a blanket over it and cover everything from my sight.

I'd dressed, eaten a small breakfast of fruit and cheese and strode to the Temple at first light deep in thought. Micus followed at my heels carrying my things as silently as a shadow as he detected my dark mood. I made a detour past the boarded house and stood in the street reviewing its position once again. Fusus' son's delight at the opportunity to own a town house on the Clivus had reawakened my thoughts about the dwelling where I now stood. A Gallic looking slave was tending the garden, his fair hair and sun-browned skin giving him away as such. I called to him and he moved across slowly suspicions aroused by my friendly face but obviously unsure of my intentions as he carried his hoe across with him and remained safe a few steps behind his mistress's fence. He looked me up and down and then to Micus at my heel. I was clearly someone of importance by the look of my clothes and Micus' expensive sandals, which I saw him look at.

"Is the mistress home?" I asked with a finger pointing to the flag. "I might have an interest."

"She's abed, Master," he said with a bow and with a strange lilt to his voice which showed his heritage. "Can you come by later? She rises late now she has..." his words cut off and he glanced to the door behind him. "Now she has no husband," he said quickly.

I understood his fears and was about to say so when the door cracked open and a young girl looked out, her Gallic flame-coloured hair tied into a single knot on her head. "Go back Flora," called the gardener, it isn't the man with the eggs." He turned back to us. "The delivery is late and my daughter does the cooking," he explained.

I nodded. "Shall I come back in two hours, three?" he nodded. "Three then," I said as it was still early and I wished to give the lady some time to dress and prepare the house, but not too much as an untidy house may be easier to shake my head at and suggest it would cost me a lot to repair or at least clean. I turned and was about to leave when I thought of something. "Is she moving to the country?"

It was a question which would help me frame any price discussions as houses in the country were cheaper and I might use this information to negotiate the price down a bit.

"She's moving to Fidenae," he said quickly. "A new start, She has family there."

It seemed like a practised answer, short and curt and I wondered how many people he'd had to tell. Maybe there were a few others interested. I might have to act quickly.

I was nodding and looking at the vegetable plot, some healthy looking crops. "Will you be staying when she leaves?" I was wondering if the slaves might be part of the sale as he was clearly good with the gardens.

"No. We are all going together," he said indignantly and I wondered if I'd accused him of slavery when he was, in fact, a freedman.

Sensing his darkening mood I thanked him hurriedly and moved on, quite pleased with myself despite the fact that I might have upset him. The house really was on a good plot and if I could get a good price I felt sure that my father would pay, after all I'd gained him a decent dowry for Fabia as well as relieved him of the cost of adding stock to my new farm following the payment of the ruby I'd received from Fucilla. My mood darkened, though, as I considered that we may not have any future if I couldn't get this case resolved soon. Fusus wouldn't wait forever, and it sounded like vultures were already starting to get a sniff of a meal from this situation if Scavolo's trip through the latrines was anything to go by.

Micus asked me about the house as we walked up the Jugarius and came to the Vulcanal. I explained that it was just something I was considering and said it looked like a good place. I decided I better get a goat for Vulcan or a lamb as my fortunes were truly starting to turn, but then worried about the cost and bit at my thumb nail until it started to bleed. Idiot.

I was surprised to see several people were standing and chattering animatedly at the Temple as we approached. I wondered what had happened to bring such a crowd out so early and strode over purposefully. Athitatus was arguing with a tall, bearded, man. Nesta, Hector and Caelius stood like guards, arms crossed, at his side. The stranger seemed non-plussed by the ensuing argument and at his shoulder were two other men, one short and strongly built and a blonde-haired fellow with a missing ear and a scar down the side of his face which suggested he was an ex-soldier or at least had been lucky that whatever hit him didn't remove his head from his shoulders. It gave me a shiver just to look at him and I couldn't stop staring until he turned in our direction and I instantly turned my face towards the Flamen to avoid his glare.

I joined the crowd to listen and get an understanding of what was happening, although I was also careful to tuck my purse away just in case the pickpockets were hanging around. Micus stood beside me with a frown and started to edge close to me, maybe that scar and missing ear was affecting him too. He tugged at my elbow and I turned to him.

"Master," he whispered. I bent to his height. "I could find out more about the house if you want me to? Maybe what price they want or what debts they have?" His face was alight at having something to do.

I gave him a short moment as I chewed my lip before acknowledging his request.

"Be very careful. I don't want people to know you are trying to find out information. Go to that cloth shop, tell them your Master walked past and might be interested in a new tunic or a gift for his lover, and get some prices, but see if they know anything about the house. And see if anyone has any stories about the priest walking the roads at night or saw anyone with a cart or heavy sacks late at night. Thank you, good thinking," I said to his beaming face. The lad was turning into a proper little spy and I watched him circle slowly on the other side of the Temple before he turned back along the Jugarius.

I returned to the continuing discussion in front of me and listened for a further few moments. There seemed to be a lengthy debate related to slates, hands waving at them and talk of expensive timber, and I soon remembered that Athitatus had told me he was meeting a building contractor today and so I started to lose interest in what seemed to be haggling about costs and prices. I people-watched for a while but stopped listening soon after and wandered back to the Lotus Tree, seeing further devotions of flowers and fruit had been laid at the base of the sacred object. I looked to the vegetable patch where I'd started to dig the previous day and saw that my pathetic attempts to dig for silver had been smoothed over. The rows of vegetables reminded me of the house along the road and I was just considering if I would change the layout of the garden as a voice startled me and made me jump.

"Secundus," he was on first name terms as he greeted me. I turned to Caelius, his lip curling to a smile at my expression of welcome.

I nodded. "Tell me," I inclined my head towards the vegetables which ran along a straight furrow and would be in the full glare of the sun when it reached above the trees which ran intermittently along the edge of the road. "Should they be in full sunlight or mostly shade?" He gave me a quizzical look so I justified the odd question. "I might be buying a small farm," I said to his slight inflection of understanding.

"The real farmer amongst us was Titus, but Hector has taken over his duties since his death. He would know more than I, but I understand that as long as the water is added before or after the full sun, it doesn't matter for a small garden like this."

Hector joined us and nodded a welcome, to which I replied with the same. I showed my understanding to the answer but my interest had moved as something was coming back to my mind. I pointed to the Lotus Tree.

"I see you receive devotions each day." He answered that they did, and often they included fruit, nuts and berries, some of which they burned as offerings to Vulcan and the rest was used for the priests. It was common practice.

"I hear you have a new benefactor who is going to pay for the roof," I said quietly. "He must be a devotee of the temple," I had said it in the hope that they would agree and might give me more information.

They didn't reply.

"Is he a local man?" I had waved towards the Capitol inadvertently and realised I should not have done so and quickly turned my raised hand to scratching my head. They both stepped back a half-step, assuming I had lice and turning down the corners of their mouths in unison.

"We were told it is so, but we don't know who it is. The Flamen is the only man who knows who it is."

I nodded. Then my thoughts sharpened to another question as I could see them closing up again. "Tell me about the berries of the tree. I'm not sure if it was you who said that Titus had sucked on too many Lotus berries. What did you mean?" I was looking to Caelius.

Caelius' mouth turned down once more and his features became guarded, as did those of Hector, but he answered. "The berries can be squeezed to create a juice to make you drowsy and receive visions from Vulcan. It is well known that the Flamens of old used this in times of disaster to see portents and augur the future." He'd turned toward the figure of Athitatus, still arguing with the contractor, as he spoke. "Our Flamen cannot abide the bitterness of the juice and it makes him sick. He often asked Titus to complete this act for him as he seemed to have a special connection with Vulcan when under the influence," it was said with a shake of the head which suggested to me that this was not seen as the proper behaviour for a Flamen. I made a mental note of this fact.

"So Titus was drinking the berry juice because the Flamen asked him to?"

Caelius gave me a fearful glance. I could see in his face that he suddenly felt he'd said too much and turned to Hector as if he had just noticed he was standing behind him or needed his reassurance in some way to continue speaking. I noted a narrowing of the other priests gaze as they faced each other before he replied.

"I think that is something for you to discuss with the Flamen. I do not know why Titus was given this honour, but he enjoyed the berries too much" he shrugged. "Anyway, Secundus Sulpicius," it was more formal now. "What can we do for you today? We have much to do as you can see" his expansive gesture towards the men arguing over the pile of slates and rubble didn't need further explanation.

"Can I ask," I said as I rubbed my chin, thinking through what I'd written on my slate this morning when I'd awoken. "On your return from Ostia, why did you travel in the dark? And why were you in a hurry to return?"

They looked at me as if I'd gone as crazy as Titus. "We must complete the ceremony of light each morning," said Hector. "We were hurrying as we needed to return before dawn. We were making very good time when Nesta twisted his ankle and slowed us. The Flamen was anxious that we might miss the appointed time."

I stood and gave him my best *I don't have a clue what you're talking about* look, to which he replied, head shaking slightly as he did so.

"The priests of Vulcan begin the day by lighting candles to bring in the morning. It has always been that way and will always be so. Vulcan requires the light to turn darkness into day. This is the first time that the ritual has not been completed by the Flamen in centuries." He was now shaking his head and turning towards the figure of Athitatus. A flare of anger crossed his face.

I seized on both their glances in the direction of their leader. "So the Flamen was angry and that is why he was lashing out at you when he arrived? It isn't a good portent for him," I said, watching them closely and thinking of how the people would interpret this information if they knew of it. They flinched at my words and turned cold stares to me.

Caelius spoke this time, rubbing his smooth chin slowly as he did so. "You must speak to the Flamen if you wish to understand his motives. This has been an unlucky year." The words were spoken harshly and followed quickly by the statement "we must get to work," which suggested that I would get no more from them.

"Thank you for your time," I said with a quick smile. "Oh" I raised my hand to my lips. "Might I ask how often Titus and his father met, were they close?"

It was Hector who replied. "Titus and his father did not speak for over a year. They had some fall-out," he shrugged as if he didn't know the reason why or would not tell me. "It is Athitatus that you should speak to regarding this as there was bad feeling between them. We were never told why."

I looked around at the Flamen as both men turned away. Every road was leading me back to the head man.

****

It took some time for the builders to leave and for Athitatus to be alone, during which time I kicked my heels and wandered about the site looking at the newly cleared areas as well as spending a moment or two looking at the vault and tapping different areas of the wall and floor in search of a secret hideaway, of which there was none. I finally caught up with the Flamen after several rebuffed attempts, convinced by this time that he was, successfully, attempting to avoid me.

"Athitatus, I have a few questions that must be answered," I said impatiently as he turned away at my latest approach.

"Can you not see that there is much to do?" His voice was harsh as he jabbed a finger at the remains of the Temple before turning away once again.

"Fusus will be at your throat as much as at mine if we do not find his ingots," I answered sharply whilst trying to be as quiet as I could to avoid the ears of anyone close by.

At this he faced me indignantly. "I've had the messages," was his grim-faced reply. My quizzical face told him that I had no idea what he was speaking of. "Fusus has made it clear that I am to be held personally responsible for the missing ingots if they are not recovered. I got his message just now about the signing of the tablet on the last day of delivery. Forgive me if I don't bow to your feet and do everything you say. I am not sure that you and that fool Scavolo can find his missing silver," he added sharply.

"What message?" He shook his head and turned on his heel dismissively. "Fusus has not sent any message," I called to him as he strode past the vegetable patch. "I was with him yesterday and he said nothing of it."

"Then he is playing you for a fool, Merenda. He will not let up until his ingots are found and you, nor I, will stand in his way. If you cannot find these ingots then..." he was shaking his head with a haunted look in my direction and his teeth ground in his jaw as he stared at me for a silent moment.

His features turned to stone before he strode away. I ran alongside, like a child following his mother, to ask more questions.

"Who brought this message, what did it say?"

He puffed out his cheeks in exasperation at my hounding his footsteps and then stopped dead, turning baleful eyes to mine.

"Fusus wants his ingots, you know that. He is prepared to raise a legal case against me personally, to bring up old scores and family ties to get back what he obviously thinks we," at which he was waving an expansive arm at the Temple "have stolen from him."

We were now close to the guard who nodded at our approach, three or four citizens standing and looking at the burned-out site and chatting quietly. Nesta appeared, with Hector and Caelius close behind, each man lifting their chins to hear what was being said as the Flamen and I were clearly arguing. I tried to hush the old man but he was now bent on telling me exactly what he thought of Fusus and whatever threat he'd implied through this *message*. Marcus and Regicius lifted their heads from their work tilling the soil too as his voice carried to them.

"You can tell Fusus that I have resigned my position at the Temple and sent word to the college of priests to pick a successor. I will not be his scapegoat and I accept no responsibility for the fire and the theft of his silver. There is more to this than we know Merenda, so you need to cast your net wider to catch this fish. We all know that you believe we are implicated, but whoever did this did not have an inside man in the Temple."

He was almost in my face as he finished, chest heaving with anger.

"Fusus has his son digging around in your wake. Watch him, he is a dog who will wag his tail and bite you when you think he is your best friend. Much like his father."

"I know nothing of which you speak Athitatus."

"Then you are more of a fool than Scavolo," he added, looking up to the by-standers, all of whom had turned at his raised voice.

He pulled me aside and continued in a harsh whisper. "You think I have not been searching as you have, Merenda? These ingots cannot have been moved overnight, you know that and so do I. But I am now tainted. I am *unlucky*, it is a *bad year for the Flamen of the Vulcanal*. I know what they say. They move in like crows to peck at my eyes," he said, bringing vivid pictures to my mind.

I now understood what the priests had said when mentioning that they have been searching too.

"I guess as you have from your questions that you believe the ingots cannot have been moved far and that Titus must have been involved." He bit his lip in anger for a second, his eyes dark as I considered how he knew this. "I believe you are right but I know nothing more but I have set things in motion." He started to walk again. I followed like a puppy with my tail between my legs.

"Then share information with me, Athitatus. Work with me to find Titus' killer and find those ingots. It's in both our interests." I tried to keep my voice as low as I could.

He ignored me as we came to the fence and the guard lifted his chin at our approach but his eyes were wary of the continued conversation. The priests turned to one another with raised eyebrows and the guard looked at us with concern at the determined look on the Flamen's face.

He turned to see the priests and by-standers watching intently before he let out a slow, resigned, sigh.

"You are being played like a lyre at the festival, boy. You don't know who you are dealing with and what the consequences of pissing off Fusus will be. Mark my words, he'll find a way to implicate us all in this and it'll end as badly for you as it has for me. I've had to resign my position, been made to look like a fool and been the first Flamen to miss the morning ceremonies in as long as the records have been written. He will drag you under the Tiber and drown you quicker than a snake can strike with its fangs." His face turned to a scowl as he looked me up and down with scorn. "Favoured of the gods," he was shaking his head. "I see no evidence of this in any of your ridiculous questions or actions."

The anger in his words jabbed at me like a bee sting. I was about to reply when Caelius, who had come across, spoke loudly as he pushed across me to face the high priest.

"What do you mean resigned your position?"

Athitatus stared at him, lips tense and brows furrowed.

"You can't just walk away," he was now waving his arms expansively as his voice carried across the temple, "from this. From Vulcan."

Hector joined in as the old priest closed his eyes and I watched his chest rise and fall as he sucked in slow, deep, breaths. "This is typical of you. Give up when the going gets tough, just walk away. You did the same with Titus."

His nostrils flared angrily as he spoke.

Regicius was by his side and stepped across to the Flamen, grabbing his tunic by the shoulder, which Athitatus shrugged off with a strong hand and turned a stern face to his fellow priests. I was shocked at what I'd just heard and stood by as their frustrations boiled over into physical aggression. I stepped back once, allowing Regicius closer access to the Flamen and glanced around to see a small crowd of on-lookers was now gathering, as usual the possibility of a fight causing excitement.

"You really have become unlucky, just like he said. This is all your fault."

I watched intently as Athitatus ground his teeth and his eyes moved from one to another of his priests. I wondered who *he* was, but assumed he meant Titus.

"We should never have gone to Ostia. That was another mistake you made. You should never have listened to Titus. If you weren't so hung up on his moaning and whining..."

Nesta had his hands on his hips as he raised his voice to interject. "Arguing here will do us no good," he reprimanded. "You should have discussed this with us before, Athitatus. Not here and now. Such disrespect to your brothers," he was shaking his head and I could sense the indignation within him as all eyes turned to the watching crowd.

I noticed that Caelius was watching me closely as I glanced from man to man. The old guard was grinning at the fracas and licked his lips in anticipation.

"Let's go to the house and discuss this. The Vulcanal must choose our new priest, not those pricks from the Regia."

It was Caelius who had spoken, his words bringing nods and movement from the priests as they all knew that the College of Priests, under the Pontifex Maximus would put their own man in place if they had the chance. Usually the Vulcanal priests would appoint internally before informing the College of the change and the priest had recognised that they needed to rescue whatever dignity they could gain from this situation. The resignation without a successor was a break in protocol that even I knew of, and I was as far from an expert in these matters as any man in the street. Athitatus looked to me and his chin dipped slowly as he stared malevolently at me, his meaning clear. I could see that he felt I'd tricked him into speaking and revealing his resignation of his position before he'd spoken to his own priests.

I wondered why he would do this? What was going on here? I watched him turn to follow the rest of the group and a thousand thoughts ran through my mind as my vision landed on the stone altar and the dark stain of blood at its foot. I fumbled in my pocket for a coin but came up short. I needed to make a devotion to Vulcan, he was putting me in the right place at the right time. Something was changing in this mystery and I felt my heart skip a beat as my senses started to prick. The priests were arguing, starting to fall apart. Someone would break, someone must know something, and the fact that they had been searching as well surprised me.

I was deep in thought and only realised that the guard had come to my shoulder when he spoke.

"Pricks aren't they?"

I looked to him and noted for the first time that he had thick grey eyebrows which shot out from his brow like twigs on a branch. They moved as he spoke, the leather cap he wore on his head, a relic which he obviously treasured as it was well oiled and shone as if he had polished it every morning for the past twenty years. His dark eyes were warm and friendly, laughter lines emanating right down into his cheeks like ridges on a mountain.

"They have secrets they won't tell, that's for sure," I replied quietly. And then something came to me. "Sorry," I said. "What's your name?"

"Flaccus Havitus, sir," he said standing stiffly to attention as he said it. "Served with your father and Scavolo when they were babes," he grinned broadly, then dropped the look in case I thought it was too familiar.

I ignored it. "How long have you been here, Flaccus?" I asked. "Did you come on the night of the fire?"

"The next morning, sir. I've been here every day since. Keeps me out of mischief with the wife. Nothing much else to do these days," he said with another wide smile.

I placed a hand on his shoulder as my thoughts ran to owing a second devotion to Vulcan as he was surely guiding my actions again. "Tell me what you saw on that first morning, who was here, what was said, did you see or hear anything that was odd?"

I raised a finger to stop him talking as I continued.

"Did you see anyone carrying heavy weighted sacks or boxes at all, anything that might indicate people moving items out of the Temple or," I was looking around the road where we were standing. "Anyone out of place, strangers or men standing in groups who suddenly went into action? You know what I mean?"

He pushed out his bottom lip and nodded as his lids narrowed in thought. "I understand, sir," he replied. "On that first day there were a lot of people hanging around, that's why Scavolo wanted me here, to stop idiots getting in the way." He rubbed at his nose, which held a small wart on the right nostril. "I can't say that I remember any groups of people looking out of place," he added slowly as his eyesight started to range around the vicinity, clearly trying to pick out anything in his mind's eye. "There was a small group of women, I think they live over there as I've seen them several times since," he was jutting a thumb over his shoulder towards a tenement block. "Kids everywhere. Maelius was here with his lot," he was shaking his head. "Usual crowd of locals come to see what was happening. I had to keep a few of the younger ones back as they were searching for anything worth stealing, you know what I mean. Scavolo was here moving things around, getting that body out of the rubble and sorting the movement of the iron. The priests were angry, telling everyone to keep away and the Flamen was shouting at the others."

I was going to ask what he was shouting about when Flaccus added, "there was a small group of men hanging about," his eyes were wide now. "They were over there," he was pointing towards the Via Sacra and they went off towards the Boarium. "Only appeared late at night, just before sundown. Wore heavy cloaks of a dark colour but I couldn't tell what. A man and two youths I'd say, two skinny lads. One was a bit taller than the other, who was quite small and the cloak reached right to the floor. I guessed they were looking for anything in the rubble so kept an eye on them. They did move off with a couple of sacks at one point though but I don't know where they got the sacks from."

This raised my eyebrows. "Show me where they came from," I said as I moved in the direction he'd indicated.

Over by the turn into the Sacra Via were two large houses, one of which was surrounded by a low wall. Two slaves were standing talking, one leaning against the wall and at our approach they scurried off, glancing back over their shoulders as if we had been coming to find out what they were up to.

"They were here-abouts," said the soldier, his head turned left and right. "About here I'd say." He was by the edge of the wall now and looking along the Jugarius and then back towards the Vulcanal.

I leant over the wall as it only rose to the middle of my thigh. The space behind was grassy and muddy, with the low walled barrier continuing from my right to connect to the building. It created a narrow alcove that appeared to have hardly been used by the amount of rubbish and broken pottery shards that filled the floor and the smell of piss. On this side of the building there were no windows until the third floor so nobody would look over this area, a good place to hide something. I stepped over the wall as Flaccus watched me with a frown.

"Does that look like the ground has been flattened?" I asked.

He leant over and nodded. I let out a sharp breath. The space directly up against the wall and out of sight of both the Temple and the block of flats behind appeared to be flattened, as if heavy weights had been placed on the ground. There was flattened grass and several heavy footprints were impressed in what mud remained where the grass had worn away. I'd found where they, because it was clearly more than one man, might have placed the ingots. It may not have been them all, but this was possibly where they'd been hidden to collect and move later.

"Describe these men," I said to Flaccus, whose smiling face had gone, replaced by a serious frown.

IX

Having spent some time with Flaccus and seen no sight of the priest's return I headed back to the Temple of Jupiter deep in thought. Graccus and Maximus were together in my room when I entered, laughing about old times. It seemed they had the same tutor for several lessons and had played various tricks on him which they were recounting. My glower shut them up as I entered.

Graccus wiped his sleeve across his face and Maximus stuck a finger up his nose. Great!

"What's up?" asked the nose-wiping boy. I glanced to Maximus who was wiping his finger on his thigh. "He's alright we can trust him," came the quick reply.

If the fact that Graccus, who I believed spread news of the missing silver to Milo, felt that I could trust Maximus, who was inspecting the finger that had been up his nose, then this suggested I should take every precaution I possibly could with this newcomer. I took a deep breath and welcomed him graciously. I took the small wax tablet with my notes from my pocket and stared at it with the expectation that it would furnish me with new ideas. It didn't. I looked to the cupboard and cursed, remembering that Scavolo and Novius had drained my reserves of wine. I then realised I'd not completed my bargain with Vulcan and still hadn't sacrificed anything which would appease his possible anger. The feeling that things were turning away from me fell on me again and I felt my stomach churn. I had a few copper coins and one Greek silver stater, which was the last I had in my personal allowance for the month. Here I was, a landowner who hadn't even received his land deeds but could lose everything if I couldn't solve this case.

"Maximus," I said as I fumbled in a cupboard drawer for the remaining coins I kept hidden and hoping Scavolo hadn't found them as well. "Could I ask you to get a chicken from Philus please, tell him I need it for a sacrifice to Vulcan. I'm sure he will be able to pick me a suitable bird. Take it to the Vulcanal for me please and wait for one of the priests before you hand it over. Tell the old guard, Flaccus, that I sent you and he'll look after you."

The boy was delighted to do so and skipped out with my coin.

As soon as he'd gone I turned to Graccus. "What did Brocchus and his family have to say?" I'd been thinking about the reason I send him to the horse-faced boy's house as I walked the last slope of the Clivus as it was one loose end which nobody had yet looked into as far as I was aware.

"They wish me to give you greetings and pass on their continued thanks." I waved away the comment. "I asked them if they knew of any recent contracts for the hire of wagons or carts in recent weeks or since the fire." My eyes were wide as I waited. "They said they have heard of nothing."

"Nothing?"

"Nothing!" came the response to my high-pitched reply.

I was convinced that someone would be planning to move the stolen goods and who better to know if such a request had been raised than the wagon business that the Brocchus family owned. They weren't the only ones in Rome but I guessed they would know if anything was happening across the city. Maybe I was wrong.

"And nobody has asked about buying new carts either." It was the other question I'd requested he asked. I sighed. Another closed door. "He did say that the only business with enough wagons or carts that carries goods that he wouldn't know about is the grain business of..."

"Spurius Maelius."

The answer was out of my mouth before he could say it. Of course the man would have his own fleet of wagons which transported the grain he bought in Etruria and sold across the city. I was mindful that I now seemed to have possible links with the Flamen and Spurius Maelius to investigate as well. This case was becoming more and more complex.

"Yes. The Brocchii say he has at least ten Sarracum," he said, meaning the larger four-wheeled wagons.

I considered this. He'd need at least two to move the ingots that had been lost and yet it seemed oddly convenient that he lived so close, had business dealings which might be affected by Fusus' new venture and also seemed to be the only private individual in Rome with enough wagons to move the ingots.

"Would he really get involved in something like this?" Graccus simply shook his head.

I explained what I'd found, the Flamen's outburst, the words of the old guard and the space behind the low wall being a possibility of a storing place for some of the ingots. I rambled for a few minutes about the Flamen and whether he was implicated and looking for a way out by resigning his position so suddenly. I also mentioned that Maelius must somehow be a part of this mystery.

"Whoever did it they could have moved them a few at a time each night but it would still be a big effort to do so and nobody saw anyone except the priest. A single Plaustrum could do it." This was the two-wheeled cart that farmers used to transport their goods. He was right, it would be an easy job to hide it under a cover and walk it out of the city. And yet it would have to be done at night after the deliveries had been made and so the period of time to move the ingots was incredibly small and the options to move them seemed more and more difficult to manage. I rubbed at my chin. Add to this the fact that carts were invariably noisy and fickle and it became more and more difficult to see what had happened and how the stuff had been taken. If the ingots were stored over the wall and moved one or two at a time during the day then Havitus would surely have seen them, and he said that he hadn't seen anything except on that night. My thoughts went back to the old man on the Jugarius, had he seen a single man with a cart or two men carrying sacks or boxes? I'd have to go back and talk to him when I returned to meet his neighbour and view her house.

Graccus was clearly having the same thoughts as me because he continued the conversation.

"If it were the priests, how would they get it out of the strong room and to the low walled area? It would have to be two of them at least, and on the night of the fire there was only one as everyone else was on the return journey from Ostia. And" he continued "we are assuming that Titus was the thief and that his accomplices turned on him. We don't even know if that is the case. On top of this is the fact that two men moving those ingots alone would take a considerable time and if there were more, then someone must have seen them."

He was right. Were we looking at this case from the wrong position. I told him so, which made him smile. "All we know is that the ingots were delivered over three nights and that somehow the majority of them, including all the silver, were gone when the fire happened."

I thought about going back to the temple and digging up all the vegetable plots as it seemed to me that the ingots could not be far away and my efforts to find them had been pathetic.

"If the thieves hid them they could have moved them by now, especially if there were three of them as Havitus says. If they took them one or two at a time during the whole day then it could be done."

He was right again. I was biting my nails once more and chided myself as soon as I realised. It was a bad habit and I needed to stop it. We'd finished exactly where we had started, without much of a clue as to what had happened.

"If we *are* looking at it in the wrong way, what have we not considered?" I rubbed my temple as I stood and walked around the room slowly. "What if Albinus Fusus didn't deliver the ingots and is in allegiance with the priests?"

"Unlikely," Replied my fellow investigator. "That would take some organising with all the men who had transported the ingots, and" his head movements showed he was suggesting it was a bad idea and would be a waste of time spending any energy exploring. "He has nothing to gain from it."

He was right and I knew it. "So, if Flavius Aetius is the thief he cannot have acted alone. Would he really murder his own son? Who are the three men that the guard saw?"

As always I had more questions than answers. My thoughts went back to the offering to Vulcan and I hoped Maximus was acting quickly.

"The three people could simply have been walking past, put their sacks down in a safe place to see what was happening and then carried on once they'd seen enough." I raised my brows at this, it was a good suggestion.

He sniffed and wiped his nose before picking at it. I tried to ignore his actions but watched as he flicked whatever disgusting item he'd found up his nostril onto the floor. It was a good line of thinking for sure but we had absolutely no clues as to who these people were. I explained about the Flamen's ring and the signature, which interested him.

"Maybe the Flamen is sending us down blind alleys. If he is implicated then he could be tricking us to make it seem he is innocent."

"Maybe that *is* why he's resigned," said Graccus. "He's going to slip away and take the ingots with him."

I nodded, it had occurred to me too. "Then he is very clever and very good at acting," I said quietly as my mind churned through all the different aspects of the case. "But how could he move the ingots? And he was on his way back from Ostia when the fire happened."

"Well, that's what the priests said. Has anyone checked that all the priests actually went? We only have their word that they did. If they are all in this together it is an easy lie to tell."

We both stared at each other for a moment. "We need to check that, but I am certain they would have told us if that was not the case. Has Scavolo's man sent a report from Ostia which tells us anything new?"

"I'll check," said Graccus, making a note on a slate.

"What are we missing?" I said to the room at large as I came to a stop by the window. "The main issue we are facing is how the ingots were moved and to where." Graccus agreed. "And why was Titus murdered before they set the temple on fire? It only makes sense if he knew his attackers." I rubbed at my chin again. "I think we need to get Scavolo into a room with Athitatus and ask him some more detailed questions. I hate to say it but the Flamen is starting to look like he is implicated in some way. If Scavolo puts the fear of the gods into him," I shrugged. "He may crack. There's more to these priests than we know and certainly more to this situation than they are letting on."

I had another thought.

"Can you investigate the report from Ostia and if there isn't one which says how many priests went there, can you find out what people know of their visit, what time they arrived, what time they left? Also," I was alive with thoughts now. "Can you check the flats beyond that wall, see if anyone saw anything. Take Micus," I said quickly, "he's good at finding things and people will talk to him. And Maximus, take him too but don't let him know that Fusus lost his ingots." He was nodding his understanding. "And we still don't know what part Maelius might have played in any of this."

Graccus undid his sandals and started to rub his feet, which were filthy. I looked at him more closely. He looked tired. I wondered if he forgot to use his fine imported sand today as I noticed his usual red-faced glow was in short supply. I lifted my chin in contemplation that the old man Athitatus, could hardly lift two slates never mind an armful of bronze or silver and I didn't know if Titus, who was not too dissimilar in age, was weak or strong. "It took five men half an hour to carry those ingots into the temple. I cannot see how two men, especially two old men, could move it. Even if they moved it to that place over the wall, how did they transport it and where to?"

We both had more questions than answers and the fact that the priest had suggested he had started his own investigation because he felt I was incompetent was starting to annoy me as it pecked at my brain like the crows that Athitatus had mentioned so vividly. And what had Athitatus meant when he said that Fusus' son was now investigating as well. I ground my teeth and picked at a nail in thought before staring at it in frustration.

I walked the room in silence for a few minutes before speaking. "I think we should call on Spurius Maelius and see if he is agreeable to visitors."

"It'd be better than sitting here on your arses all day talking shit like two old women," said Scavolo as he appeared in the doorway, making me jump with his loud intrusion. "And I'll come with you to Maelius', they know me. I have a few things to tell you about on the way as well. Let's go," he ordered.

We were on our feet and heading for the temple door before Graccus had time to lace up his sandals. He hopped and skipped as we crossed the square outside, Scavolo on a mission and striding out in full military manner.

"I left one of the lads in Ostia to keep an eye on things," he said as we passed a group of people heading to the Temple of Jupiter. I noted a few of my father's clients heading in the direction and then I saw the widow again, the one I had seen the day before outside the Vulcanal. She caught my eye with a glance and I saw a flash of red hair under her hood, which she had pulled up tightly around her face at my glance in her direction. I didn't get chance to see her features but she reminded me of someone, I wasn't sure who.

"I had a report last night that a man was trying to hire two carts to move heavy goods from Rome." My jaw fell and I looked to Graccus. "Arrius," he continued, who must be his man in Ostia, "followed him but he says he slipped away in the port as he must have been seen shadowing him, prick."

We turned the corner onto the slope of the Clivus and walked briskly down the hill.

"I've sent Novius to get Titus' fathers' slave and take him to Ostia. I don't think any of us actually know what Flavius Aetius looks like other than the basic description that stupid slave gave us. We've kept the slave in the Carcer so I'm sure he'll enjoy a day out to the seaside."

He was right, the description we had could relate to every other man in Rome. I still had so many questions and I was running these through in my mind when Scavolo stopped and hammered on a gate to our left. The house of Maelius was not more than a good spear throw from the Temple. I noted that the walls ran for a further hundred paces down the hill and a further two hundred or so paces backwards until it reached the sheer wall of the Capitol Hill in the near distance. At our back was the road and the edge of the cliff which overlooked, at this juncture, the Temple of Saturn. I noted the wide gateway which would easily fit a large wagon or two, even three with horses, at a push. For a town house it was a good place to live and made me think, once more, of the meeting I was to have later today on the Jugarius.

The gate cracked open a slither and a face appeared, a very handsome lad of about sixteen or seventeen, with olive green eyes and dark eyebrows peered out.

"Yes, Masters?" he asked in very clear Greek, the language of trade.

"We're here to see Spurius Maelius," said Scavolo, in his most basic Latin.

The boy frowned. "Do you have an appointment? The Master is a busy man. I am sure I can get you some time with him tomorrow afternoon or the day after," he replied with a bored expression.

"Tell your Master that Gaius Scavolo from the Temple of Jupiter Optimus Maximus is at the gate, lad. I'm sure he will find the time to see me."

The boy looked at us as if he very much doubted it but closed the gate and we heard a shuffling sound as he disappeared off. Scavolo tapped his nose and winked. I was confused but said nothing, obviously missing whatever clever move he'd just made. Surely enough, whatever it was that had evaded me got us in. The boy was left at the gate and a wide-hipped female now escorted us, she'd told us her name but I forgot it instantly as I stared at her large breasts for too long and got a slap on the shoulder from Scavolo as he shook his head at me with a wide grin.

"Your father wants you to visit Dentatus the tutor," he said at my indignant look. "You need some lessons in diplomacy and tact," he said to justify this statement as I had never heard of the man and had jumped to the conclusion that Dentatus was some sort of illicit tutor in sexual behaviour. His broad smile suggested he had gleaned this from the slack jaw I presented to him. "To stop *that*," he added firmly, jutting out his jaw as he lifted his chin towards my stupid face. "If you're going to move up in the world we need to get you sorted."

He was right but I didn't need him telling me. I sulked all the way to the door and even across the Atrium as we followed the hips of the slave into the house. I didn't need this prick telling me what I needed. We were led to a rear room which overlooked a long garden bordered by trees and overshadowed by the high cliff above. Nevertheless it was a pleasant view and it brought me back to the present moment.

"Scavolo," It was the Master of the house and he greeted my companion loudly and with open arms as if they were the best of friends. I was surprised. I expected an older man. I had no idea why, but the way people spoke of him I expected something out of a bad dream, a bent-backed, hooked nose and shifty-eyed demon. This man was tall, athletic and handsome, exactly the opposite of my inner thoughts. He had a smooth chin and trimmed hair with lively light-brown eyes. His lips were full and he looked like he spent a lot of time smiling if the laughter lines at his eyes were any judge of his character.

"And, if I am not mistaken it is the boy who found the killers of Lucilla of the Arturii."

He was appraising me with his bottom lip out and a nodding head.

"Come, come you will have to tell me all about it. The gossip is *pathetic* and I never know what is true and what is not." His inflection on the word reminded me of an orator or an actor. "And" he was looking at Graccus, whose nose was dripping after the walk. "Don't tell me, I'm good with faces," he was saying as he tapped a finger on his lip and appraised my friend. "You must be Porcius' son," he said. "Grantius isn't it?"

"Graccus, sir," my friend spoke and bowed, before he wiped his nose along his sleeve. I saw Maelius notice it but he looked away quickly with a slight frown.

I was going to speak but he carried on with the impetus of a horse that's jumped the fence and was heading for the hay field. "Here, sit. Flavia, go get the decent wine for our guests and ask cook to do some light snacks. Oh, and bring your lyre and play for us, please."

He was all action, arms and words and I felt exhausted by his energy already. The girl bowed and disappeared with her light blue stola flowing behind her. I noted two burly men appear at the door, clearly he wasn't as friendly and open as he seemed to suggest as these guards glared at us distrustfully.

"Gaius, Gaius it is a pleasure to welcome you into my home. Have you re-considered my request? You know you'd be welcome."

Scavolo gave him a scowl before replying. "I am happy in my role for the Quaestores," he said with a false smile.

Maelius let out a feigned sigh and dropped his shoulders theatrically.

"Well you know I could use someone with your abilities, you know the plebeian tribunes need a champion and you could be that man with your connections." He inclined his head and drew his chin to his chest, looking at my former boss with wide questioning eyes for a second.

"No?" he laughed as if this game was one that they played at every meeting. Scavolo was tight-lipped but had a gleam in his eye, nonetheless. "One day Gaius, one day." He turned to me and I dreaded what he'd say next. He obviously knew who we were. I wasn't surprised. A man of his wealth and connections would have several men in his pay who fed him all sorts of information. He probably knew the colour of my underwear. That gave me a start and I rubbed my crotch slowly. He noticed but smiled.

"Ah, the wine" he was off to the door in a heartbeat, taking the jug from the slave girl and bringing it across to where we had just sat, on wide comfortable chairs with leather backs, the best imports. The jug was a heavy silver with a large single flowing handle. As he lifted one of the cups that the slave had just brought in on a tray I noticed the sailing ships and sea creatures adorning its side.

"It's exquisite, isn't it?" he said, having seen me looking at the jug. "I got it from Corinth." He poured the wine himself before handing the cup to me. "Odysseus," he said, the picture of the man on the cup turned to me as I took it.

"Impressive work," I replied. It was. The detail on the engraving was of the highest quality. I sipped the wine as he handed out the drinks and I nodded at the quality of this too. It was strange that the Master of the house was pouring drinks for his guests, but I realised that it had put us at ease and given him control of the conversation. I was as impressed with his style as I was with his taste in silverware and wine. The slave began to pick at her lyre, the quiet tones easing us into a relaxed mood as I took in the room, allowing my gaze to wonder from object to object. It was sparsely furnished, suggesting modesty but also wealth as every item was an imported treasure. Dark urns covered in various scenes picked out in red clay sat on highly polished wooden tables, drapes near the windows and doors were brightly coloured and heavy, the best quality.

He handed a silver cup to Graccus, who was bowing like a slave, and then asked. "So, to what do I owe the pleasure of your company?"

The question was to me.

"It's about the fire at the Temple of Vulcan."

"Terrible business," he replied fixing me with his best stoic face. He was clearly good at this and I wilted under his cool, unblinking, gaze.

"We wondered if you or any member of your household had seen or heard anything of note in the days before or after the fire which might help in our investigation to find the missing state ingots?" I'd been clear to keep the matter to the missing state items and avoid any other inference to Fusus.

"I see." He sipped his wine before answering in a measured tone. "I was awoken by one of the guards and we rushed out to help as any concerned citizen would have done. It was chaotic and I cannot recall anything other than the noise, smoke and excellent work that the local people did to put out the flames. Terrible business," he repeated, returning a questioning gaze to me once more.

It was a calculated answer, giving no details whatsoever. "Did you notice anything out of the ordinary at all?" I asked.

"Other than ten foot high flames and people rushing up and down the streets to find water, no," His response ended with a smile and then back to his stoic best. I was floundering, and wondered if Scavolo might come to my assistance, but it was Graccus that took over.

"Sir," he was deferential, which seemed to please Maelius. "When the priests arrived can you tell us anything you noted which might have been strange or out of place in their actions? We had a report that the Flamen was striking his fellow priests," his brows were raised in expectation as he made the request.

Maelius tilted his head before responding. "The poor Flamen must have been out of his wits. Can you imagine returning in the early hours of the morning and finding your home almost destroyed by fire? What a bad state of affairs it is for him. he missed the ceremony too I hear. Very unlucky," His head was shaking. "No doubt he panicked and let out his anger on those around him. I cannot say I saw him do anything that I would not have done myself should I have returned to find my home ablaze."

It was another noncommittal answer. "Did you see any men moving heavy boxes from across the street?" asked Graccus. It was a question I was going to ask once I'd softened up Maelius a bit and I noticed Scavolo move his head at the asking.

"Men carrying boxes?" he turned a shrewd look to myself and then to Scavolo. "I wondered why the son of the Quaestores himself was looking into this matter. It seems strange to have the force of the mighty Scavolo and yourself," at which he bowed his head "involved in looking into this case of a pretty minor amount of iron stolen during a fire."

A small curl of his lip crept up his face as he looked directly at me, playing with me.

"Is there more to this matter than meets the eye?" His question caused me to fix my face, though in truth I felt like I'd set it into a scowl, which brought a further glint to his eye as he picked up on my expression. "I can honestly say I saw nothing more than the fire." He turned towards the wall where one of his guards stood and flicked his chin in his direction. "Lars," the man was clearly of Etruscan stock. "Did you see anyone carrying boxes on the night of the fire at the Vulcanal?" The guard was suggesting not by the movement of his head, the other guard similarly agreeing with him. "Sorry, gentlemen," he added with a shrug of his shoulders. I noted the intelligent appraisal he gave to us all and realised that we may have given him more than he had given us as a short silence stretched and he sipped at his wine slowly.

"May I ask if you had heard of the priest Titus walking the streets at night and upsetting the local neighbours?" It had come to me as I sat and sipped at the excellent wine, I needed to know more from this man as he was clearly only telling us what he thought we wanted to hear.

"Ah that," he smiled. "Yes, I know that complaints were sent to the Flamen but the old man ignored them all. He really has had a bad year, hasn't he?"

He deflected the question well, but not well enough. "Indeed." I replied. "Did you see him at all, staggering in the streets and singing?"

His eyes flicked to Scavolo and back to me before he answered. "Yes, of course. Who could avoid the drunken fool."

"Was he drunk?"

"Or intoxicated on that berry juice they drink." His tone suggested disgust at such activity.

"Did you see him yourself?"

He took a calculating look at me and I saw his lips curl slightly as he realised I wasn't as dim-witted as he might have thought and was also able to play these verbal games before he replied. "I did."

I let the silence stretch for a second or two and my eyebrows rose in expectation of his continuance of what he had seen, but he was too clever to do so.

I nodded slowly, sipped the wine and lifted my eyebrows in appreciation once more before I asked. "How did he seem to you? Where was he when you saw him and where was he going?"

I could sense his thoughts working through what I was asking and why as he answered. "We saw him on a few nights when returning from visits to clients. He was singing," he shrugged. "Shouting that Vulcan was bringing his vengeance on those who had erred from the old ways," he shrugged more slowly this time. "On one occasion he tried to stop our party and tell us that we needed to pray to Vulcan to avert fire as it was surely coming to cleanse the city from our wanton ways. He was clearly mad." He finished by inclining his head and raising his eyebrows to me to check if I had more to ask.

I did. "Did you always see him by the Temple or further along the road?"

His lips pressed together before he spoke, a glint in his eye at my question. "Mostly at the Temple or close by. At one time we met him along the Jugarius near Marcus Metilius' house. He was shouting at a slave beyond the fence about fires and praying to Vulcan. We kept out of his way, on the other side of the road."

I knew the name Metilius but wasn't sure why. "And was he always alone?"

He inclined his head again with his ingratiating smile which was now starting to annoy me. "I was in my carriage, I hardly saw him unless I opened the curtain," he replied. Of course, I'd forgotten he wouldn't have been walking. "Lars," he asked towards the wall again where the silent men stood like two birds sat on a fence listening to our every word. "Did that priest ever have anyone with him?"

"I only saw him with that old man at the gate arguing once, never saw him with anyone else, sir."

Maelius nodded to me as if that was all he could tell me. "Which gate?" I asked to the guard, looking to Maelius first for the Master to allow me to do so.

The guard received a nod from his boss and replied, "the house next to Metilius'."

I had a strange feeling I now knew which house they were speaking of and who they spoke of. "Isn't Metilius dead, who is living at his house?"

"His widow lives there alone. She's his former slave." He was shaking his head at this. "Dreadful business. Poor man threw himself into the river on Lupercalia."

My jaw slackened and I saw Scavolo scowl at me as Maelius maintained his stoic features but I could see him laughing at me behind his eyes. I rallied as best I could. "And the man next door, why was he arguing with him?"

"I'm sure he would know that but we do not. Probably because the idiot priest was being too loud in the dead of night and disturbing the peace or pissing on his gate post, which I heard he did as well. From what I hear these issues had been raised to the Flamen several times but he did nothing about it. Terrible business, what an unlucky year he's had. Poor man. I'm sure the college of priests will have to do something about him."

I could see him spreading this gossip in the Forum to his cronies. It annoyed me, but I wasn't sure why.

The mention of the house and widow had reminded me that I had a visit to that exact house, the one that must have belonged to Metilius. "And did you ever see the priest pushing a cart or carrying heavy sacks?"

Maelius appraised me again, his intelligent eyes searching me for more information before he replied. "I see," he said quietly. "You think he was implicated in some way. Moving the state's ingots." I saw his lip curl slightly as he inflected the word. Did he know more than he was letting on? Did he know that Fusus had lost so much of his wealth in the fire? I tried not to show any response on my face but wasn't confident that I did or didn't. The bastard was good at this. I glanced to Scavolo who was back to his statue-like best, and Graccus was sitting with wide eyes and a scared expression, giving away everything that I was trying hard to keep under wraps.

"Lars?" he asked the man at the wall again.

"Nothing, Master," came the quick reply.

My short silence at his words seemed to give Maelius the impression that our time with him had ended and he rose from his seat.

"Well, that was very interesting Secundus Sulpicius," he said, placing his cup on a small table. "I do wish you luck in your investigating, you seem to have lots to do. If there is anything more I can help with please do ask. I'll let the door man know you are welcome at any time." He was looking to Scavolo, who had stood whilst I remained seated for a moment. "You really must come over to one of my evening parties Gaius," he was saying, first name terms and that light-hearted tone of voice evident once again. "Bring your wife and eldest son, he must be twelve now, or more?"

Scavolo was answering but my mind was racing at what I'd heard. The old man had told me he'd argued with Titus but he'd not mentioned others were on the road at the same time. I needed to speak to him urgently, he could hold further clues to this mystery. The music stopped, the slave with the lyre receiving a round of applause from Maelius, which we all followed.

"And you too Graccus Porcius," Maelius was saying. "I haven't seen your father for such a long time. Yes, yes I'll arrange it, we could do with a night of laughter and poems," he was saying expansively to the room as if the room itself would hear and start to organise an evening event for everyone to come along and have fun. "It has been a pleasure to finally meet the man to whom the goddess Minerva has given her grace," he was saying to me, clearly he knew about Fucilla's dream and it irked me, but I still didn't know why I was taking such an approach to my host. "I have been impressed with your questions," he added as he bowed slightly and motioned towards the door. "But I really must get on, I have another engagement that needs my presence and as this meeting was unannounced I'm sorry that I cannot chat for longer." He was ushering us out as he spoke and we all mumbled our thanks.

As we reached the door and the slaves were bustling us towards the exit I turned to Maelius as another thought came to me. "Might I ask one more question, please?" He agreed with a head movement. "Did you know Titus, the priest who died defending the Temple?"

He hesitated for a split second before his shrewd eyes changed back to his stoic best. "Yes, yes of course, we know everyone along the street," he answered. "Poor man, what a hero, what a hero," he was waving his hands and looking to the skies. "Poor man, poor man, what an unlucky year for them all," he added, though he continued to move us towards the exit through the Atrium.

"And his father, did you know him as well?"

"Of course I knew him."

His short response suggested he was holding something back, and his false smile didn't hide this fact either despite his excellent stoic training. "You know then that he is missing?"

My question brought no affirmation or denial to his face but he replied that he did know that the man was missing before adding to my surprise, "and if I find the bastard before you do, I will gut him."

X

I'd hurried to the house, late for my meeting after leaving Scavolo and Graccus to pick up the pieces from what Maelius had told us as we left his Domus. It was another piece of this complex puzzle akin to a tale from the Sphinx. Maelius had told us that Flavius Aetius had rented a wagon from him recently and not returned the item despite several requests. He didn't expand any further and we were ushered quickly from the premises after that revelation. As I made my apologies, citing an important meeting but not sharing what it was, Scavolo had agreed to set up a meeting with Athitatus to lean on him and see if he cracked, and also confirmed that the reports from his men said that all of the priests except Titus had visited Ostia. We'd set a time to meet back at the Vulcanal and parted ways, with Scavolo saying he would find out what Fusus' son was doing sending messages to the Flamen that might interfere with our investigation.

The road was busy and I had to avoid several laden carts in my haste, pushing past people who'd moved to the side of the roadway to allow them access and getting the odd curse for pushing against the flow of traffic, which I ignored. I watched the carts being pushed in and out of the Forum laden with fruit and wine, vegetables and nuts as well as pottery and cloth and none of them seemed to be hiding stolen silver. I also scoured the road for Micus but couldn't see him anywhere, hoping he had some information which would help me with my bargaining at the house, but with no sight of him I pushed on to the property regardless. At the gate I was greeted by the garden slave, or freedman as I couldn't decide which he was, who looked as if he had been standing waiting for hours though I was hardly late at all in reality. He opened the gate to allow me in and I thanked him.

"Welcome sir," he said with a bow. I bowed in return and looked across towards the old man's chair, which was empty. I really needed to see him as soon as I could. "Please follow me," continued the Gallic-faced man. I looked at the vegetable plot as we passed by, well-tended and full of green leaves, the soil clearly good for growing crops. I was disappointed as it meant the price would be higher. Away to the right by a shed was a dung heap. It, too, was well maintained, a sign that the gardener was good at his job. *A tidy muck-heap means a tidy gardener* I'd heard one of my father's slaves tell him many years before; odd how these things popped into my head at the strangest moments. I appraised the walls of the house, part brick and part wood. Again, well maintained and no settlement or other cracks were visible. I could feel the price rising with every step I took towards the building and I was starting to worry that my gift to Vulcan wasn't large enough to support my quest for this house.

At the door we were greeted by the red-haired girl I had seen previously, her blue eyes looking to me quickly before they dropped to the floor. She was pretty, round-faced with a healthy glow about her. Her skin was pale and her hands looked soft. She hid her remaining features under a heavy wool dress and thick shawl, which I didn't think was needed as the day was early and the sun was up. I wondered if the house was cold or damp, the first opening for any price discussions that I'd seen so far. She welcomed me into the Atrium, which was a wide square with an archway and several doors to the walls at each side. The archway seemed to lead to a corridor with light flowing through from above and I wondered if it was open to the sky. The floor was stoned, which was a sign of quality. The price was rising again. The girl closed the door behind me as we entered and then disappeared off to my left as I walked behind the man through the archway and into a wide corridor with a roof suspended on arched porticos through which light and air entered the space. It was very cleverly done and would keep both the rain off in the winter and allow the sun and light in to dissipate heat in the hot months. I was starting to think that the house might be outside my price range.

I was shown to a side room of about eight or nine strides square with several small stools and a large table, a dining room. It was clean, aired by three small windows high in the walls, shutters open, and with a long low table against the wall at the rear. An iron brazier stood in the middle of the room which would be used to heat the area if required but stood empty, so maybe the house wasn't cold after all. It was an impressive little room and would easily seat ten or more people.

"I will announce you to the mistress and her associate," said the man. "May I please take your name and your family status," he asked. Of course, it was a very formal process and I should have considered that they would need to confirm that I wasn't just some trumped up squirt trying to get a look over the house before I snook in at night and robbed the place. I gave him my details with a smile and he inclined his head, clearly impressed with my family status, or so it seemed though he had a glint in his eye, which I was unsure whether it was joy or fear, which confused me for a second.

Moments later he re-appeared with a wry smile and beckoned me forwards. I was put out by the sudden change in his features, but nevertheless followed him as requested. On entering the room I understood instantly why he had given me that smile. Sat in front of me was the widow with the red hair I had seen near both the Temple Of Vulcan on one occasion and also this very morning on the Clivus, and sat beside her, with a stylus and pen and a stupid grin on his stupid face was *Philus*.

The lady stood, I bowed and the man introduced her to me. "May I introduce Bravia Mugillensis Metilius and her scribe from the Temple of Jupiter Optimus Maximus. Though I hear that you know each other," he smirked. I felt like kicking him.

"Madam, it is a pleasure to meet you although I am sorry that it is in such difficult circumstances," I said. Her lips smiled thinly. "Philus," I nodded, he bowed. I should have realised that the woman would have to have a scribe from one of the Temples to complete any negotiations over the sale, it was what was done and men like Philus knew both the laws and the documents which needed completing. He wouldn't finish the documents as that would be a priest or lawyer (often they were the same) but the Temple would underwrite the process and documents would be stored in the City vaults for the future in case anyone made a claim to the land or property. It made a modest income for my father in his year as Quaestores and I knew Philus was good at his job despite being a prick.

"Secundus Sulpicius," started the Temple man. "The mistress has some questions before she shows you around the house. You may ask any questions you have as we move around the Domus once we have completed these formalities."

His brows rose for confirmation that I understood and I nodded, to which he ticked a box on his slate. I glanced to the red-headed lady, who was slim and sat stiffly although she did not look at me at all. She had a smell of fresh flowers which was welcoming, her hair was tied tight on her head and ran down her back in a thick braid. I was impressed with the scent and thought of Fabia, wondering where she got the perfume and if I could buy some as a gift for my wife-to-be. Philus was staring at me as I was staring at Bravia. She reminded me of someone, and it wasn't just the slave girl who had opened the door, because they could be sisters, although I realised immediately that was just the red-hair and I hadn't really compared them both – a simple mistake to make. I blushed slightly before he spoke, she appeared not to notice my staring at her or was too polite to say so.

"I have appraised the mistress of your background," at which his eyes rose to me and he seemed to smile, I wasn't impressed by this but tried to ignore his movements as I am above such things. "And of your recent alignment to the clan Vibulanii."

It was another blow to my pocket I was sure and I tried not to show this, feeling like my angry face was giving me away as I tried to breathe silently whilst inside I was wanting to tell the prick to stop pushing the cost up as well as get on with things as I was very short of funds and time. I nodded again, my neck suddenly stiff. The lady didn't turn her face to me once, she remained quietly poised on her chair and faced the small window which was behind my left shoulder. Once again I realised that these future sessions with the tutor Dentatus were going to critical as this slave girl turned mistress was a better Roman stoic than I.

"Why are you considering this house?" Asked Philus, stylus poised.

What a stupid question. I was hoping for a bargain.

"I believe the neighbourhood to be fresh and airy, the soil is good and it is between both the Forum and the Boarium so ideally suited for a public and private life."

It was a rehearsed answer and one I knew that sneaky bastard Philus would be telling Scavolo later. He turned to the lady, who made the slightest dip of her head. He ticked his slate before speaking again.

"Are you considering a family and if so how many children?"

It was another odd question, but it came from a woman so of course she would be looking at this from a female point of view. I was quick-witted enough to know that if I could play to her heart strings I might get a few thousand off the price for appearing to be a noble husband who wanted a strong family.

"We have not yet discussed the details, but I would be wary to impose too much on my future wife." I was making it up as I went along but the pang of sadness from the loss of my own family were there in my voice so I let those tunes play out. "I lost my wife and child in childbirth recently," she had turned her eyes to me at this and I could see her interest piqued. "And I would not want to lose another. I would let my wife choose the timing of such things if possible. We are young enough not to rush to such decisions."

It seemed like a good answer to me. The lady seemed to understand, her lashes blinking with a tear at the thought of death, whilst Philus curled his lip in a sneer at my weakness of spirit. I didn't care what he thought if it got me a better deal.

Philus ticked the latest box as the mistress inclined her head and then looked at me long and hard, bringing a frown as he stretched the silence. I was worried what he would ask next, but surprised when he said, "and have you ever beaten your slaves?"

My mouth dropped, and I saw them both notice before I clamped it shut.

"Never!" I said quickly, as if such a thing was far too much below me but suddenly realising why she had asked such a thing. I'd just been told that she was a former slave herself, she would not sell the house to a slave-beater. "In fact, you will know yourself Philus that I recently purchased new sandals for a young slave boy in my father's house as he had none. Much to the displeasure of some," I added with a knowing smile at his downturned lips. "And only recently I asked the Temple to feed several slaves who had struggled through that awful rain we had and were to return home soaked and hungry. If it wasn't for my actions those men could easily have caught a chill or even worse succumbed to fever if I was not so caring."

I dared Philus to deny my claim as I puffed out my chest.

The lady looked to Philus this time, and he nodded before ticking the box at her movement to do so. "And a last question." The bastard was enjoying this. "How quickly could you prepare the funds should a sale be agreed?"

Fusus' ingots ran through my mind as I caught her glance to me. "That depends on the price, but I have no hesitation in saying that an agreement through the Temple of Jupiter Optimus Maximus could be resolved within seven or eight days."

I knew that usually a sale would take one or two cycles of the moon at least and that my links to my father and his role as Quaestores would add some measure of security to the transaction in their minds. If I could find Fusus' ingots I was sure this could be agreed, but if I didn't... I dare not think how much of a fool I'd look.

She nodded.

Philus nodded.

I nodded.

It was going well and I hoped that my gift to Vulcan had been delivered by now and he was by my side bringing me luck.

"Then let me show you around the house Secundus," she said in a light voice. By this she meant that the man of house, the gardener Cursius as I learned he was called, was to show us around and she and I would follow with Philus making any notes which might affect the price. He walked with a slight limp as he set off but I noted that his shoulders were broad from all the work he had done over the years.

He was a half a head taller than me with a good head of hair which was now greyed to almost white and was close cropped but clearly showed that it had been fair in his youth as I had noted when I first saw him in the garden. We'd circulated through several large rooms and I was starting to see myself living here, when we came to the kitchen area. It consisted of three linked rooms, one large with an enormous iron oven and two smaller rooms for washing and cleaning. There was also a heavy door which was locked with a thick padlock, no doubt to keep the slaves from the wine, and used to store foodstuff and drink. I nodded at the sensible precaution and glanced around the area to try and find a way to reduce the price in some way.

"No Lavatrina?" I asked.

"No," replied Cursius flatly, as if washing was a thing that evil men did. I noticed the sweat patches under his armpits as he turned towards the rear door, his grey hair thinning at the back of his head.

I nodded to Philus, who made a note.

"I would have to go to the expense of adding one," I said to make it known that it was something that was lacking. "Do you have your own water supply?"

"Yes," said the gardener, which pleased me. "I will show you when we inspect the grounds."

I thanked him.

The main kitchen was large and I touched the iron cooker, which was hot as it should be, three doors set into the frontage. It was old but clearly well serviced. "Any cracks in the iron?" I asked, looking closely and seeing nothing, but knowing that a split in the iron could mean replacing the whole thing, and that would be expensive job. He replied that there was not. I was disappointed but didn't show it.

The price was still rising.

The view of the rear garden was good from where I stood, with the crest of the Palatine Hill visible beyond the high fence and the roofs of the houses which stretched beyond it dotted in the distance. The situation was very good. We moved towards the back door, which was reached through another archway and a wide corridor. At the entrance to the corridor was a square wooden box which held, from what I could see with a quick glance, a wooden club, a rusty spear and two large swords. It was good to keep weapons close by in case of thieves and I nodded at the security measures as I knew we kept a similar box just behind the door at home.

The rest of the entranceway was wide enough for two to stand shoulder to shoulder and the space was so well designed that seats had been built into both walls with shoe and boot slots constructed into the oak seating. At the end of the seats and next to the door were two deep recesses on both sides with coat hooks so that the hanging garments did not block the entranceway. At the foot of each was a gulley to catch rainwater. Whoever had designed this house had done a fantastic job. I tried not to be impressed lest I gave away my excitement.

I noticed a row of sandals, well-oiled despite age and clear usage. They were obviously for someone with large feet and embellished with numbers, these ran from two to four and I wondered if this was for use for specific days of the week. I had large feet and from where I stood these seemed to be my size. I wondered if Minerva was smiling on me and remembered that I owed several devotions already today. I was pleased to see that they fitted the slots very easily. I glanced to the gardener's sandals which were of a cheap leather and stitched in several places where they had worn. Maybe these were the former Masters which hadn't been replaced.

Two long dark-blue cloaks also adorned the pegs, beside a few smaller coats, one of which looked like it was wool-lined and expensive and was well worn. I noticed the number one sewn into the sleeve of one of the cloaks and guessed it corresponded to the sandals, although the number one pair were missing from below. The quality within the house and garments really stood out. One cloak had mud trailed at the hem and the other had a dirt patch across one of the arms so they had obviously been worn whilst gardening recently. A third cloak, brown in colour, hung on another peg and this garment had several patches sewn into the neckline where it had worn.

I noted old sweat patches stained the cloak at the neck and thought of the man in front of me, so assumed it was his. Looking up I noticed that the beams in the ceiling were carved with dolphins where they met at a joint, and the skill of the woodwork was exquisite. Again, I tried not to show my excitement at these details.

Cursius had opened the door and stepped outside, looking back at me impatiently. I followed. A covered walkway which would allow the door to remain open and still keep the rain from the entrance was built over the door. Another sign of the quality of design.

"The mistress will await our return," said Cursius as Bravia nodded and returned to the house, her skin too pale for the sunlight, or so I assumed.

After a short walk across the grounds we came to the rear fence, which was a hedgerow to head height with a wooden fence along the back. Just prior to the hedge we came to a stop and Cursius bent to pull at a trap door. He had to dip his left shoulder as his hip was clearly giving him some pain, but he managed to pull at the door with evident strength. Once open I could smell what this was and wrinkled my nose. The good news was that it was sufficiently distanced from the house that the stench would not reach the domus.

"The cess pit is linked to the Cloaca Maxima," he said with evident pride. "The former Master had a channel dug which goes through these trees and then reaches the drain about a hundred or so paces over there," he was pointing into the distance. "In the winter the waters flush it all clean and in the summer the smell almost disappears unless the Cloaca itself blocks."

I was impressed again and said so, realising my mistake quickly and snapping my mouth shut. I needed to get the price down. "Was the former Master an engineer?" I asked.

He didn't answer and I wondered if he'd heard me before he finally spoke, having by this time closed the trapdoor over the hole in the ground through which piss pots would be carried and emptied. "He had many skills and was a fine craftsman. He built the steps which take you to the top of the tower in your Temple," he said slowly. I understood what he meant as the steps up to the top of the temple of Jupiter Optimus

Maximus were a magnificent affair with two Gryphons at the base and winding steps which finished with the head of the god carved in oak.

"I didn't know," I said, looking to Philus, who similarly looked like this was news to him. "Did he build anything else around the City."

The man looked up at the house and then across at the expanse of the city beyond the hedge. "Several of the finest houses were designed by him. People sought him out for the best quality house developments and designs. He was a genius and made improvements to the Cloaca as well as to the old developments in some of the Temples, but he was not a kind man." His gaze fell to me and then to Philus. "I'm sorry," he said suddenly. "I cannot speak of him. The mistress will not allow it."

So, he was a slave, and there was something here that I didn't understand and he didn't want to divulge. Maybe the dead Master had been a brutal owner and had beaten them all, hence the odd questions I'd endured moments before. So why marry the slave? Was the red haired girl at the door her daughter? It hadn't crossed my mind but now it did and I looked more closely at the Gallic man, his blue eyes and fair hair staring back at the house. If they had bad memories attached to the house then maybe they could sell it to me quickly and cheaply. If they had skeletons in their cupboards then the only thing I was interested in was whether it might reduce the price.

****

Milo gave me a strange look as I approached but then waved to me and pointed towards a table at the rear where Micus was slurping at a bowl of steaming broth. "I've added it to your account as you said to do," he said jovially, following me to the seat, although I didn't remember leaving the invitation to feed the boy more than once. I let it pass, the lad looked like he needed to eat and my mind was distracted by the meeting at the house. "Same for you?" he asked. My head movement sent him off to add another bowl to the growing list I would have to pay for at some stage in the future as I was unsure how this *account* system worked.

"Master," Micus had risen and bowed as I approached, just as a good slave should do.

I waved him to sit and placed myself to look at the roadway. "Eat first," I said with a nod towards his half empty bowl. Milo, who was already returning with my meal, was waving towards a customer to sit and I noticed that his store seemed busier than usual. Three people sat on the table next to us and another table held two ladies, one of whom glanced to me as I sat. I thanked him and took out my spoon, licking it clean before I stirred the contents of the bowl. On the table in front of me was a small statue of Minerva, the clay approximation of the goddess cheaply done to say the least but still clearly an image of the deity. I glanced around and noticed that the other tables and his store front also held such small statues. This was new and it took me a moment to realise what it meant. I shook my head, the bastard was profiting from my situation and my presence. Just as Maximus' grandmother, or whatever relation she was, knew about me from the *ladies at the temple*, then others must have heard the tale too. I bit my lip as I watched him serving the newcomers and I saw that three of the people at various tables were surreptitiously glancing in my direction.

I ate slowly, my mind a fog of information and fear. I'd been impressed with the house and then shocked at the price that was suggested to me. Despite trying not to react it was obvious I had done so as Philus narrowed his eyes and tensed as I looked to him aghast at the figure he'd given me. I'd said I would consider it and reply within a day or two and left hurriedly, worried that I'd wasted my time and theirs as the house was well above any expectations I'd made regarding the price. I assumed my gift to Vulcan wasn't good enough and trudged dejectedly, head down, back toward the temple of Jupiter, stopping at Milo's as my belly was growling. Thoughts of Fusus' anger came back to me as I walked. Something was eating at me and I struggled to catch whatever small bug it was that was burrowing into my mind. The house was a distraction. That was what I had concluded in my slow walk. If the mystery was solved and my fathers' fortunes were secured (and my own along with them) then I could return to pursue the house. Until that point I had to close that door and focus solely on the issue of the ingots and the death of Titus the priest.

I looked up to see Micus sat silently watching me and waiting.

"Go on," I said, giving him the go-ahead to tell me what he'd learned.

"The cloth-seller was a hard nut to crack," he said as he pushed the empty bowl aside and his eager face turned up to my own. "He sells clothes and shoes to the Temple, so he said, and he is busy on their new contract for tunics, cloaks and sandals as they were all burned in the fire." That was interesting and I knew they had been burnt but not who was replacing them. I remembered the gold thread on the collar of each priest as he spoke and something else continued to burrow into my thoughts. I lost the thread of it as Micus resumed. "And he says that he cannot start any new commissions until that job is finished in two weeks."

I was slurping at my broth, a rich mixture of vegetables and chicken laced with garlic and herbs. Micus hurried on.

"I said that my Master was considering buying a local house and asked whether it was a quiet location," he shrugged "and if there were any problems that I should let my Master know about, but he was a shut door and wouldn't say anything. He kept saying I should go as he was busy. But I hung around and talked to some of the customers. He got angry after a while." I was smiling at his persistence. "And told me if I didn't go he'd set his dog on me. It was a small thing with half an ear," he was now smiling back at me as his shoulders rose to suggest that the dog was a pampered waste of space as most of them are these days. "I left and went up the street asking if anyone had seen anything on the night of the fire or the next day but nobody had. So, I went back to the cloth shop." I'd finished my broth and rubbed my hands together as he continued with his tale. "I said I'd heard about a mad man in the streets at night, someone calling down the gods and speaking of fire."

I appraised Micus once more, he really was good at this stuff. I decided to buy him a new tunic for his effort and persistence.

"He got angry again and told me to push off, but I said that there had been a fire and asked why this didn't concern him, surely as a local storeowner he must be worried about such things. I asked him if the street was unlucky." I was even more impressed with his line of thinking and questioning and realised my jaw was slack once more so snapped it shut, nodded firmly and tried to adopt my best stoic gaze.

The boy stopped talking and gave me a quizzical frown, obviously confused by my change of features. "Go on," I said encouragingly.

"He started getting crosser, telling me to go away and never come back. He shouted for the dog but it stood and barked and then lay down again. I asked why he was being so angry, which made him even angrier. The man from the garden across the road, the house you looked at Master. He came out and was watching us as the cloth-seller was starting to shout at me so I stepped back a little so he could see me, you know you said it's good to have a witness." I had said this to him when we'd walked to the temple one morning, just so that he never put himself into any trouble when asking questions on the street. "And I asked again why he was so angry, all I wanted to know is whether he'd seen anything strange on the days before or after the fire." His eyebrows rose as he finished his story. "He tried to hit me with a broom so I ran away."

I put a hand on his shoulder thanked him and then sat and thought about this for a moment. A light rain started to patter on the floor. Those tables which were open to the elements soon emptied as people finished their broth at speed and scattered like lambs from a wolf. I was happy in my new, exalted, location under the roof and said to Micus that we'd wait for the rain to finish before we left.

The reaction of the cloth-seller wasn't uncommon, people got angry for the slightest things these days. But it did seem an over-reaction for such innocent questions. Maybe I needed to speak to the man myself and dig a little deeper into this. Then I decided that I'd send Graccus to see if there was any possibility that the location could be being used for storing missing ingots. It was within the scope of my original idea for the distance involved in moving the ingots. I could always accuse him of threatening my property, Micus, if Graccus saw something he thought might be of interest. I was thinking this through when I realised I still needed to speak to Athitatus again as there were several gaps in this mystery that I still needed to fill, not least the gold ring which sealed the agreement for the ingots whilst he was away.

It was with these things in my head that I found myself having walked back to the Temple of Vulcan with Micus at my heel once the rain had stopped. The floor was wet, but no puddles splashed us as we wandered to the roadway and along to the Vulcanal. Two priests were digging the garden and one was moving stones across to a low wall where a craftsman was starting to rebuild the foundations. The stonemason was a thick set man with a heavy leather apron over a rough woollen tunic. He was kneeling and hammering at broken stones to dislodge them as the priest piled new stones behind him. Athitatus had clearly agreed that his priests would do some of the work to reduce the costs. I smiled at this, tight bastard. I saw Havitus chatting to a woman with a basket of fruit sat against her hip. She wore a long green cloak with the hood pulled over her head so must have been there for a while and not realised the rain had stopped. I wandered across. He noticed me and lifted his chin in recognition as I approached. The woman glanced over her shoulder at his movement and her red hair flashed. It was the slave girl from the house of Metilius and I nodded but she turned away before I reached the two of them and had bustled away with her head down before I reached the spot and the old guard greeted me.

"She didn't seem so happy," I stated with a lift of my head towards the retreating girl, who turned along the Sacra Via.

"She was here on the night of the fire," he replied. "She's been back every day with a small devotion," his hand was pointing towards the Lotus tree. I nodded my understanding. "Poor girl," he added.

"Why so?" I was perplexed by his words.

"She was sold to a brutal Master, whips them for all sorts of things. Naked as well, you know the type."

I did. I tightened my lips and felt Micus shuffle his feet at my side. Metilius must have been a hard man for all his skills as an architect. "Is the Flamen here?" I asked, looking around but not seeing him.

"They all came back about half an hour ago but I can't say I remember seeing him," came the reply as he threw a thumb over his shoulder. I was about to turn away when he added "and the son of Furius Fusus has been here asking for him too. He was shouting at the priests, telling them they'd pay for their mistakes. He's a nasty piece of work. What's he got to do with anything?" he was asking me the question as I let out a startled sigh. Yes, what was he doing poking his nose into the investigation.

I shook my head. "I have no idea Havitus. I better go and find the Flamen."

The house on the hill was closed as tight as a bank vault and despite several loud knocks nobody answered. I sent Micus to find Graccus and tell him to meet me back in our room at the temple and then went back to the Vulcanal. I was soon standing at the rear wall looking up and down the street when a voice startled me.

"Standing on the fucking street looking up and down won't find anything." It was Scavolo and two of his men. "What have you found out? Anything?"

"Albinus Fusus is kicking up a stink. He's been here shouting at the priests." I was shaking my head.

"I know that," he grimaced. "Pricks been up at the temple telling your father he's not doing well enough in the investigation and he's taking over if we don't find something by the end of the day." It wasn't good news. "That's why we're out here walking the fucking streets like whores looking for business during a plague." It was a rough analogy but suggested that they'd found nothing either. "We've been looking for Athitatus to bring him in for questioning."

"I have too. There's nobody at the house and he's not here," I replied to his cold stare.

Scavolo rubbed his face vigorously. "Maelius has put in a legal claim for Flavius Aetius' house in reparation of a debt owing," said the head man of the temple.

"What?" I was incredulous.

"The fucker owes him loans from about eight or nine months so he says, not just that cart he hired but several other items that add up to a substantial sum. He's already written twice to the man but now he wants the house before it gets sold at public auction if he isn't found."

It made sense. The Twelve Tables were quite clear on the debts issues, but it also complicated this mystery. Where was Flavius Aetius and what had he spent the loans on?

Scavolo was scouring the road. "How the fuck did they move seventy five ingots out of that place without anyone seeing anything? They must have had an inside man, and it looks like it can only have been Titus and possibly his father," he spoke quietly. I was still shaking my head at the fact that we didn't have anything which gave any clue. "We've marched up and down this road just like you said and found nothing. It's almost as if the gods themselves have taken it."

I agreed and bit my lip as I turned back to the remains of the temple where the guard Havitus was looking towards us. The place was starting to take shape again, the floor space cleared, the walls starting to be rebuilt and the altar was adorned with fresh flowers and a candle.

"Are you sure Albinus Fusus wasn't implicated in some way?" I asked with a glance around to make sure there were no ears listening. He replied with a shake of his head and a mumbled answer that whilst he couldn't rule it out it just didn't seem plausible. "Then as we've said several times they had to be moved either in the days or nights they arrived or they are hidden close by," I reasserted. "And how did the people who stole it know about Fusus' ingots? It can only have come from the temple itself, maybe through Titus' father or one of Fusus' men. The only information we have about any unusual activity is that a priest, and we are assuming it was Titus, walking the streets at night and calling on Vulcan to desist from setting fire to the city. There is nothing else. It's as if someone has snuffed out the candle and we are all in the dark. Someone must know *something*," I said in exasperation.

"Look," it was one of Scavolo's men. "Isn't that your lad?" We all followed his eye line. It was Micus waving at us urgently from along the road. I rushed off, the others following my lead and we were soon at the corner of a small side-road which held three houses along three sides of a square. At the doorway of one was Athitatus, shouting angrily at a tall man in richly coloured robes. I recognised him from Milo's earlier as he had sat at a table and was eyeing me up for a while before he left just before the rain.

"Got him," snapped Scavolo.

"Flamen!" called the former centurion as we approached. Athitatus turned in shock and then fear raced across his face as he saw us approaching. He mumbled something to the other man, who hastily retreated and closed the door. "Get inside, get that bastard," barked Scavolo and both of his men raced ahead as Athitatus lifted his chin and started to exclaim anger at our sudden arrival.

"Shut up you prick," growled Scavolo.

"You can' speak to me like that," replied the priest as our two men hammered on the locked door before one moved to the side and started to climb the wall.

"I can speak to you any way I want now that you've resigned your position. Hiding something in there are you?" he lifted his chin to the doorway.

"None of your business. And you know the law," he replied angrily. "You can't accuse me without proof."

"My lads will find proof, don't you worry." He gripped the old man's arm tightly. "You need to come to the temple. On the authority of the Quaestores we have questions to ask you," he said formally. "And Secundus here is my witness," he added quickly.

The Flamen tried to shrug him off but failed as the grip that held him was like iron. The door behind us crashed open and our man was inside, shouting and swearing at whatever was there awaiting him.

"You'll pay for any damage," said Athitatus with a glance at the broken woodwork.

"Not if we find what we're looking for we won't. It'll be you who pays then," came the quick response. "Secundus, get in there and see what you can find, those two will wreck every bit of evidence if they're not held back. Then come back to the temple. I can handle this," he added with a condescending look at the High Priest

I hadn't responded quickly enough so Micus pushed me forwards and we both ran into the house, me stumbling, Micus racing lithely. The atrium was small, square and low ceilinged, a contrast to the house I'd been in this morning and which still worried at the back of my mind. Three doors were open and I followed the noise, avoiding discarded pots and tables which were half-broken in the chase that must had occurred. The house wasn't very large, with no courtyard or central space and only four rooms. The last of these came to a walled garden of about ten paces square. The space was overgrown with weeds and smelled strongly of piss. Three men were writhing on the ground, the coloured robes giving as good as they got against Scavolo's men who had floored him and lay on his back to wrestle him to submission. Thinking quickly I turned to Micus. "Go and search inside quickly, see if you can find anything of value, any hidden items from the temple. *Anything*" I suggested.

I moved across and started to call the man to stop fighting, that he'd been caught and under the authority of the Quaestores, I'd taken that lead from Scavolo, he was under arrest. He told us to fuck off, so the two guards continued to punch his head as he fought back, hardly landing a blow and getting two to one for his poor efforts. Prick. Eventually he stopped fighting back and one of the two men took a length of rope from his waist and tied the man's hands tightly at his back.

"You'll pay for this you bastards," called the brightly robed man through a fat lip which dribbled blood onto his chest.

I shook my head. "Under the law of the Twelve Tables a man who resists questioning when called can be forcefully retained," I said with a slight smile which brought vigorous nods of approval from the two men who held him.

"Bollocks!" came the reply. "You entered my house without being called to question."

I shrugged. "If you hadn't slammed the door in our faces I am sure you would have heard my request, wouldn't he?" I replied to the evident glee of Scavolo's men as they agreed wholeheartedly that I had said this. "Take him, I'm going to look around the house. Oh, and get the man from the temple, Havitus, to come and stand guard here. Can't have anyone coming in and stealing anything whilst he's being questioned."

The man swore all the way out of the house, cursing me and Scavolo and suggesting that my balls would be on his dinner plate by nightfall.

XI

Athitatus had said nothing by the time I returned to the Temple of Jupiter despite both my father and Scavolo being like a lion at his throat. We left him with a guard and retreated to my father's room for an update.

"The house was almost empty of any furniture," I said, explaining that we'd searched every room to find only a single bed and very little of anything else. I told them we'd searched every corner, looked for loose stones and searched the one small chimney for secret doors but found nothing. It was another mystery. Why had the man reacted so violently to an empty house? I'd left Micus with Havitus and told him to continue searching and report anything he found.

My father rubbed his chin at my words. "I need you to speak to the Flamen Secundus, we'll speak to the other man. See if you can loosen his tongue, you've been good at it before."

It was praise coming from my father and I accepted it with a nod. They left and I realised I was suddenly thirsty so headed towards the kitchen area at the rear of the temple, finding Philus sat at a table and chatting to another slave. At my approach he jumped to his feet and bowed. Before I could ask for water he spoke.

"They'll take five thousand less, Master," he said with a thin-lipped smile.

I pouted my lips at the sudden words, taken aback slightly as the house had momentarily slipped my mind. "That's good to know," I replied making the assumption that he believed I had sought him out with my answer to the meeting earlier. So there was a bargain to be had after all. I wondered if this was an opening gambit and there was more to come. "I'll let you know later," I replied calmly. "Can I have some water and a small bowl of fruit."

He bowed and set off to gather the items, returning quickly and placing the items on the table.

"When are they planning to leave the house?" I asked.

His gaze to me was calculating. "In two or three days," he replied. "They need to finalise their transport arrangements now that they have a potential buyer," he bowed again and gazed at me with a glance which suggested he had given away too much information and then departed hastily in case I quizzed him some more. So they were planning to move, which made my bargaining position stronger; it seemed there were no other bidders. I rummaged in my empty pockets and then remembered that my monthly allowance was due in a day so any devotions would have to wait. Nevertheless I sank the drink quickly and took my small fruit bowl to the altar and gave half to Jupiter Optimus Maximus and asked for his guidance in the matter of the house of Metilius.

Graccus was waiting for me in the corridor when I returned to the room where the Flamen was held, a jug of water and small cup in hand for the incarcerated man. He waved me away from the door guard to speak in silence, casting furtive glances which raised my eyebrows and caused me to quicken my pace.

"What is it?"

"Albinus Fusus is here and causing a scene. He knows the Flamen has been brought here and wants to question him. He's pushing his weight around but they can't find Scavolo or your father to sort it."

I knew where they were and guessed it would take a few moments to find them. "Quick!" I exclaimed. "Come with me." We rushed back along the corridor and to the room where the guard was standing outside. "Don't let anyone in except my father or Scavolo," I ordered him as he pushed the door and we entered.

"Athitatus," I said to his bored expression as he turned his face to ours. His eyes were heavy, as if he hadn't slept, and his mouth turned into a frown. "Fusus is here. He wants to speak to you urgently. He's in an angry mood. We need you to tell us things so that we can work out this mystery and clear your name."

I was talking quickly to draw him into our discussion. I'd used the family name to make it sound as if the old man were here and not the son. It had more weight, especially for a man of his age and standing who would not see the son as his equal.

"We need your help," I urged, moving hurriedly with my plea and hoping that by suggesting we were on his side and believed he was innocent of any crime I might get truthful answers to my questions. He was sighing and narrowing his eyes in suspicion but I pushed on. "Titus signed for the ingots on the last day. He must have used the Flamen's ring," I said this as I looked to his hand to see that he still wore it. "If he wore it how did you get it back?"

He looked at me shrewdly before answering. "I guess there is no point in hiding it, I believe you will find out eventually. There is a secret drawer in the altar. Only he and I knew of its location because he is the first priest, the oldest. I explained it to him when he took that role and moved up the line of succession. He would have been the next Flamen if he had not been murdered." It was something I didn't know but it made sense that they promoted from within and had a system to do so. "I agreed we would go to Ostia to stop the incessant bickering about the dreams and bad omens he was having and he agreed to sign the contract and then to replace the ring. He had replaced it when the seal was made and I gathered it when we could get into the remains of the temple on our return and the altar was cool enough to get access. It is one small light in an otherwise dreadful situation," he said as he span the ring on his finger nervously.

I rushed on as noises were coming from the corridor outside already. "Tell me of Titus and his father. How was their relationship?"

His eyebrows rose at this. "Flavius is an old friend of mine, we grew up together. When Titus turned twelve he was dedicated to the temple as the family had no other children and Flavius worked as a blacksmith for us, he was very good. Titus didn't want to join and argued against it as he had some relationship with a girl from the Quirinal that his father wanted to put a stop to," he shrugged "but that soon ended as he had to obey his father's wishes and the rules of the priesthood, as you know."

He smiled mirthlessly at this as the priests had to swear to celibacy in the same way that the Vestals did, although there was no threat of being buried alive for breaking Vulcan's rules. It was one reason the Vulcanal struggled to attract new priests to their order whilst orders such as the temple of Saturn seemed to be growing rapidly as they happily took on family men.

"So they didn't get on?" I asked.

"No. In fact any time that Flavius visited the temple Titus would avoid him. It was a difficult situation as Flavius and I remained on good terms and he often gave devotions and support to the temple. I would say that Titus never forgave his father for assigning him to the role as a priest. Recently his father was trying to reconcile their relationship. He is getting old and has no heir you see. But that hasn't gone well."

The noise outside was growing louder.

"Did they meet? What happened?"

"They met on the street once and began shouting at each other, accusing one another of terrible things. After that I tried to intervene and set up several meetings which turned sour within moments. It would all be fine until I left them to discuss things alone, and then within moments they'd be at each other's throats. The hatred from Titus was too strong. My old friend was distraught afterwards and asked if I could release Titus from his duties, but it cannot be so without banishment from the city which would serve nobody."

"And Titus..." I was looking at the priest now as something was clicking in my mind. "He was drinking too much berry juice, having visions. Did you sanction this? What were his dreams about? Is there anything you can tell us about how these ingots could have been moved?" They were random questions, too complex to answer in a hurry. The door behind us was pushed and words exchanged which suggested the guard was doing his duty of blocking entry.

"Who knows?" he answered shaking his head. "He only had the juice when we completed our ceremonies, as did some of the others on occasion but he did store a few jugs of the stuff in the temple. His visions were clearly given by Vulcan as he saw fires leaping into the streets. He could tell us when the weather would change and he seemed to have a very clear idea of what the future held for us all. I wish I'd listened earlier. But he wasn't drinking the juice very night as some seem to believe. His anger at his father had disturbed his mind I think, certainly more than the juice of the lotus tree."

"Did any of the other priests or any other men stay late at the temple? Could any of them have moved those ingots?"

His head movement was suggesting not. "There is nothing I can tell you. Titus slept there for the nights before. I locked the gates to the vault myself and the key was in the secret place in the altar. Only Titus and I knew it was there. The ingots were there every day when I returned. I checked every day." He looked up at me from his seat, silver stubble showing on his chin. "Well the shape of the two piles was there. I am sure you and I now realise that the thieves kept the outer ingots in a square but the inside was hollow. If Titus had an accomplice and they moved them," his eyes were angry now "none of the priests saw it happening and despite all our searching we have found nothing, as I am sure you have or you wouldn't be asking me these questions. I know as little as you do Secundus despite all my searching." He spoke in a resigned tone, his shoulders drooping. "And now I will likely be banished." His head dipped.

The guard outside was now raising his voice to stop the group who were outside entering and I recognised Albinus Fusus' voice responding furiously. Athitatus shook his head at the noise. I looked at him again and something made me ask, "did Titus let himself go in the last few days?" His face turned a questioning gaze to me. "Not washing his hair or face. Not shaving. Wearing filthy clothes or not maintaining his usual standards? When you saw him each day did he seem different in any way?"

"No. he was a meticulous man. He never let his standards slip."

"They will ask you why you were so angry when they found you just now, who that man is and why he slammed the door and tried to escape. Is there anything you can tell me that about who he is and why you…"

He spoke across me with a mirthless laugh. "He is a private investigator Secundus Merenda. I asked him to search for clues to the mystery as I felt you were incompetent. He will say nothing to your men and you cannot accuse him of anything as he is under the protection of the temple. Oh," he added quickly. "You or the temple of Jupiter will have to pay for his door as well."

He gave me a cold stare to suggest that I dare to disagree with his assessment. I tightened my jaw and saw the vision of my balls fried and placed with salad on the bastard's dinner plate.

The door crashed open.

****

Athitatus had told me something I had missed. At least I now had one part of this mystery solved, and it was a game changer. It made my thoughts whirl with excitement as possibilities now opened which I had not contemplated previously. I started to reconsider everything I'd learned to this point and what it meant. And yet there were so many parts which didn't add up. Graccus had missed it, but my mind was now spinning with the news. I'd rushed back to my room and grabbed a slate to scribble my notes before I decided I had better pay a devotion to my patron goddess as well as Janus and even Jupiter for the opportunity of the new beginning which set me on my new path. Despite this revelation I felt I couldn't trust Graccus after the Milo incident. I held it close to my chest as I sent him to find Maximus and get the lad to come back again the next day as I felt guilty that the boy had hardly done anything whilst with us.

Not long afterwards I stood at the temple of Minerva, asking if Fucilla was in attendance today, but she was not. So I placed a caged chicken on the altar and asked the priestess if she could give it to the head priest who was performing the duties for the day and complete a reading quickly as I was in a hurry. She was a sour faced old woman who looked me up and down with distaste written in her features, clearing thinking I was atoning for some sin or abuse against plebeians or even worse. I ignored her harsh face as she turned and took the gift. The priest looked bored, his face alight at the bird as it was given to him and he turned his quick-eyed face toward me. He was smiling when he received the offering as it was a healthy bird and he would eat well tonight once he'd removed the liver and heart which would be offered to the goddess. I'd asked for the liver to be read and he quickly dispatched the bird, the blood captured in a cup as the animal was sliced and the liver and heart removed quickly.

Another priestess, a young dark-haired girl with large brown eyes and thick eyebrows gave a much more favourable view of the temple as she maintained her gaze on me for an uncomfortably long moment. When I glanced to her she met my eyes with interest and a modicum of sensuality which surprised me. I swallowed nervously as it was something I wasn't expecting. This seemed to make her smile as her full lips curled before she turned away in time for the priest to start moving the liver parts with his silvered knife.

"There is a lot to understand here," he said slowly and with wide eyes as he wiped his hands on a blood covered cloth, the red life-giving liquid shining brightly. "You have the favour of the goddess, she guides your footsteps," he said. I tried not to shake my head as it was clear that my devotion was to gain favour and he was also surely aware that I had been involved with the temple when solving the death of Lucilla as it was obviously big news; well certainly big enough to bring people to Milo's to stare at me. I placed myself into that bored expression that I hoped showed my status, but at that moment a thought relating to the night at the temple of Vulcan hit me like a stone thrown from the Tarpeian Rock. Was it the goddess giving me insight?

"You see it don't you?" said the priest who had clearly seen the expression on my face change.

I stared at him, my mouth now as wide open as my eyes.

"The goddess has given you a sign. Take it. The path is narrow and difficult but she guides you Secundus Sulpicius Merenda."

I'd not given my name so he obviously knew who I was and what I was doing. Had he simply played the usual game of giving the supplicant a half-truth with double meaning that could be interpreted in several different ways or did he know what I had just seen in my mind's eye. Two things had now fallen into place very quickly. I almost stumbled as I stepped back. The young priestess turned an urgent face to the priest as he beamed a wide smile, my stupid stumble adding to the drama of the situation. Heads turned from around the temple, people seeing this movement as a sign from the gods. If the priest had stumbled or dropped his knife it was a bad sign. The supplicant slipping, falling or having some sort of reaction was a good omen. The priest knew as well as I did that my stupid slip had instantly raised his standing in the temple, and the news would spread so the wider religious factions as well, and his wide smile told me that whether or not he'd made up his reading it had meant something to me and was worth its weight in gold ingots to his career.

I held out a hand. "Thank you sir. You have helped in ways you cannot understand," I said as his bloody hand was wiped on the cloth before he gripped my hand with a shrewd look in his eyes. I was learning quickly, just as my father had said *pay the plebs and the plebs will pay you back*, I thought to myself *pay the priests and the priests will pay you back*.

"Marcus Decitus Drusus," he said with a nod of his head. He understood it as much as I did. An ally for the future for both of us.

Outside the temple the sun was drawing the day to a close. I considered returning to the temple of Jupiter to see what had occurred after I'd left Albinus Fusus shouting obscenities about Athitatus stealing his inheritance, but decided I needed a bath before much needed sleep. Thoughts ran through my mind as I rounded the Palatine Hill and started my journey towards my father's house. The road had been updated in the Etruscan style, good flat stones and a deep channel at the edges to take away rainwater and rubbish. If the Etruscan's had given us anything of value it was their road building skills. I made quick headway despite the busy traffic of people, some pushing hand carts others carrying poles with sacks attached as they headed to their own homes. As I approached the house I saw Micus at the doorway. He waved quickly and then disappeared inside. It wasn't long before I was greeted by my mother at the entrance, a strange occurrence indeed, and I noted several unknown slaves hanging about near the kitchen.

"Secundus," she almost spilled her wine as she greeted me. "Come and sit with me."

I was about to decline but knew I'd get the tutting and sighing treatment so half-smiled and followed like a dutiful son should do, wary at what was coming next. The brazier was blasting heat and the smell of wood smoke permeated the garden as we exited into the large square in the centre of the Domus. I was reminded of the house on the Jugarius and the covered porticos as we stepped into the cool evening and I realised why Micus had rushed away and I was greeted at the door by my mother. Five faces turned to me. Five mouths opened into beaming smiles.

"He's here," said mother with a pained expression that suggested they'd expected me hours before and I'd somehow neglected my duty to them by turning up later than my appointed hour when in truth I had almost returned to the temple and certainly had no idea that I was awaited by this gathering of old crones.

They all clapped and two stood to greet me.

I turned a frown to my mother. Her eyes told me I'd better play the game.

I bowed and greeted everyone. My mother then listed the old ladies who sat around the brazier. It appeared they were a group from the temple of Minerva who had popped round for a meeting about helping out poor orphaned children, which I guessed was a request for funds from my family. I'd forgotten their names as soon as I was told them.

"I've just been to the temple to make a devotion," I said jovially. This raised excited titters and smiles. "Marcus Decitus Drusus completed the sacrifice in a most professional manner," I said as if this meant anything to them. "He's an impressive fellow."

This set them off into a whirlwind of discussions about good priests and bad and the role of female priestesses. I found them debating why a female priestess could not sacrifice to the gods if the gods themselves were female. I had no answer but agreed that it should be something that was given thought. I was waning under the chatter and constant requests for my view and was delighted when Micus appeared to announce that my father was home and requested my presence. I bowed to them all, kissed my mother gently on the hand, which I hadn't done for years and left them to continue to devour the family wine vaults as they certainly had an appetite for the stuff by the look of their re-rimmed eyes.

Father was in the Lavatrina. Sul was next to him splashing water on his face and Scavolo was leering at me from the small tub before he ducked under the water and them let out a spray of water as he came back up for air.

"You could have rescued me earlier," I said indignantly, seeing that they must have been there for a while.

Father laughed. "The old crones need to see the goddesses chosen man, Secundus. You know that by now. It's costing me a fortune in wine but we've had two dozen eggs and four sacks of flour as gifts from *the ladies* this past week so a few minutes of your time is well worth it."

Scavolo grinned at this and splashed the top of the water. "Room here lad," he said to my baleful glance. I undressed slowly as he carried on speaking. "As I was saying to your brother, we found out that the man with Athitatus is an investigator. He's been searching the streets for news about the fire and what happened as well as the missing ingots. The Flamen paid him." I nodded at this as if I didn't know it, keeping back my own news. "He's found nothing either."

"This case has to be solved or that prick Albinus will take over," said my father, changing the mood in the room dramatically. Sul glanced to me and Scavolo scowled at the room at large. I slipped into the water, it was deliciously hot.

"I'll rub your back," said Scavolo immediately.

I turned at his request and felt the rough sponge rubbing forcefully over my shoulders. My father continued as I clamped my teeth tightly shut.

"This fucking thing is going to ruin me," he started. "How did they get those ingots out of that vault?" He was staring at me now, and I hesitated long enough for him to continue speaking. "All we know is that the dead man's father is missing, that the ingots are missing and that nobody knows a bloody thing about it. Athitatus says he knows nothing and the whole fucking thing is going to fall on us like a bolt from Jupiter if we can't solve it quickly."

Scavolo was enjoying his role as my back scrubber but answered, "We know that there must have been someone on the inside, otherwise how did they know about the ingots being stored at the temple. We know that Flavius Aetius knew about the ingots because his slave told us he did. If he knew, who told him? How did they get them out? Well the gods only know that one. Secundus is right, they must be somewhere close. We walked up and down that street today and found nothing. We asked at almost every door and got blank stares and silence." I thanked him with relief as I took the sponge as soon as he stopped and wondered if my back was now akin to the red mess of Graccus' face when he used his imported sand to tone his skin and give him a healthy complexion.

My tub-mate lifted his chin and turned his back to me. "Just there," he pointed at his shoulder blade. "Be hard. I like it hard," he said before continuing. "We went past Metilius' old house, it's for sale," he said.

"Since his death the house has been seen as unlucky." It was Sul who spoke in reply.

"Unlucky?" I asked.

"That's what I heard. He got drunk and threw himself in the river and drowned at the Lupercalia last year. Then the next day the building he was working on had the roof collapse and two men were killed." he shrugged. It did seem like a bad omen.

"Prick," replied Scavolo. "Always was."

"You knew him?"

"Of course I did. He was part of the Hastati. Good spearman for a short arse."

"Short arse?"

He looked at me as if I was stupid. "He only came to my chin. Little man but strong as an ox and to be fair he gave a good account of himself in the ranks. He was a prick when it came to business though, telling everyone they were idiots, looked down his nose at everyone," he chuckled at his own words. "He was super clever. He'd solve mathematical equations in his head and then tell people they'd cut the wood to the wrong side or shape and telling them they were stupid. He was hard on everyone. Proper little bastard at times."

It was another character assessment from Scavolo but one that interested me on several fronts.

"How do you know he was drunk on the night he drowned?" I asked as I had another thought come to me.

"He was seen wobbling around, shouting and singing," said Scavolo. "Why?"

"And how long has that house been for sale?"

Sul looked to my father before he answered. "Almost a full year," he said with a frown. "Why? Do you think it has something to do with the ingots?"

Everyone was looking at me now. I let out a slow breath and contemplated telling them my thoughts about the two things that had come to me today but didn't as I could only foresee problems if we rushed to a conclusion without proof, just like they had done with Brocchus.

"I don't know," I said. "But Athitatus told me that Titus used his ring to seal the delivery of the ingots and then placed it in a secret drawer within the altar and that they kept the keys to the vault there as well. He collected the ring the next day after the fire."

I'd deflected the question of the house as best I could but made a mental note that I needed to close this loose end as quickly as I could, and that if the house was seen as unlucky and had been on the market for so long then I could possibly get another few thousand off the price at least. I looked to my father and wondered if I could get a private moment with him and discuss the price.

"So the ring was there all the time and Titus used it. That closes that question," said my father with a glance to his head man, who was now scrubbing his groin with the sponge I'd handed back to him. "And if the key was there all the time anyone could have opened the lock and moved the ingots. What does it mean for the investigation though?"

"It means that only Titus and Athitatus were aware of the final delivery and that Titus did his duty and then replaced the ring. If he was intending to steal the ingots and leave, why would he leave a heavy gold ring? It must be of great value just for the gold alone." Everyone nodded. "He also told me that he had tried to broker discussions with Aetius and his son, as the boy was given to the temple in his twelfth year and had been unhappy with the decision. Titus hated his father from that day and wouldn't listen to any request from his father to make up. It was something to do with a girl he was in love with at the time. They'd argued and fought recently and the Flamen had tried to help out but it had caused more problems than it had tried to solve," I added.

"The priests have their own code when it comes to their artifacts and treasures," said Scavolo in answer to my previous point. "I guess that he saw the ring as a sacred object and wouldn't take it. You know what they're like," he said to my father, who had been a priest for many years.

He nodded agreement and I wondered what that meant for him. Was he not as devoted to the priesthood as it seemed? He'd spent most of his life in various roles and only become Quaestores due to his patronage of temples and work within them. Politics was new to me and I was still struggling to understand what motivated people, including my own father.

"I wonder if we need to think of this as two separate mysteries," I said slowly. "If the death of Titus was not related to the stealing of the silver, then would we look at it differently?"

"What do you mean?" Asked my father. "They are clearly related."

"What if they were not and that by assuming that they are we are missing something?"

"Explain?" said Sul, his face alight with questions.

"If the silver was stolen but nobody died and there was no fire what would we do?"

Everyone sat in silence for a moment. Even Scavolo stopped his vigorous rubbing of his genitals. "We'd get everyone in for questioning and find holes in everyone's stories until we found the culprit."

"But we can't do that because it is Fusus' ingots and nobody except the High Priest and Fusus' family knew about the transport so we have to keep it quiet in case it leads to questions being asked about his finances."

"It complicates matters that is for sure."

My father was rubbing his chin now as he could sense what I was suggesting with my questions. "But you are right. Only Athitatus knew of the exact delivery dates until the first one was sent. That was a deliberate ploy to ensure that nobody was able to make any plans to intercept them. And nobody knew there were any more than just the one delivery, Fusus told me that himself only yesterday. They only moved the ingots with a few hours' notice so that nobody was aware so much silver would be in the vaults."

"So there must be a spy in the household who has sold their story to the thieves. They needed time to prepare the theft, it is impossible to move that many ingots in a single night so they must have been ready on that first night and Titus must have been involved. It is unthinkable that they had to sneak in and out whilst he was walking the streets, it would complicate matters beyond limits," I said in response.

"No," replied Scavolo. "Fusus and his son are insistent that nobody knew from their end and that they trust everyone."

I bit my lip as the links I'd made started to align into a single chain. "Nobody?" I turned to the man at my side.

"You can't still think that Fusus' son is complicit in this?"

"It does make sense," replied Sul.

Before Scavolo could reply I asked another question. "But let us think then how the fire and death would be dealt with if there were no stolen ingots."

"We probably wouldn't have investigated much as there was a dead body and stories of him walking the streets claiming Vulcan was sending fire to burn down the city. The man was clearly mad and I guess we would have concluded that he set the fire himself. It's unlikely that fool Novius would have seen that he was murdered as you did."

He appraised me with a calculating glance.

I sat back and nodded, although I felt the rebuke that Novius must have been given by the tone of Scavolo's words. My father looked at me shrewdly. "Gaius is right. We'd never have known he was killed," he added. "The fire would be seen as being set by him due to his madness. It would have been a closed case and added to Athitatus' unlucky year."

"Then all we need to do now is work out how the killer and the thief, for they could be two different men, joined these stories together. I bit my lip for a moment remembering what had come to me at the shrine of Minerva.

"Scavolo, I have something I'd like you to do for me." He looked across at me with a worried frown. "How strong a case does Maelius have against Flavius Aetius?"

"Hardly a thing really, but he has some documents which are signed," he shrugged. "Though without the second copy it isn't clear that he'd win anything in a court."

"But Aetius is missing and his only heir is dead. If he has a document which says he loaned the money and carts..." I replied coldly, letting them make their own conclusions to my unfinished sentence that suggested he would win.

Scavolo looked to my father and they both raised their eyebrows.

"I'd like you to investigate this claim and get into his store to see whether he has ten Sarracum, for that is the number that the Brocchii family tell me he owns. They'd know, it's their livelihood." My father glanced to me with interest as this was another fact I'd not informed them of yet.

"I see," said Scavolo. "Get in, see if he has anything missing that might mean his claim is valid but also to spy on him."

I tightened my jaw before I spoke, unsure what information I should let them know as I was not sure myself of my conclusions. "I have a theory," I said, bringing all faces to me. "On the night of the fire who was at the site helping to put out the fire with all his slaves and men?"

"There were a lot of people around from what we've heard," said Sul unhelpfully.

"You mean who had the numbers to pick up a few sacks of bronze or silver and sneak them away in the chaos?" said Scavolo. "Clever bastard."

I nodded. "But it is only a guess, we cannot be sure."

Scavolo let out a hiss as he sat on the ledge to the side of the pool. "You're right though. He could easily have had his men running up and down pretending to fill buckets with water and taking hidden ingots back to his store up the Clivus."

My father's face grew dark. "If he's taken those ingots I'll string him up myself," he muttered.

"We cannot speak of this," I said quickly with a glance to each one of my bathing companions. "It may be wrong, but it is the best guess we have made so far. It's too much of a coincidence that he was there and has the men to have been able to move the treasure. If you can get in and see what he has, check if anything is covered or hidden away."

Scavolo nodded.

I was about to tell them my other piece of logical guesswork when someone hammered on the door so urgently that we all turned sharply.

"Master," it was my father's head slave, a man by the name of Closus who I very rarely saw or had dealings with. He pushed open the door and with wide eyes exclaimed "you must come, all of you, there has been a man found dead."

"What man?" called my father, half out of his tub already.

"The Head Priest of the Vulcanal, Athitatus. He is dead," he replied flatly.

XII

His body looked pathetic in the darkness.

The man who had been so often angry and yet so full of life had been dragged into the undergrowth and dumped, his face turned up to the sky in a parody of praying to the gods whom he loved. I felt a tinge of sorrow as my mouth stretched tightly and I let out a short breath. Memories of Lucilla and Perdita flashed across my mind as I looked down on his prone form. The whites of his eyes were rolled back in his head and his arms and legs lay at odd angles.

"We let him go just before sundown as you asked," said Novius to Scavolo's question as we stood over Athitatus' body. I noticed Scavolo shake his head at his man. "He was angry that we'd wasted his time but otherwise he was fine and he didn't seem to be in a hurry to leave, he kept asking about when the other man would be released as he wanted to get his help to clear his name. He's still locked up."

That interested me. So Athitatus was still claiming he was innocent. So what had led to his death if he had nothing to hide? I looked at the scene where the body lay. We were in the trees near the foot of the Tarpeian Rock which was directly below the Temple of Saturn and not far from the Vicus Jugarius from where we'd just come. Once again this road seemed to have something to do with this case. The body had been dragged through the dirt to this point, we could clearly see the trail, and been dropped, which led to the strange body angle, legs crossed but arms splayed outwards. His windpipe was sliced neatly, just as that of Titus had been cut. Was it the same man that killed them both? I knelt and touched his body, he was still slightly warm and so couldn't have been dead long. The trail of blood suggested he had been killed elsewhere and moved here to hide his body. I'd have to check that out as soon as possible.

"Does he have his ring?"

Novius dropped his candlelight to the Flamen's hand and we all stared grimly at the mess that was left of his hand; his ring finger had been removed. "Looks like they couldn't even be bothered to try and take it off," he said with a shaking head.

We stood in silence for a moment before I said loudly, "we need to follow his last movements." I was suddenly thinking aloud. "If he was released just before sundown then it cannot have been more than an hour until this point in time. He's still warm. So where did he go?" I turned to Novius. "Who found him?"

"A lad down the street. The dog came out for a shit and started barking at something and ran into the trees."

"Is he here?" I asked as a small group of onlookers had already arrived at the scene and were stretching their necks to see what was happening.

"Here, Scolius" called Novius into the dark.

A small boy appeared, his father at his side to protect him. I nodded to the boys parent as they both looked at the dead man and then to me and I asked, "did you see anyone else out here when you chased your dog into the trees?"

The lad looked like he was going to piss himself in fear and gazed to his father, who gave him a stern stare and flicked his head towards me indicting the boy should answer his betters.

"The dog ran into the bushes and then I heard a falling sound and someone running."

"Did you catch a glimpse of him at all?"

"No," he replied. "It was dark."

We all nodded at that. "Did the dog chase him?"

He looked at me quickly before averting his eyes. "No. He was too busy here." His face fell to the floor and I noticed that Athitatus' leg had been bitten in several places.

"Can't blame the dog," said the father, clearly worried that the attack might be raised in some form of legal claim.

"You don't need to worry on that account," said my father dismissively, arriving and taking control immediately. "The man was clearly dead and the animal cannot be blamed for any action against a man out after dark."

This brought a flash of relief in the face of the older pleb, his knowledge of the laws clearly lacking.

My father turned to the boy. "Which way did the man run?"

The lad pointed to the right, towards the Tarpeian Rock. A flick of the head sent two of Scavolo's men off into the woods at a trot, bright torches burning as they disappeared through the trees.

"Thank you," I said to the boy and his father. They left slowly, looking back at the dead man and then up at my father, his thick robes of office hastily thrown over his shoulders and still dripping wet hair.

"Novius?" The temple man looked up at the mention of his name. "When you released the Flamen, did he say where he was going?" He was suggesting not by his head movement. "Then I suggest we go to their house on the Clivus and see if he made it home. He must have been out in this direction for a reason, he can't have simply wandered out here at dusk without an explanation."

Scavolo and Manius joined me as we trudged slowly back along the Jugarius and past the ruined Vulcanal. I looked at the dark structure, its famous altar still visible in the ruins as we passed by. I considered what we knew so far as I glanced across at the site. The death of the priest, the movement of the ingots and now the death of the Flamen. It had been an unlucky year for Athitatus, but how much of it had been his own doing? His actions had seemed rushed, his decision to go to Ostia seemed a strange one, and then the decision to resign his position.

I was shaking my head as we circled to the steps which led to the priests house. Scavolo hammered on the door despite the late hour and within moment's a worried looking slave cracked the door a slither and peered out at us, his eyes searching as if he was expecting someone else. It was the man I'd seen before. "Let us in" called the ex-centurion "in the name of the temple of Jupiter and the Quaestores. Fear showed in his face as he briefly glanced over his shoulder, where I could see Caelius had appeared in the corridor, a half-eaten apple in his hand.

"Who is it?" he asked loudly.

"Scavolo!" shouted the man at my right. "Let us in you pricks, we have bad news for you."

I touched his arm and whispered "don't tell them yet. Let me speak and see if they know of his movements first."

He nodded agreement, though I sensed he'd prefer to rush in and bash everyone, as the door was opened and I led the way into the small corridor. We were greeted by the faces of the priests as they sat around the table in the room in which I'd interviewed Athitatus. I tried to note if any of them had splashes of blood or dirt on their hands or clothes as I nodded to them all, but everyone seemed clean and they all wore the same brown tunics so I assumed their blue clothing was being washed after the day's work.

"What's this about?" asked Caelius indignantly, clearly their spokesman and a good actor if he knew what had happened to his head man.

"Have you seen Athitatus this evening?" I asked calmly.

"He came in earlier complaining that you'd arrested him but then he went out?" said Hector, his face a picture of surprise at my question. "Why?"

"Did he say where he was going?"

"No," replied Caelius in confusion. "Why?"

"He had a note," came a small voice from behind me. I turned to see the slave looking at me.

"What note?" I asked.

"It came this afternoon. I don't know who brought it, it was pushed under the door with his name on it."

"Do you still have it?" He hesitated at my question, eyes darting to the priests who were glaring at him. "Did you read it?" he looked frightened but I knew house slaves often read their Master's letters or post to check if it is important.

"Come on, did you read it?" said Scavolo as he rounded on the slave, who stepped back against the wall in fear. "Well?" he added loudly as the man took a few fearful seconds to answer.

"It is here," he said shakily, moving quickly to a small alcove where several slates and wax tablets were piled. I saw names and dates on some of them, probably letters from home, shopping lists and so on. He fumbled with the slates and then handed

Scavolo a small non-descript wooden tablet on which the name of the Flamen was scratched.

Scavolo opened it and then passed it to me. Inside it simply said

You double crossed me. Meet me at the rear of the temple of Saturn at dusk. FA

I stared at it for a long moment as thoughts streamed through my mind. This couldn't be right, surely!

"Did you see any signs of who left this for him?" I asked as I stared at the words. The slave suggested not as he cowered at Scavolo's glares. I shared a moment of eye contact with Scavolo but I knew something that he didn't and so I kept my features as calm as possible despite my mind being alight with thoughts. "How did he react to this note?"

"He was angry," he was shaking his head as he spoke. "Then he went to get changed, threw the tablet down," he nodded towards the pile from where he'd retrieved the document and then shrugged.

"Did he speak to anyone before he left the house?" I asked to the assembled priests at the table. "We need to know?" I said urgently.

"Why?" asked Caelius again.

"Just answer the fucking question," snapped Scavolo, who had now stepped into the room and was circling the table like the Hercules circling the Erymanthian Boar. Caelius scowled at this and started to stand but was forced back into his seat by the temple of Jupiter's head man, Manius at his right shoulder.

"It's a simple enough question, shouldn't be too hard for you clever bastards," he said slowly as he eyed them all viciously, daring anyone to answer back.

"He didn't say much at all." It was Regicius who had spoken. "He complained about being arrested. Changed into a clean tunic and left almost immediately. He never mentioned that" at which he pointed at the tablet and glanced angrily at the slave. "I did ask him where he was going, but he just shrugged and said he'd be back soon. Why are you here?" he now added. "What's happened?"

Scavolo glanced to me and I inclined my head.

"Athitatus is dead," he said flatly.

The priests rose as one, mouths open, eyes wide and gasps filling the room. I watched them all, looking for signs that might give away any one of them, but I saw none. Every man was full of questions, hands over their mouths in shock and tears in their eyes.

"What happened to him?" It was Caelius again, his question directed to me.

I let out a short sigh. "He was murdered. Somewhere near the trees at the base of the Tarpeian Rock less than an hour ago." Caelius sat heavily, Nesta placing a hand on his shoulder as his tearful eyes glanced around at his fellow priests. "I assume you've all been here and nobody's been outside in that time?"

Their angry faces at the suggestion gave an indication that they understood my question and was soon followed by verbal assurance that none of the priests had left the house since they returned from the temple.

"Did he say anything else? Anything at all. The smallest thing could help us find his killer," I asked the question as I continued to watch them all, looking for any falseness in their actions but still seeing nothing. They were all continuing to shake their heads. I glanced to Scavolo who stepped back towards the door raising his chin as if we should leave.

"Do any of you recognise this writing?" I asked suddenly remembering the tablet in my hand. I held it out.

"It looks like that of Flavius Aetius," said Caelius" his eyes wide. "Those are his initials and he often wrote to Athitatus and signed his notes that way."

"Would you agree?" I asked the slave. He nodded quickly.

****

Scavolo and Manius had been to Aetius' house at the bottom of the Clivus Capitolinus but it was shut up tight, as we expected. I'd returned to my room at the temple to find Philus blurry eyed as he opened the rear door to my knocking as it was now close to midnight. I'd explained what had happened and asked him to find something to eat for four or five men as the men sent to search for the Flamens murderer would be arriving soon. He rushed off to do so after a few quick questions at which he'd gasped when told of the death of Athitatus.

I'd started to write my notes on a wax tablet, bent close under two candles to get enough light to do so, as Scavolo and I discussed what we knew. His men arrived soon after in a single group, exhausted and talking loudly after their march up the hill. They were pleased to find Philus with trays of grapes, dates, watered wine, flat bread and some cold cheese as they appeared in the corridor by the kitchen and helped him to bring it to the room.

I raised my eyes to Novius as he entered. "Any news?"

"Nothing. No sign of anyone anywhere near the temple or in the trees. Nothing more than a few tracks which suggested someone ran off towards the Jugarius." His glum face was etched with frustration. "We carried the body back. It's in the cellar," he said to Scavolo.

I suddenly remembered something and stood, turning to them both. "Is the body of Titus still down there?" Novius said it was and I nodded to them to follow. "Bring as many candles as you can, I have something to show you," I said to the assembled group as I headed off into the rear corridor and down towards the steps which led into the cellars. I could smell the body of Titus, given its own room because of the stench, from fifty steps away and pulled a cloth over my nose. "When do you bury them?" I asked.

Novius was somewhere behind and answered, "they usually get taken by a family member. I'd forgotten he had no-one so you're right I'd better get it sorted."

I was glad he hadn't despite the reeking stench as I was about to show them what I had learned from my conversation with Athitatus earlier. I stood over the body, which had been wrapped in a thick cloth and peeled back the layers slowly as my eyes watered at the smell of death. Flies lifted to the burning torches and candles as I moved back the cloth and I noted the white skinned maggots burrowing on his burns as I pulled away the damp clothes. Trying to ignore it, and feeling as if I was about to puke, I clenched my teeth and spoke hurriedly.

"I spoke to the Flamen before that prick Albinus burst into the room and started accusing him of stealing his silver and he said something that made me re-consider what we knew. I tried to discuss it earlier but I wasn't certain so held it back," I had turned to Scavolo, his eyes shining and mouth tense as he listened. "We all know that the priests are very fastidious," I said as I pulled back on the cloth and lowered my candle, with it's pathetic light, towards the neck of the body. "More light," I said and several hands closed in around me to illuminate the corpse. "What do you see?"

Novius looked confused. Scavolo narrowed his eyes, but nobody answered.

"Titus was a particular man, as all the priests of Vulcan are. You've seen how they use creams to keep their faces young?"

It was a question to the group and received several grunts from the assembled men. "They wear their hair in that knot down their backs and..." I opened my palm and faced it toward the head of the dead man.

Scavolo grimaced but didn't seem to understand what I was getting at. Novius shuffled his feet and I felt Manius and another man edge closer to get a better view at whatever I was using my palm to indicate.

"Fuck." It was Novius.

"Yes, you see it don't you?"

"It's not him?" he said incredulously.

"Not who?" asked Scavolo.

"Titus," we both said in unison.

"What?" he pushed Manius back a step as he edged closer. Scavolo was the only man not wearing a cloth over his face but he had to wrinkle his nose as he pulled his dagger and scraped it across the slit throat. "What do mean not him?"

"The beard" said Novius. "They all scrape their chins every day. It's part of their rituals," he said with an appraising glance to me.

"What?" asked Scavolo again, his brows furrowed.

"That is what made me rethink everything earlier. If I am not mistaken, Scavolo, this is the body of Flavius Aetius and not that of Titus. Titus is still alive."

My father was in shock at the revelation. His wide eyes were followed by a creased brow as he took the tablet that Scavolo handed him, signed *FA*. "So, someone wants us to think that Flavius Aetius is still alive and by the look of this tablet has tried to suggest to anyone who finds it, that Athitatus and he were in on this together?"

"Exactly!" said Scavolo. "And they killed him to close that loop and make it look even more like Aetius had done the deed and absconded with the silver."

My father looked at me for a long moment, his face fixed but his eyes shining brightly in the flickering light.

"But they don't know that we know that it's not Titus that is dead."

"So you think it's the priest Titus who did it?" My father had shifted his position in his seat and placed the tablet on the table.

I clenched my jaw before answering. "If it is, he's working with someone else?"

"That bastard Maelius," snapped my father.

"We don't know that" I said slowly.

He huffed at this, clearly his mind made up as to who was behind this series of murders.

"All we know is that Titus is probably still alive and he is likely the person who both stole the silver and committed Patricide." The significance raced around the room as eyes narrowed at the words. In our laws Patricide was one of the worst forms of murder and would lead to strangulation, beheading and having your body left out for the dogs to eat. "We must use this knowledge to our advantage," I said to Scavolo.

He nodded. "I'll go and visit Maelius at first light. Get there early and see whether he has anything hidden in that store of his or if he has all ten of the large wagons. If he tries to block me I'll tell him his case against Aetius will be buried under last week's latrines and never dug up again. He'll believe me," he smirked. I believed him too. It was exactly what the senators did with juicy bits of information that didn't work in their favour.

"Keep a look out for locked doors too, or signs that Titus might be holed up there," I added to his gaze in my direction.

"What about Albinus?" It was Novius who asked the question and it brought several nodding heads in response. The son of Fusus had been kicking around the temple at the Vulcanal for most of the evening before and had had them dig up some of the crops as well as lifting two of the stones in the vault to check that nothing was hidden under there. It had raised many conversations around the Forum as many of the bystanders had watched this happening. My father told us he'd received a note from one of his friends with a query as to why Fusus' boy was digging around the Vulcanal. The news would soon get out that Fusus had lost his silver and that wouldn't go down well with our investigation. We needed to act even more quickly now to try and close this case as Albinus Fusus kicking up a stink was sure to cause even more problems.

"Well, we better try and catch some sleep even though there are only a few hours till Gallicinium when the sun would rise. You can stay here for the night, Philus will find you a blanket," he said to all of Scavolo's men who nodded at the offer.

On our way home, which was a good twenty minutes' walk and I was beginning to wonder why I hadn't just curled up in my room with a blanket as my father pressed me for thoughts on why Titus would kill his own father.

"Such an act is against nature," he said sternly. "And the laws preclude it with the most severe of punishment. His whole family and tribe would suffer the consequences," he added.

"He has no-one left in his family," I said through the fog in my head as I was still trying to understand what we'd seen this night and what twists to this plot Vulcan was giving us. "His father let him go when he was a boy and he has no connection to the tribe. If he had then it may be different as you say, but he has only the hatred he felt when he was given to the priesthood against his wishes."

My father huffed at this, suggesting he couldn't understand how anyone could go against their father's wishes. "But to go against the family is the lowest form of dishonour."

I remembered Scavolo's words *piss off with daddy's gold* as he persisted to bemoan the state of modern Rome. "But father, you know as well as I that people act in a state of madness, driven by the will of the gods, when they face these dangers. How many men have stood before you on the Comitium and had no thought beyond their own immediate situation. Few consider the implications of their actions."

He looked over his shoulder towards me before speaking. "All men consider the implications," he said slowly. "They just choose the wrong actions."

I shook my head. "I don't agree. A man put in a tight corner will fight like a dog to get out with no thought of the consequences. If the gods Phobos and Deimos place fear and dread in your heart there is little that runs through a man's mind other than panic. Panic breeds action and action leads to implications beyond what rational thought dictates. Each action creates a new set of reactions. Titus has been guided by Nemesis, by revenge held in check for years. Something triggered the desire and opportunity to act and his only thought was to achieve his revenge, without thought of the implications. Nemesis drove him through the years."

My father looked at me with a shrewd glint in his eye. "You're turning into a scholar," he said with a smirk. I shook my head at the rebuke. "So the man is not responsible for his actions, it is the will of the gods?"

"I didn't say that."

"But if Deimos puts dread in your heart and you flee the battlefield, should you not be punished? If the gods will it, then you have no choice in the matter even if your actions lead to the demise of all your fellow soldiers."

He was enjoying this, the bastard.

I walked in silence for a moment as thoughts jumbled around in my head and tried to fix themselves into a coherent sentence. "We are both right," I said, resigned to the fact that my father was too clever for me to play word games with; you didn't get to his level in society without being good at this sort of intellectual sport. "But as you say the critical fact here is that Titus knows the law but has chosen to ignore it because Nemesis, or whichever god is driving his thoughts, has turned him to madness."

"Then the gods are to blame again, not the man," he said almost in triumph at my pathetic argument. "Titus is weak. He cannot control his own emotions and has gone against the laws of the gods and of man in murdering his own father. His actions were in spite of his knowledge of the consequences and he will suffer the full weight of the law when we catch him. The gods haven't directed him to act, his own weakness has given him the desire to act."

We'd reached the slow rise towards home now and the track became steeper. "But that is the point, father. His actions suggest that he doesn't think we'll catch him. His actions are clearly designed to try and put us off his track whether it is the gods directing him or not. If we didn't know that the body was that of Flavius Aetius we'd be looking in another direction right now and thinking differently. If Janus was tricking us into a different set of thoughts we'd leave Titus alone and focus on his father and that would give him the opportunity to escape. He's fighting to get out of a corner, irrational thought and actions will follow. That is how we will catch him father. He will make mistakes now that he believes we think his father killed the Flamen."

We approached the gate and one of the men had run ahead to knock and announce our arrival. My father rubbed his chin and gave me an appraising glance. "Then I was right," he said. "He has chosen his actions and dishonoured his family in doing so. He understands the implications and has chosen his path. Under the law he has no defence for murdering his father."

I nodded, he didn't. "One thing is for certain," I said with a dour glance back along the road we'd walked. "If he thinks we are looking elsewhere then he will run for the hills, with or without the help of the gods. We need to double the men on the roads and check every cart for those ingots." Another thing came to my mind and I smiled as my father turned a questioning gaze to my changed facial features. "And in answer to your question," I said. "If it is not the gods guiding the actions of men, how is it that Minerva guided me to the murderers of Lucilla Arturii?"

This brought a smile. "If a man follows the laws and heeds the implications, the gods will support his actions. It is the will of the gods that gives direction but the actions of men that create opportunities to be exploited in the world," he said philosophically.

The gate opened and we trudged in, my legs starting to ache at the walking I'd done today. I left my father to discuss the day with my mother, who was waiting at the door with a glass of wine in hand despite the late hour.

XIII

It was far too early when I was dragged from my slumber, I couldn't honestly call it sleep as I twisted and turned for what remained of the night. Micus and I were left behind the marching group as they set off at a fast pace towards the Forum and the Capitol. My feet dragged like I'd been walking in thick mud all day and my arms felt like I'd been lifting heavy weights at the gym for hours as I yawned again and again. Gods, only a few weeks ago I'd be up all night getting smashed out of my skull on cheap wine and then up and about again with only a few hours of sleep. If this is what work does for you, you can keep it. It was no wonder people like Graccus were driven to using fine sand to rake their skin to a red pulp in an attempt to try and look healthy, it was probably part of the ritual of simply staying awake. I yawned again and then nodded to Micus to take a left turn and head towards the Jugarius and the house of Metilius. I wanted to see if the old man was at his gate and I was sure I'd soon catch up with my father's group as it wasn't too far of a diversion.

The road was empty as we approached the houses on the Jugarius, with a fine blue sky just visible above the light mist as the morning was dawning with the suggestion of a bright and warm day. I considered a devotion to Vulcan as we would pass the temple and was fumbling in my pocket as I walked to see what coins I had on me, if any. Birds sang in the trees on either side of the road as we came within a few houses of the place I wanted to see and I noticed that the cloth shop had lights in the windows and the shop keeper was out on the road waving his arms at something above him. His head turned in surprise as he saw us in the distance and he seemed to suddenly change his actions, making them more urgent and waving wildly at the swinging crane that was reaching outside the upper window and was likely moving cloth from storage to store front. His actions had subsided by the time we arrived and I noted that he'd closed up the doors and all the shutters were closed. Odd, I thought, but he probably thought we were up to no good being out at this early hour. I was standing outside the shop when Micus spoke quietly.

"Is that the man you wish to speak to?" he asked as an old man appeared from the doorway of one of the houses ahead of us. He had a basket and a knife and proceeded to cut some ripe olives from a tree, inspecting them before taking them and placing them into his basket. We hurried across and I waved at him as he frowned in our direction at my movement.

"Oh, it's you again," he said with a half-smile. "Do you need more information," he grinned with the expectation of more bronze.

"I do as it happens," I said with a warmth that belied my empty pockets. "This is Micus," I said as he looked at the boy. They greeted each other with a nod. "Can I ask you about the nights that the priest was causing a disturbance on the road?" He looked up, thrust out his lower lip and nodded. "I understand that Spurius Maelius and his men saw the priest here a few times late at night. Did you see them as well?"

"Maelius?" His brows were creased.

"Yes, he told me himself. Said that the priest was causing a commotion and arguing with the locals. Did Maelius get out of his carriage and speak to him? He said as much," I lied.

The old man rubbed at his chin and gave me a calculating glance. "Maelius told you that?" he asked looking to Micus, who nodded slowly as did I. He clipped another olive from the tree and placed it in his basket.

Something was troubling him. I guessed it was the thought that a man as powerful as Maelius might not be happy to learn that a local had been gossiping about him to strangers.

"Yes. I spoke to him yesterday. He said he'd come across the priest a few times along the road between here and the temple." I had to play this right as there was clearly something here if the guarded look on his face was anything to go by. I turned to look back along the road, the slight decline giving a good view over the houses towards the Forum Halitorium. "He also said that he'd come across a local man, which I'm guessing was yourself, arguing with the priest about the noise and had come to your aid." It was another lie but I had nothing to lose.

He looked back along the road to where I'd turned my head before he answered. "I didn't need any help," he replied coldly. "Bastard priest kept pissing on my gatepost. He deserved a good kicking and I was about to give it to him when Maelius and his lot turned up."

I raised my eyebrows and nodded knowingly as if Maelius had told me the same story whilst in my chest I felt my heart start to hammer at my chest. Once again I felt the need to send a devotion to the gods but I also heard my father's voice in my head suggesting that it was the actions of men, and not the will of the gods which created our opportunities.

"And what happened next?" I asked with a glance to his gatepost, suddenly sensing that slight smell of piss once more that I'd attributed incorrectly to the old man.

"Well Maelius shouted at his men to drag the priest away. The bastard was a strong bugger though and they took a while to get him up the road. He kept shouting and cursing about fires. Maelius came over and apologised though. Nice fellow," he said with a curt nod.

I agreed. So Maelius had lied to me.

"And they took him away, back to the temple. That was good of him," I said with my thoughts working through what I'd heard. I looked over at the house next door and felt a slight anxiety as I noticed the red flag had been removed. I assumed that is because they thought I was buying it. The shame of having to drop out of the sale if I couldn't find Fusus' ingots burrowed into my mind. I definitely needed to make a devotion to Vulcan.

The old man saw my glance. "Saw you going in there. You buying?" he smiled with narrowing eyes.

I turned a smile back to him and shrugged. He obviously saw everything that happened on the road. "It's expensive," I said in response before looking up at his house. "You selling up?"

He laughed at this. "If I did the lad would kill me. It's his inheritance," he said. "He lives in the Subura at the moment. Rats nest of a place," he added shaking his head, "but closer to his work. Good road this. Brings a good price with the position and being close to the Boarium and Halitorium too. I'd have him living here but he wants to make his own way in the world, you know what I mean?" he looked me up and down to suggest that I was similar and age to his son. "Get a good view if they throw someone from the Rock too," he added, inclining his head towards the Tarpeian Rock which was visible along the road towards the Capitol Hill.

Something clicked in my mind. "Did you see anyone out here last night?" I asked. "There was a body found up there."

His jaw fell slack at this. "Really? Last night? Who?"

"Not long after sunset. Probably an hour into dark but I don't know who it was yet. We're going there now aren't we Micus?" I said in reply, deciding that I'd better not say who had been killed. Micus nodded quickly.

"It was fairly quiet, has been since that priest died in the fire," he said slowly. "*He* came back from the fish market late, it was almost dark," he said inclining his head towards the next door house. "Cursius. He goes late to get the cheap stuff they sell off before it goes off. Had a good sized portion by the look of it too." He rubbed at his chin once more and I turned to the house and considered this for a moment, Cursius might have seen something. "And Maelius and his lads went past towards the Tiber, in his carriage. Partying again no doubt," he was shaking his head as he spoke.

That got my attention. "Oh!" I said. "How many of them?" he was suddenly guarded again. "If they saw something which would help find the killer then it'd be good to know how many I need to speak to," I replied to his frown.

His mouth tightened but he finally replied. "The carriage and three others. Those two big buggers and another one."

I nodded my thanks. I needed to speak to Cursius and mentioned that to Micus before I turned back to the old man. "Well I must be getting on my way. Good day to you," I said with a smile and noting his glance towards my pockets as I appeared to be leaving.

At that moment my father's words floated through my mind; *pay the plebs and the plebs will pay you back*. "And thank you," I said as I thrust out my hand. "I will send a quarter sack of grain with Micus later today in thanks for your information."

He gripped my hand like a long lost son and held it for several heartbeats, thanking me a little too long for my liking but apparently sincere in his gratitude.

****

Milo greeted my arrival with a wave towards my *usual* table as we came into view of his shop at the top of the Clivus and I suggested to Micus that I needed something to eat. I noticed that the statues remained and that despite the early hour he had one other customer, an elderly lady wearing a thick shawl which covered her shoulders and head. Milo was chatting animatedly as he turned hot bread in a pan over the fire and then crushed a couple of cloves of garlic on a slate before adding it to the bread with some oil. My mouth watered as the smell drifted across. He waved to Micus, ladling some hot wine into a cup and held it out for the boy to collect and bring to me.

I sat and considered what I'd learned from the old man. Maelius had lied. Why? His men had manhandled Titus back to the temple on the day before the last delivery of silver from what I could gather, but he hadn't told me this when questioned. What was he hiding? The wine was perfect and warmed my throat before Milo appeared at the table and checked if I wanted hot bread as he didn't have much else on the go at the moment due to the early hour. I was just nodding when I heard a call from the corner, it was Graccus, with Maximus in tow and they headed across quickly lest they miss out on the food order. I could see the slate filling at my cost as they approached and I nodded to four flatbreads, a small one for Micus to which he beamed as he had missed breakfast too.

The two men took off their woollen cloaks and sat on them to keep their legs warm as the stone seats were cold.

"I have some news," I said quietly as I bent my head to avoid Milo listening, although he seemed consumed in chattering to the old lady. Graccus wiped his nose in anticipation and I saw Maximus move his arm towards his face, intent on picking at his own orifice. Nevertheless I resumed with my news, explaining how the Flamen had been held prisoner, released and found dead in the trees near the base of the Tarpeian Rock. It received shocked gasps from both of them, followed by slurping at their drinks before Graccus wiped his nose on his sleeve once more. I stared at the silver line on his tunic in despair as Maximus made to pick at his nose again, giving a long prod which even Micus screwed his eyes at. I then recounted the story from the priests with regard to Flavius Aetius' note and how I'd shown my father, Scavolo and his men the dead body of Aetius and concluded that Titus was still alive. Again this brought astonished looks from both men, followed quickly by the upending of their cups.

"So Titus is the thief and the murderer."

"It would seem so," I replied to Graccus' statement as I continued to stare at the long trail of silver on his sleeve which flashed as he lifted his arm. Something was nagging at my mind as he did this, but I couldn't put my finger on what it reminded me of. "We think that Maelius and Titus are working together," I said, glancing to the shopkeeper who was turning the bread in his pan whilst still chatting to the old lady. "Scavolo is going to visit his house this morning and see if we can find anything."

A thought came to me. "Graccus, you should go with him. bring any news directly back to me," I added, with a feeling that whatever Scavolo found he would report to my father first and they would decide what to tell me when they had thought through any plans or stratagems that their new information would give. "You go too Maximus," I said to his nodding head and words of thanks.

The food arrived and Milo handed me the slate to sign, which was almost filled so I shook my head and ordered three more cups of wine and a water for the boy. I rammed the food into my mouth as quickly as I could as I had a sudden sense of urgency. Were the gods driving my actions or was it my own internal hunger? I smiled at my memory of my father's clear thinking and my own indecisions. I remembered I owed a libation to the gods and so I suggested to all that we saved a small amount in each cup that Micus could take to the Vulcanal and pour an offering to a closure of this mystery. Everyone thought it was a good suggestion and we ate quickly, chatting through the discussion I'd held with the old man, whose name I couldn't remember ever asking, and the fact that Maelius had lied.

It was Graccus whose comment made the most sense as he said, "he'll be finding some way to profit from all of this. It's not just about turning you away from his door, it's about ensuring that he isn't implicated in any way so that he can retain his position." It made sense. But if he was attempting to muscle in on Fusus' grain deals then surely there was a simpler way to do this than to murder two men. Maybe my father was right, the opportunity had been presented to him by the gods and he'd made the decision to break the law and chance his arm. I couldn't put it past the man, but it still seemed far-fetched. What links did Titus and Spurius Maelius have, if any? Had Titus found out about the debts his father owed and somehow gained access to Maelius in this way?

"Graccus," I said, turning to my friend who had just finished his last mouthful of bread and was wiping his hands on the skirt of his tunic. "We need to know more about how Titus and Maelius are linked. Ask around, did Titus visit his house at any time?" I held my breath for a second as my mind ran through options. "I'm going back to the Vulcanal to ask the priest some further questions as well. If they know what relationship Titus and Maelius had they may unlock some of the clues to this mystery." I looked to Micus, who was staring at me intently. "You better go home before you're missed," I said slowly to his disappointed face. "But I have a job for you after you take the wine. Drop in at the house on the Jugarius and speak to Cursius, the head slave of Metilius' house. Ask him if he saw anyone out last night when he came back from the fish market." The lad beamed at this. "Bring the news back to my room at the temple. If none of us are there leave a message with Philus." He nodded his understanding.

I was soon back at the Vulcanal, my hands on my hips as I looked at the neat rows of stone that had been built over the past day. It was good quality work and at this rate the temple would be back in place in no time at all. Hector was busy watering the rows of vegetables and I noticed Caelius behind the Altar on his knees so walked across.

"Caelius," I said to his back.

"Ah, Secundus Merenda," he said, getting up from where he was cleaning the floor with a thick scrubbing brush. I noted that the flagstones behind the altar were scorched and he was removing as much of the thick black stain as he could do. "What news do you have for us?"

"Very little I am afraid," I said sadly, suddenly remembering that behind this mystery life still continued and the priests must have hundreds of questions to ask. I looked around at the almost tidy scene. "You've done well to get the temple cleared."

He sighed slowly. "Athitatus pushed us to get things tidied. He said it was what Vulcan would want," he was shaking his head and I could see tears building on his lashes. "Despite this year he has been a good Flamen," he added quietly.

I nodded. "Scavolo and my father are out searching for clues of his death. As soon as I know anything I'll send a message," I said, knowing full well that I'd forget to do so, but it was the thought that counted. He seemed pleased by that. "Who will take over as Flamen?" I asked, the thought coming to me.

"We voted when we discussed it with Athitatus." I remembered them all going to the house to do just that. "I will be the Flamen elect until the Pontifex appoints a new man," he said with some resignation in his voice.

"My father knows him," I said before I'd though through the implication. Were the gods directing me? "I'll speak to him and ask for a good word to be put in for you," I said with a small incline of the head to suggest it was a small gesture and I was unsure what weight it would carry. He nodded slowly. "Might I ask a few questions?" I said to his momentary silence.

"Go ahead."

"Has anyone thought of anything else about Athitatus' return and leaving last evening?"

He was shaking his head. "Nothing. We discussed it and came up with nothing new. We came down here late last night to light a candle in his name and then said prayers to Vulcan. When can we claim his body?"

The suddenness of the question caught me off guard. "The temple man Novius will be able to tell you. If you send your house slave to ask for him he will arrange it for you." I looked around the scene. "I hear Albinus Fusus was here yesterday."

He was shaking his head again. "The man's an idiot. He pulled up flagstones, dug up the crops. Does he not think that we had already checked all of this," he said. "But of course his kind never do," he said before looking up sharply. "Apologies," he said, suddenly realising his mistake in blaming a patrician for being overly aggressive and ignorant. I waved away his remark.

I looked towards the broken gateway to the vault and inclined my head. "When will you get the gate fixed?" I asked as we wandered across towards the sunken treasure vault from which the ingots had been taken.

"I will redo the iron work in the next few days, and Nesta is going to learn. We think we should listen to the old ways and start afresh, keep the best of the old ways of Vulcan as well as try new things. A new vault, deeper and with double gates." He placed a hand on the thick stone walls which remained at head height in this area and we both looked down into the darkness from where the ingots had been taken.

The chain and smashed lock remained on the floor and I peered at them as a thought came to my mind. I bent and picked up the chain. It was weighty and old, but solid in its construction. The lock, too, was sturdy but had been hit several times to break it. None the less the mechanism looked quite clean and the connector didn't look damaged. "Caelius," I said with a sudden thought crossing my mind. "Look at this. Do you think the lock was broken?" I asked.

He gave me a quizzical frown but took the heavy iron lock and turned it in his hand. "I assumed so," he said as he stepped back a fraction and held it to the light. He pushed at the clasp and then at the broken edge whilst shaking his head. Then he pushed the closing bar into place and wiggled it slightly. It came loose but his tight mouth told me what I needed to know. Titus had opened the lock and then smashed it afterwards. It was a clue we'd all missed. "This lock was not broken before it was smashed. The mechanism is still in place, it was opened before it was smashed," he said with a deep frown. "It was Athitatus, wasn't it?" he said with a long sigh.

Obviously they'd put two and two together overnight and decided that Athitatus and Flavius Aetius were responsible for stealing the ingots and burning the temple. His shaking head and angry eyes told of what the priests believed. I couldn't tell him what I knew and so with a tight jaw I nodded quickly. "There is a secret door in the altar," I said. "Do you know of it?" He looked confused by this question. "Athitatus told me of it. Titus placed the Flamens ring there when he signed for the ingots," I confirmed. I turned back towards the altar and asked, as we approached, "where might it be?"

He came across and bent to the altar searching for a moment before he pressed at a figure of Vulcan and the stone effigy moved slightly. He shook his head. "All these years I never knew where they kept these things," he mumbled.

The figure of the god pulled out effortlessly by pinching the head and neck, which protruded slightly, between my finger and thumb and an empty slot behind the stone was revealed. Sadly there were no objects or clues within and he replaced it before turning to me.

"Do you have the Flamens ring?" he asked. I shook my head, explaining that whoever killed Athitatus had taken it, avoiding the unpleasant truth about half of his hand being missing as well. He bit his bottom lip at that and looked down at the altar in sadness.

"I must go," I said after a few moments silence. "Thank you," I said with a glance towards the altar and vault. He nodded. "I will remember to mention you to my father. It might have some weight," I shrugged.

"I believe that the Pontifex will put his brother in place," he answered. "We are prepared for it." He sounded resigned as he turned and knelt back to his work once more.

I now knew one more thing, something that could have been useful a few days ago and was now too late to do anything with. The gates had been opened by Titus and the ingots taken without having to force the lock. It was obvious now that I had the knowledge of the priest and his actions but it led them to believe the worst of their former head priest. It was no wonder that nobody had heard the lock being smashed. I felt sorry for the dead Flamen, his unlucky year none of his own doing. I was at the corner of the Clivus Capitolinus when a thought struck me that the lock had a further significance. I stood for a moment looking back at the altar and the gateway but whatever was digging into my brain didn't connect as I was too far to distinguish whatever image on the altar or whatever significance being at the temple had played with my mind. What was it that I had missed? Was Minerva sending me another message? Or was it Vulcan trying to guide me? Or was it just a lack of sleep? I stood for a while staring at the Vulcanal as people began to pass me on their way to temple of Jupiter to make devotions or towards the market in the Forum to buy goods. Whatever significance it was, was lost on me. I tapped my lip slowly thinking that I needed to carry a wax tablet to write significant thoughts or they would flitter from my memories like the seeds of a flower floating in the breeze. I decided I needed to make a libation to Minerva and headed back up towards the temple to find some wine which would serve for that duty.

****

Philus greeted me with a frown as I crossed the hearth of the temple of Jupiter Optimus Maximus with the appearance that he'd been awaiting my arrival. I was immediately taken aback by his dour expression as he bowed quickly without taking his eyes from mine and then straightened to offer me his most serious face.

"I have bad news Secundus Merenda." he started.

My heart sank, was there some tragic news that I'd missed in my haste to visit the temple and talk to the priests? Was it my father? What had happened? I gaped at him, he was clearly shocked at my expression as his face turned pale. "What? What's happened?" I said sharply.

"The house." he blustered, his face a picture of surprise at my outburst. "The lady has decided not to sell. She has asked me..."

He continued speaking but my ears turned deaf at the suddenness of the relief that flooded through me. I was so consumed with this case and the two deaths, both violent and horrible, that I had immediately jumped to the conclusion that the killer had crept into the temple and attacked my father. My mind ran back over the previous months when I had cursed him for his arrogance, ignored my family as they complained about my state of mind and constant drinking, blamed the gods for my losses and then blamed everyone else as I was imprisoned in my room to avoid the anger of the wider familial elders. All of the emotions and anguish of the period since the death of my wife and first child flushed through me like a river running through the Cloaca. I sucked in a long breath of air and my wide eyes stared at the face of Philus, who simply stared back at me as if I had gone mad.

"What?" I asked quietly as my ears and eyes started to function again. "What?"

"They have decided not to sell the house just yet." he repeated with a worried expression.

"Not sell?" I was flabbergasted.

"Yes Master."

"Not sell?"

He stared at me with a look which suggested I was the village idiot asked to solve a mathematical conundrum. "Yes Master." he replied again, his hands clasped tightly lest I let out my anger at him.

Someone shoved past me and grabbed my arm, pulling me along like a wooden horse on a string. "Come on, prick. We've got some serious shit to think through. Philus get us a drink and some food and then get the Quaestores."

It was Scavolo who almost dragged me into his room. I glared at Philus as I was pulled along, the anger at losing the house suddenly dawning on me. "Bastard was out when we got there." started Scavolo as my father appeared in the room looking as tired as I felt. My mind was racing to catch up and I remembered where he'd been. "It took us a while to get in but eventually we did. That knobhead Farrius followed us around like a puppy and stopped us poking our noses where he didn't want us to." Farrius must be one of Maelius' men, but I had no clue as to who he was so simply sat and listened.

"But these two did their bit and kept wondering off which gave me time to peek around a bit when he went off after them." he said with a nod towards Maximus and Graccus, both men showing pleasure in his praise. "We checked the store and the yard. He has eleven wagons, so one more than you thought." he glanced to me. "If he lost one to Aetius then he had twelve." He was now looking to me for confirmation. I didn't know what to do as I'd relayed the information from the Brocchii, but that was certainly not confirmation of how many wagons he actually owned. I raised my eyes in agreement.

"Then things got shitty." he grinned. "The bastard came back and was clearly shocked to see us crawling over his yard." I suddenly remembered that the old man from the Jugarius said he'd seen Maelius going out on the previous evening. He'd obviously stayed out all night. I suddenly wondered if his carriage could conceal ingots, a thought I'd had before but had been dismissed. "He kicked us out on our arses with a few curt words." he was grinning now "and a flat denial that he asked us to investigate anything to do with his claims against Flavius Aetius." He slurped at the wine that Philus had served whilst he was speaking. "He's on his way up the hill behind us to kick up a stink Marcus, so I thought we'd better get back quickly and prepare."

"What else did you find?" I asked quickly.

"Fuck all." he said flatly.

I grimaced at his choice of words. I was about to ask another question when we heard shouting from outside.

"That'll be him." said Scavolo, standing, downing his drink, pulling his tunic tight and smiling to my father, who grinned back at him. They were like two boys playing a game in the Forum.

I gaped.

Scavolo scowled at me. "We need to get you to that fucking tutor." he said sharply as I snapped my mouth shut.

****

Milo was surprised to see me as I appeared at his bench and sat, my back to the road. "You look like you bet everything on the blues and the greens came in," he smiled. "Wine?"

It was still early, a little after sunrise and yet I felt that the day had stretched from yesterday with little repose. I nodded despite the early hour to start drinking and he served it with a cup of water for me to dilute. I drained it neat. Placing both hands on the counter and frowning at me he let his eyes flick around the road and land back on me after he'd confirmed that there were no spies listening at my back or shady characters standing at the corner watching.

"Bad day? Want to talk about it?" His beetle-like eyebrows danced as they rose high above his eye sockets. "Have another one, on the house," he added as he poured another, though I noticed this one was only half the measure of the one I was going to have to pay for.

I shook my head and sighed. To be honest I wanted to let it all out and discuss exactly what had happened, but I felt Milo was probably not the right person to have this conversation with. "I've been up all night on this case of the Vulcanal," I said slowly, sipping at the free drink and looking to his pans, which bubbled away with an aroma that made my mouth water, to see what he might have that I could consume. "It's turning out to be a lot more complex than it seemed at first."

"Fish in that one and this is vegetable broth. Both will give you a good start to the day as they're not too heavy. This one has plenty of garlic and herb to wake you up," he indicated the closest with a wooden spoon, taking the lid off the pan and stirring it as he noticed my look towards his wares. I'd seen his pictures of a fish and some vegetables drawn on the front of his counter as I'd arrived so it confirmed the choices. I inclined my head at the feast within and he quickly upended a bowl and ladled in a good measure.

"Go sit in your usual seat," he said as my head acknowledged the gesture and I moved between the increased number of tables and chairs towards *my table*. I looked back at the space and was surprised to see that there were now at least three more tables squashed into the small space. Additional, crude, figures of Minerva, and also now a spattering of Jupiter shaped statuettes, sat on each table. I licked my spoon and started on the vegetable broth. As usual it was very good. Salty and fresh. I looked back at Milo as he filled two bowls from his pan of the fish dish and took some coins from a well-dressed woman and her slave, a pretty young thing with light hair and a thin waist. The mistress looked across at me for moment, catching my eye before she turned away quickly and the two moved to sit close to the front of the shop area. I was staring into the sky, which had lightened quickly now, with a hundred thoughts clouding my judgement when Graccus and Maximus arrived, both of them getting glances from the two females, who then bent their heads together. I was intrigued.

"Two more Secundus Sulpicius?" came the shout from the counter. I nodded slowly, expecting the slate to be almost full by now and in truth wondering when I could get the money to pay it, if at all. I could hear Milo extolling his friendship to myself and Graccus and how we'd solved the case of the Fuller's daughter. The women giggled and turned wide eyes towards us. I looked down, I didn't want them staring at me. Graccus was oblivious but I noted that Maximus turned to stare at them with a broad grin.

"Well?" I asked.

Graccus shook his head so slowly I thought I'd have finished my broth before he actually made his point. Maximus was digging into his nasal cavity with his face twisted in concentration and I dropped my chin to my chest and let out a hiss of air. "He's gone now."

"Who's gone?" It was Milo with the broth.

"Maelius," said Maximus as I glared at his loose tongue.

"He's a good man he is," asserted the storekeeper. "What's he been doing? Is he linked to your case," he asked with raised eyebrows.

My glare at Maximus wasn't missed and Milo smirked. Maximus flicked whatever he'd found in his nose away over his shoulder and Graccus slurped on his broth as he picked up the bowl and set his lips to the rim. "No. Something else. He was at the temple looking over some figures on transport for us, he knows more about it than we do." My lie brought narrowed eyes from Milo for a second before he nodded sagely to suggest that he knew better than to accept such a pathetic falsehood. I tensed my jaw, Scavolo was right I needed to see that fucking tutor.

Our silence sent Milo away, and I noted that the same old lady from the day before had arrived at his counter and was looking in our direction. Both of the younger ladies had stood and greeted her. Milo was ushering them to a table for three much closer to where we sat. Two traders also arrived at his counter, their bags looking laden with goods as they placed them on the floor at their feet and asked to taste a little of each of the wares he was selling. I remembered he'd not asked me to add my seal his slate and decided to increase my speed to see if we could get away without paying. It was a vain hope, but I was feeling in a bad mood.

I thought back to what had happened, and what had put me into such a bad mood. Maelius had appeared with two of his advisers, both of whom spoke like lawyers and both of whom seemed to suggest that by entering their clients house under false pretences their client was somehow due compensation. My father had danced rings around them as I sat in silence and watched Maelius closely. He sat with a permanently false smile as Scavolo informed the lawyers that in his opinion Maelius had asked for the temple to investigate the loss of his wagons to Flavius Aetius.

"My client is clear that he did no such thing. Is there a written request?" asked the bald-headed one, his brown eyes calm and collected.

"It was a verbal request," responded Scavolo, adding nothing else and sat with the most serene face I'd ever seen him wear.

Lawyer two checked his wax tablet and was shaking his head. "My client remembers no such request," he added, with a protruding lip. Maelius sat looking bored.

"I remember it clearly." Scavolo talked in facts. "On the day we visited Spurius Maelius' house we were just leaving and a question was asked as to whether he knew Flavius Aetius. At that point your client," a gentle nod was sent in his direction "suggested that he did and that if he found him he would *gut him*. I think that was the correct phrase used?" The question was to me. I inclined my head to show that it was as eyes flicked to me and then back to the ex-centurion. "At that point your client explained that several debts are owed to him by Flavius Aetius. I suggested that we were investigating the case as it may have links to the fire at the temple of Vulcan, to which your client stated that if there was anything he could do to support the investigation and return what was owed to him he would appreciate our help and also would be more than willing to support."

It was well said, and it was what *had been said*. Maelius didn't blink once during Scavolo's sentence but interlinked his fingers at this point.

Baldy looked at his slate for a second. "Yet that conversation didn't offer access to my client's house."

Scavolo raised his eyes to this. "Anything to support the investigation," he said in mock surprise, with a slow look towards my father, who was equally as good at this stoic game as Maelius and simply sat in silence with no expression on his face. "Technically we never entered the house, only the yard and store. We had a need to check the type and number of missing wagons and had asked for your client on arrival. There was no subterfuge," he added with a frown.

Lawyer two was older, grey haired and portly. "So a simple misunderstanding?" he suggested, a glance to Maelius, who didn't react.

I saw an opportunity. "Indeed," I said, bringing several surprised looks toward me as it wasn't the done thing to interrupt the hired workers when they were conducting business. "There are several leads relating to this man Flavius Aetius and our investigation has led us to believe that he may have used the wagon that he has rented to move items from the temple on the night of the fire."

This caused a stir in both lawyers, one staring hard at Maelius and one at me. "Are you implying that my client is involved?" stated the older man, his face now a mixture of shock and anger. Maelius seemed to be concentrating hard on a spot on the wall somewhere to my left, his features a picture of serenity as both lawyers took on a new sense of urgency.

Scavolo jumped in before I could speak again and I saw Maelius' lip curl despite his best efforts to remain emotionless. I could feel the bastard laughing at my ineptitude. "Quite the opposite," came the steady response from the temple head man. "Secundus Sulpicius Merenda meant to say that we wished to ask your client which type and size of wagon was rented so that we could include a search for the right type and size of wagon in our investigation into this matter. There is no implication that there is any involvement on the part of your client."

"But the suggestion was made," stated baldy.

I was shocked. I turned to my father, who frowned and glared at me momentarily at my inability to keep my mouth shut. Maelius saw the movement and his eyes narrowed for a second.

"No such suggestion was made." Scavolo was trying to rescue the situation. "Might I note to your client that we asked for him on arrival at his door. There was no subterfuge. His man let us in without question. At that hour of the morning we had no reason to believe he was not at home, and when we met he had offered our investigation as much support as we required. Knowing the type and size of the wagon which had been stolen by Flavius Aetius is extremely important to this investigation and that was our sole requirement for the visit. Your client is doing a public service in supporting the efforts of the temple of Jupiter as well as the temple of Vulcan. We have a mutual benefit to finding Flavius Aetius," he smiled.

Both lawyers sighed very slowly and let out a hum at the same time before looking at their slates. I wondered if they learned this posturing at lawyer school. "Nevertheless," it was the older man who spoke, his eyes fixed to his tablet as if he was considering some legal point he'd made in his wax. "My client would like it known that entering his property without his express permission is a breach of his privacy," he said slowly.

Scavolo didn't reply or respond in any way, his demeanour fixed into that statue I knew from when I was getting a dressing down from my father. It seemed to unnerve them and they sat in silence for a moment.

"A misunderstanding then." It was Maelius. He stood and nodded. Both lawyers took a lead from him and stood, nodding. Scavolo stood and nodded and then my father stood and nodded.

I sat and stared.

Scavolo scowled at me.

"Spurius, we are sorry you had to break your day on this trivial matter," my father said warmly. "But while you're here I have something to discuss regarding the festival of Vestalia and wondered if you would have an interest in sponsoring an element of the events?"

Maelius had raised his brows to this, his interested piqued. With a stern glance towards Scavolo and then to me which suggested that I'd overstepped the mark my father left the room with Maelius and his lawyers in tow to discuss more weighty matters than that which had brought him to the temple.

"You nearly cocked that up, prick."

Scavolo's ire was bubbling over as he closed the door and rounded on me. "Don't talk over me when I'm discussing matters on behalf of your father, and don't try and play the clever bastard when you don't understand what's at stake."

My mouth opened, but he ignored my attempt to explain myself and grabbed another cup of wine, drinking it as he sat. He held a hand up to stop me talking and downed the remains of his drink before drawing himself up to the edge of his table, placing both elbows flatly in position, fingers interlocked, as if he was about to start a formal interview.

"You might be the bosses son, and you might," at which his eyes narrowed for a moment "have the support of the goddess Minerva, but you have no clue how to conduct business with people like Maelius." I could feel a lecture coming and bristled at his tone. "You don't like being told anything do you. Fuck knows what you'll be like when you get into the Equites with your brother." He poured himself another drink.

"You can't..."

"Yes I fucking can," he said with the force of Mars in his voice. "Your father has appointed me as your trainer, your guide, the voice in your head that tells you when you can eat, sleep or go for a shit. This," and he pointed at the room to suggest that he was lecturing me about the meeting we'd just held, "was a fucking shambles." He sat back in his chair, arms now crossed over his chest. "Your father needs you to learn how to act in company, how to react to situations like that and when you are allowed to speak and when you aren't." I was about to reply but he thrust forward once more. "After that little show," he waved a dismissive hand. "We now have no agreement for us to visit his house again, no opportunity to ask him further questions and he has the upper hand against your father. You made us look like fucking idiots fumbling with our cocks at an orgy."

My mouth dropped.

"And that shit has got to stop," he said loudly, pushing at finger toward my face. "If I had a silver coin for every time your face gave away your thoughts I'd be richer than Fusus and not have to look at your stupid face every day."

I glared at him, then drew my mouth closed as quickly as I could. His teeth bared.

"Let that be your first lesson. You need to get to that fucking shrine of Minerva and pray that you can find a solution to this mess or we'll all be out on our arses. Get out." His chin lifted toward the door as he drew another cup of wine. "Go on, piss off," he said sharply as I stared at him from my seat.

I realised Graccus was waiting for me to speak as these memories now faded and I felt the anger of Scavolo's words burning in my ears. He was right. I had no idea what I was doing. Despite finding the odd clue or being given some divine inspiration to see what others had not, I was as useless as a three legged donkey. My mind filled with uneasy thoughts. I'd stumbled on the killers of the Fullers daughter after believing that I'd found my killer in Ducus the goatherd. Without the gods support I was drowning without a lifeline. Were the gods now pulling away that rope, letting me sink into the cold depths from where I'd come? Yes, I'd been the only person to ask the questions which brought the realisation that it was Flavius Aetius that had been killed and not Titus, but that was only because Vulcan has signalled to me whilst at his altar. And still that information was as worthless as I am without the support of the gods. My mind whirled. Was it Janus turning against me? I hadn't laid any devotion to his name recently and I swallowed hard. Without the godly support I was a nobody, a nothing. I'd also lost the house. Why had Bravia changed her mind so quickly? Had she received another offer or was Vulcan turning his anger towards me as well? I swallowed hard once again, my throat sore and dry.

I heard Graccus sniff and saw him wipe that perpetual drip from his nose, but I didn't care. Minerva was starting to lose faith in me, I could sense it. All this time the gods had been playing with me, lifting me to a position in society in which I was not ready to operate. Scavolo was right, I was only a small part of this system and I'd just cocked up my father's plans. I sighed and tightened my lips as I stared out at the valley through which the Sacra Via stretched. I needed a drink, or several.

"What now?"

It was Graccus who broke into my thoughts. I looked at my empty bowl for a moment but the vision of an unpaid slate being smashed across my head stopped me from ordering anything else. I was about to answer when a tug at my elbow and a nod towards the roadway made me look up. I realised that Graccus wasn't asking what we were going to do, but why the man striding towards us had appeared.

"There you are you lazy bastards." It was Albinus Fusus and three of his men. I noticed Milo looking across with interest. "My father wants you," he snapped his fingers like a man giving orders to his pet dogs with a strange gleam in his eye.

"Now!" It was an order.

XIV

Fusus was as red in the face as a boxer having completed three successive bouts at the festival of Ceres. I sat with my mouth closed and breathed through my nose to keep my calm whilst I attempted to fix my face on a spot somewhere beyond the head of the man who held all of our fates in his hands.

"And you never thought to tell me of this? Albinus had to find it out in the Forum when some pleb with a need for silver started hounding him on his morning ride." The words were spat venomously at Scavolo. As the lowest rank in the room he was going to receive all the anger that anyone had to throw.

"Sir, the murder was only late last night. We have hardly had time to understand what happened, whether it was a random attack or something linked to this case," he replied steadily. As usual I was impressed and considered that I really did need to listen to him when he gave me a bollocking.

Fusus' let his sight range over the three of us one at a time, landing finally on Scavolo with an intensity that suggested he'd have him flogged if he said one more word that was out of turn. A thought struck me regarding what he'd said but I sat as still as a statue, mindful of my place after the earlier dressing down from Scavolo. I looked at Albinus from the corner of my eye, his face calm but his gaze restless as he continued to watch every movement that we made. "So, if you are right then this priest Titus is the man who stole my silver," he stated. "And he was working with Athitatus and Flavius Aetius. He then killed his own father over some feud relating to him being sent to the temple when he was a boy," he glanced to his son in confirmation of the tale that Scavolo had explained moments earlier. "And that," at which he pointed to the slate that held the note to the Flamen on the night he died "suggests that the Flamen and Titus had fallen out and Titus killed him."

It was a short version of what we knew and still that thought from a moment ago was burning in my mind. I watched Fusus as he rubbed his chin slowly and then remembered my *lesson* from Scavolo and returned my gaze to the far wall.

"That's about the rub of it," said Scavolo in response. "Our investigations," at which I noted Fusus' glance towards me "have found that the two men killed Flavius Aetius and burned the temple to hide the fact that they'd stolen the silver over a few nights."

"Then where the fuck are our ingots and where is this bastard priest?" It was Albinus who'd spoken. I noted that nobody seemed to think it was improper for him to interrupt the flow of the conversation. "Do you have any clue to that?" he added accusingly to Scavolo.

Our man tightened his jaw and shook his head slowly. "We think that they may have used a wagon that Spurius Maelius had rented to Flavius Aetius..." he was saying before Albinus interrupted him.

"It doesn't add up. How did Titus and his father make up? When did that happen? Do you know that?" It was asked harshly and I could feel Scavolo starting to lose his patience, but to his credit he held his position with the fearlessness of the military man he is, although he didn't get an opportunity to answer as Albinus pushed on with his assessment of our knowledge so far. "These three men worked out a plan, they moved our ingots each night by using this drunken-priest trick you mentioned, taking them one or two at a time to some unknown place," he glanced at me at this point. "And then on the night of the final delivery they arranged for all the priests to be away on a trip to Ostia, for Titus to seal the delivery. He then murdered his father, presumably after they'd taken all the ingots to wherever they are hiding them before setting the temple alight and escaping. And in all of this nobody, not one person, saw a thing? Nobody has any clue as to where our silver is."

His lips tightened to a straight line as he finished with a glare at Scavolo.

Several things ran through my mind as he spoke. He was almost right, but also there were some subtle differences. His assessment made me question my own account of the events and the thought from a few moments ago was still burning in my mind. I looked at the window to see that the sun was still below the trees. It was still incredibly early despite all of the things that had happened so far this morning. I glanced to Albinus as his father shifted in his seat, letting out a heavy stream of air through his nostrils as he did so.

"It isn't good enough." It was Fusus who was sealing the lid on our coffins. "You have been too slow with this Marcus," he said with a stern glare at my father. "I have creditors coming to me for silver and have little left to give them. This needs wrapping up quickly or I will have to call in my debts. And" his tone sharpened, "It will be your debt that is claimed first," he held out a hand and Albinus took a small tablet he'd concealed in a pocket and passed it across. "I believe this is what is owed," he said as he handed this to my father. He opened it, his lips pursed and before inclining his head slightly to suggest that it was correct. "Then we have two days. By the end of daylight tomorrow I want my ingots returned or the debt must be repaid," has said with a level of finality that left no opportunity for discussion.

I took a slow breath, trying to stop my heart from racing as I considered what the debt must be. The look of concern that crossed my father's face, despite his excellent stoic training, suggested we were fucked. Scavolo also flinched at the words. His future suddenly looking like it was about to turn to shit. Thoughts of Flavia and my farm ran through my mind. The gods were pissing on me now for sure and I rued the missed devotions to Janus and Vulcan as I sat in silence and stared at the wall.

Our patron stood. "And one more thing," said Fusus as he turned to face his son. "Albinus is now taking over this investigation. You lot clearly need a more direct approach. Albinus knows what to do."

The words were spoken with the arrogance of his position, the surety that he was going to lose a serious amount of money if this wasn't solved, and the fact that he wanted his own man close to the action.

I tried not to show any emotion on my face as Fusus made a point of glaring directly at me in a show of power which nobody could possibly misunderstand. The gods were surely looking at me and laughing now as I sat under his gaze and have to accept the decisions that Fusus is making for his own future. My heart sank as did any thought of future happiness. I cannot see any way we can solve this case in less than two days and find all of our patrons silver. With a calm face to the room I cursed my own arrogance at thinking that the gods gave me any credibility other than a fleeting glance in their much larger games. Fusus and his like are closer to the gods and I am just a minnow in a lake of much bigger fish. Is it Janus turning his faces against me again? Something is wrong and somewhere the gods have been disappointed with my actions for certain.

Fusus took some time to set out his plan. Albinus added his own words to embellish the anger and frustration they had at our lack of progress. My father looked downcast and Scavolo appeared to need a piss if the look of concentration on his face was anything to go by. I sat in silence and allowed everything to happen around me as a great sinking feeling filled my heart. Power was being played out and I realised that despite my father's lofty title and generous land-owning he is just a small player in these games. Scavolo was right, I am a prick.

****

Caelius balked at the demand. "You cannot do this!" he stated loudly, his voice echoing into the corridor of the house. Scavolo pushed past with ease, reaching for the collar of the slave and dragging him by the scruff of the neck into the street where Albinus stood grinning. I could see his gaze drifting over the house greedily as our two men, Novius had joined us, took the slave and manacled his hands and neck. The slave cried out at first, terror in his voice, but received a punch to the throat that silenced him instantly as his eyes bulged and he tried to suck air into his lungs through hoarse gasps.

"Under the law," I said in a quiet tone as I was abashed by the act but had been told it was my role to do so, "this slave can be questioned regarding the murder of his Master."

It was Albinus' first order once his leadership of the investigation had been commanded by his father. His words had been that we had been too soft on the priests as they knew the answer to this riddle and a few crushed skulls would loosen their tongues. He wished to start with the slave and then work his way through the priests within a few hours. It was made clear that my place was to follow like a pet and do as I was told.

"I will visit the Pontifex and tell him of this," blustered Caelius, with two of his fellow priests at his shoulder nodding furiously but with fear in their eyes.

I shrugged, knowing it would do little to stop the poor slave being beaten to a pulp and tortured until he confessed to being part of this plot and his life made forfeit. I could sense by the whimpering noises that were coming from his throat that he understood this too. Scavolo and Novius took an arm each and pulled the man along the road as they started the march back to the temple of Jupiter. I looked at Caelius for a fleeting moment and tried to apologise without speaking, but the hatred I saw in his face was enough to let me know that I would now have no answers from any of the priests of Vulcan with regard to this matter unless they were pulled in for torture if their slave implicated them in the theft of the ingots. It was a bad turn of events and one that I could not have predicted. We set off down to the intersection of the Jugarius and then turned left towards the steep climb back to the temple where the slave would be interred for questioning. Albinus and one of his friends were laughing at how easily they had taken the slave as we walked slowly back up the hill. Scavolo was marching, the slave being kicked into action and had soon gained five or ten steps on the rest of the small group who were attracting looks from locals and shopkeepers as we passed by with the slave still pleading innocence through rough gasps for air.

"Might I ask a question?" Albinus looked at me as if he'd forgotten I was there. His brow furrowed but he nodded. "This pleb who stopped you in the Forum to tell you the Flamen had been murdered, what did he look like?"

His response was a confused narrowing of the eyes but he answered with a question, he clearly didn't trust me "why?"

I took a second to respond, careful that I didn't anger him and to maintain a deferential manner. "I am surprised that anyone knew of the murder of the Flamen and also knew that there was a connection to the house of Fusus. The murder was very late into the night and you must have been up at dawn to do your exercise. How would anyone know where to find you and why would they approach you?" I'd asked these questions in a calm tone as benefitted my new status as his lap dog.

He looked back at me quizzically but with a realisation that what I had asked was correct. The thought had come to me the moment his father had said it, but this was the first chance I had to ask. He appraised me slowly in silence as we continued up the hill but then stopped in his tracks.

"Now you say it, it is odd," he replied with a look to one of his men, who I had not been introduced to so had no idea of his name. "He was of no consequence," he shrugged. "Wore a thick woollen cloak, kept his hood up now that you mention it and didn't seem to want to look directly at me," he said sharply as his recollections seemed to come back to him.

"He was quite tall. Broad shouldered, probably a farmer," said the man at Albinus' shoulder, which raised a questioning glance. "I'd dismounted to pull him away if you remember," he qualified in response to the look he was given. Albinus nodded at this.

My new boss looked down his nose at me for a moment as I was lower down the slope. "How did he know that I'd be there?" he said slowly. "And that we were linked to the Flamen's death?" His repetition of my question seemed to suggest that he had made the link in his own mind. It certainly took him a while to connect things. This worried me and gave me the feeling that I was talking to a child. I'd need to remember that in the future.

"Can you describe him?" I'd asked the question to the friend, who seemed to recollect more than Albinus, whose brain still seemed to be taking an age to get to grips with the full meaning my question.

"Long cloak, well-greased, looked expensive now I think of it. He was a broad shouldered fellow for sure. Looked like he'd been about a bit and could take care of himself if he needed to," he added with a gleam in his eye. "That's why I dismounted, just in case he got tricky," he said with a nod to his boss.

"And what did he say, do you remember the exact words?"

The man looked to Albinus before answering. Albinus was nodding for him to continue. "That he had information about the Flamen Vulcanalis if we paid him a silver coin." I nodded eagerly to get him to get on with it. "We told him to piss off but he was dragging at the horse to stop us riding off. Then he said that it related to the missing silver and we needed to know." He shrugged.

I rubbed my chin slowly as he was speaking. "How did he know that?" I asked out loud rather than to anyone.

Albinus' brain seemed to have caught up. "He wore a blue cloak and a dark brown tunic underneath which came up to his neck. He had a lined face, weathered like an old soldier. He wasn't young. I'd say forties or older. Had a thin beard and blue-brown eyes," he said with a stare at his friend before he turned back to me. "Now you say it," he gave me a shrewd glance "we should have realised about the mention of the silver." His mouth tensed as he bit his lip, teeth showing.

"It can't have been more than an hour or so ago," I said tempering my excitement at this new lead. "Someone might have seen him and know him or at least where he went after he spoke to you," I replied, raising my eyebrows expectantly. Again his brain seemed slow to respond.

"What's happening?" It was Scavolo calling from up the hill where he'd stopped as he realised we weren't on his heel.

"Go," said Albinus ignoring the ex-centurion's question and with his face fixed on mine. "But don't waste time. I need you back up here for when this prick squeals," he indicated the slave with a flick of his chin.

I nodded and turned, seeing Graccus standing some way behind us as he'd followed along when we'd come out of the meeting with Fusus. He acknowledged my raised eyebrows and turned to wander slowly back down the hill with Maximus looking back over his shoulder toward me as I followed.

****

The Forum was busy, just as I had expected as it was the start of the day and slaves would be out buying goods for their Master's breakfast and lunch. We'd split up as soon as I explained that we needed to find anyone who had seen a broad-shouldered man in a blue cloak with brown tunic that morning. I'd asked a fruit seller, who looked at me askance and shook his head before asking me to move along if I wasn't buying. Two men moved past with barrels of fish on small hand carts and a woman selling hair pins was setting up a stall on a folding table. I wondered over and smiled whilst bending over the table to look interested.

"Do you come here each day?" I asked with my warmest smile. She glanced at me suspiciously as her deep brown eyes were half-hidden by her half-closed lids. She was probably in her thirtieth year or so and had full lips with a towering head of hair in which several of her pins were prominent. I guessed it showed people how to use them and what they looked like when in-situ. "I don't have a coin today but I may be able to come back tomorrow," I suggested eagerly.

"Every day till noon," she replied in coarse Latin. "Bronze coins," she stated rather than asked. "These are one and those are three," she used a long finger set with three of four fine silver rings to point at two sets of pins which were thrust through a cloth to hold them in position.

I guessed the price had been increased because of my appearance and I could possibly barter her down if I wanted one. I fingered a couple, they were quite good quality. One with a dark green stone caught my eye and I peered closely at it, the stone shining brightly where it had been polished. I lingered before asking, "were you here early today? I wonder if you've you seen my man this morning. Blue cloak." I was craning my neck as if searching for him. "I think he might have three coins on him," I said whilst I watched her face light up.

"Blue cloak you say?" she was peering at me again. Maintaining that air of suspicion. I noticed her glance to a brute of a man by the corner who was watching a few of the stalls, probably the paid muscle who'd chase down any thieves.

"Yeah, big fellow," I said holding my arms out a bit wider than my shoulders. "He was here early to collect vegetables," I waved over towards the far wall where several stalls of root crops were laid out. It was a gamble but I had to try something.

"Did he have nice sandals?" she asked with a glance to my own which I noted were filthy from the night before when we found the Flamen.

"Yes," I said, having no idea if it were true but realising that I needed to get Micus to clean my shoes each night.

"He was here earlier when that idiot came through on his horse like he does every day, that Fusus lad," she was shaking her head at the memory.

"Prick," I said and I meant it.

She noted the sincerity in my tone and her eyes warmed as she smiled. "Your man was over there earlier," she lifted her chin towards a metalwork stall which stood empty except for a bored looking boy sat on a stool and wrapped in a thick brown shawl. "Which one do you want?" She asked. "I could do it for two," she said with a wry smile. I picked up the pin with the green stone once again as I'd replaced it when using my hands in describing the blue-cloaked man. "It's my favourite," she was into her sales pitch now whilst I was eager to get away and speak to the seller over by the wall to find out where the blue-cloaked man had gone. "Takes three hours to shine that stone," she said. "They come from Etruria, along by Lake Regillus."

It was quite a distance and I pushed out my bottom lip as I turned back to the pin and considered if it could be a gift for my mother, who wore her hair like the sellers and had many pins. It was pretty. "If only my man were here," I said as Graccus appeared in my line of sight and spotted me. "When I find him I will come back," I said to her evident disappointment as she clearly didn't believe me.

"Secundus." Graccus was at my elbow, his face shining with excitement. I waved to him to wait a moment.

"I'll do it for one, but only for today. It's two tomorrow," she said with a hurt expression and pouting lips.

I almost laughed at her teasing expression. "Graccus do you have a bronze coin?" I asked.

He looked affronted at the question but dug into a pocket pulling out a handful of small and large coins which astonished me. How many weeks had I been paying for his lunch and the bastard held a hoard of bronze which would easily buy a seven course dinner with wine. He picked out a small one and handed it over reluctantly as if I was stealing his family inheritance.

The girl smiled, took the coin and then reached across and with deft fingers stuck the pin expertly into my tunic so that it was stuck fast. She winked. "She'll like that. Lucky girl," she said as she licked her lips.

"It's for my mother," I replied with a wry smile. This made her bark out a laugh which brought a few glances to the stall from the people close by. She thanked me and gazed at me for a moment longer than was necessary before telling me I should come visit her stall again soon.

We stepped away and Graccus said, "he was here. Spent a few coins on a leather belt and a length of rope," he lifted his chin towards the rear of the Forum where he'd obviously got the items Graccus described.

"He bought something at the metalware stall there too," I said, stepping across towards the walled area quickly, Graccus in tow. "She saw him arguing with Albinus this morning," I added. "And then again here at this stall." I placed a hand on Graccus' arm as a thought came to me. "Why would he buy rope?" Graccus shrugged at the question as we had arrived at the stall. The boy stood expectantly as we approached. He was wiry, arms as thin as the pin I'd just bought with Graccus' coin and dark-haired, though he was clean shaven.

"Morning sirs," he said with a bow. "What can I do for you today?" The stall held some farming implements, a series of phalluses and several pots, pans and bowls. They were all rather crudely done and didn't seem to be of a very high quality, which I guessed was why the stall was devoid of buyers.

"Morning," I replied in my friendliest tone. "Just looking while we wait for my man," I said, using the same tack as before. I lifted a pan. It was uneven in its weight and I noted the slightly thicker edge on the right lip but I nodded as if considering a purchase. "How much?" I asked. He looked me up and down for a second.

"Three."

I replaced it.

"I could do two."

I looked at it.

"How much is this?" It was Graccus. He held up a phallus, Bacchus riding a cock. I gaped at him.

The boy looked at us, assuming we were lovers by the glance to both of us and the sneer that came to his mouth. "Four."

"Four?" The pained expression took me aback as my brows rose at the voice that had come from Graccus. He was shaking his head but he still held the phallus in his grip. "Three is the best I can do."

"One at the most. Has it been blessed?" asked my friend. I had no idea what he meant so turned a confused glance to the boy, who seemed to take it as me requesting confirmation.

The lad fumbled under his cloak and pulled out a tablet with the impression of a seal from the temple of Bacchus. I understood what he meant now. "Has to be two," said the lad with that look which suggested he was selling his own children. "They'd chop my cock off if I sold a blessed phallus for less and that's a good one," he added with a nod at Graccus' hand. My friend took out two coins and nodded slowly as he handed them across.

"Have you seen our other friend around this morning? We seem to have lost him," I said to the lad as he thrust the coins into a pouch at his waist. "Wearing a blue cloak. Big fellow," I said again using my arms to show he was broad. "I think he was here earlier just after he stopped those pricks galloping through with their horses," I waved at the centre of the Forum.

The lad looked like he was trying to gather the strength to do a particularly loud fart as his face twisted and churned in thought. "You mean the man who called himself Acco?"

"Acco?" I asked.

"Your friend, the Gaul?"

I stared at him and then looked to Graccus, who was quicker than me despite fingering his phallus as if it was giving him virility with every stroke. "Yes, large fellow in a blue cloak with a brown tunic underneath," he nodded, giving me a nudge with his elbow which set me to agreeing with him. "Where did he go? We've lost him."

"I don't know," said the lad, who was now looking suspiciously at us both. "Why?"

"No reason, we were going to have a drink with him that's all," I replied.

He shrugged and raised his chin with a smirk. "Well he was selling stuff to a few of the stalls. Said he was leaving the city soon and had to let some of his stuff go," he rubbed his forehead as if thinking was difficult.

"Leaving?" we both said in unison to the boys raised eyebrows.

He looked at us suspiciously before continuing. "Yeah that's what he said. He sold me this lot," he lifted a cloth which was covering something at the back of his stall. Then waved to a pile of metal which was hidden under it. "Good quality that, under all the rust," he said. "It's all legal," he added quickly at my changed expression. "He said he was a warrior before he was made a slave and he bought this back from his Master when he was given his manumissio. Here's the tablet," he tried to quantify his comment with a wax tablet which bore the seal of the temple of Vulcan. It was another clever trick from Titus to get more money from the old iron held within the temple.

I stared at it, my mouth as wide as a cavern. Graccus too knew the significance of this hoard of metal and his mouth had also dropped.

"What's your name lad?" I asked.

The boy's eyes narrowed for a moment before he crossed his arms over his chest. "Hiscus," he said. "Son of Hisstosius of the Aventine" he said with evident pride in his family name.

"I am Secundus Sulpicius Merenda, second son of the Quaestores Parriccidii Marcus Sulpicius Merenda and that little lot are stolen goods from the temple of Vulcan."

The lads jaw dropped.

XV

"He passed out after five lashes with the whip, soft-arsed bastard."

Novius was telling us what had happened since we'd left them to question the priest's slave. "So we drenched him in cold water and then pulled his fingernails out." He grinned widely at this, which caused me to turn my head to the bloody, ruined, fingers of the prisoner. "That made him squeal, but he soon opened up," he added. I guessed anyone would open up to anything if their fingernails were forcibly removed but kept my opinion to myself as Novius was clearly happy with the process he'd undertaken.

"He agreed with Albinus Fusus that the Flamen had planned it all. Said that the priest Titus was the thief but had no idea where he was now." He was pushing his lips out as he spoke, then stuck a finger in his ear and twisted it. "Albinus wasn't happy with that so we branded him on the forehead and he screamed until he passed out again."

Novius shrugged as if having prisoners pass out during torture was an inconvenience which slowed down his work. Visions of Brocchus, beaten to a pulp, flashed before my eyes.

"So we soaked him again and left him there for a while to think about things. Albinus went for lunch, said he'd be back just after mid-day."

I listened in disbelief. The slave had been tortured for nothing. I looked to Graccus and Maximus and waved them towards the door. "Where's Scavolo?" I asked. "We have some news for him."

"With your father doing the ceremonies for the Kalends." He glanced at my tunic oddly and I realised that the pin was still attached. Reddening I removed it and stuck it inside my tunic so that it didn't show.

I'd forgotten that my father still had all his religious duties to perform and that Scavolo would have to observe them alongside him as the temples head man. "Novius, I need you to get another man and take a small cart to the stall of Hisstosius in the Forum. His stall is against the wall on the right as you enter. He has all the stolen weapons from the temple of Vulcan."

Novius' eyes widened as he nodded at my news. "Nice," he said. "Where did he get them?"

"From a Gaul named Acco."

"Acco?" I nodded in response. "Thought he died years ago."

"You know him?"

"Scavolo captured him. Must be twenty years ago," he rubbed his nose as he responded with a faraway look in his eye.

This was getting more and more complex. "What do mean captured him? Who is he?"

"Acco was the leader of group of mercenaries who fought with the Etruscans at Caisra or was it..." he drifted off in thought and tapped his lip for a second or two before he came back to the point with a shaking head. "Well wherever it was, I heard that the Etruscans used a force of fifty cavalry to attack Scavolo's camp. He was only a young lad then mind, it wasn't his camp as such. You know what I mean," he added with a wave of his hand. "Then the foot soldiers attacked and it was a band of about thirty Gauls that did most of the killing. Big bastards with those big fucking swords they use," at which he seemed to start sweating and rubbed at his brow. "Well Scavolo fought like a lion and they ended up toe to toe, Acco and Scavolo. They say they fought till sundown before the Gaul was struck on the hip and fell to the floor exhausted. They all surrendered then. You should get Scavolo to tell you the tale, it's one of his best," he added with a gleam in his eye. I guessed that Scavolo telling me one of his war tales was the last thing the former centurion would ever want to do.

I looked at Novius, who was eating from a wooden platter of fruit and raw vegetables and realised that he must be forty or more years himself. I knew he'd served with Scavolo, as had most of the men at the temple.

"Did you ever see this Acco?"

"Only in the triumph. He was thrown in the Carcer and his family sold as slaves. His son was old enough to be hung and left on the steps," he said with a shrug in reference to the act of strangling traitors and war prisoners and leaving their bodies to rot on the steps of the Scalaie Gemoniae. "I thought Acco had died in the Carcer. Must be wrong. Scavolo will be interested in that for certain." His face turned to mine with a nod "I'll get a couple of the lads and collect the weapons once I've eaten."

We left him to his food and headed back to my room to find that Albinus Fusus had taken it over and one of his louts was sat drinking my wine, the cupboard door knocked open.

"That's mine," I said indignantly.

"What you have is Fusus' and I work for Fusus so this," at which he raised his cup "is mine." He slapped a long dagger on the table as he finished and sat back in his chair to sup at my expense, his message clear.

I stared at him for a moment before turning on my heel and heading out, Graccus and Maximus following like ducklings following their mother. I marched past my father's room to that of Scavolo, and found it open so entered and sat at his desk with a huff, my friends finding seats and sitting opposite.

"Maximus, run to the kitchen and get us some food," I said just as the lad had landed his arse on his seat. To his credit he almost bounced and was up and gone without delay.

I placed my head in my hands and rubbed at my temples. "What the fuck did I do to the gods to deserve this?" I asked aloud. Graccus looked shocked at my expletive. I realised it was as close to a criticism as is possible and quickly qualified my statement in case the gods were actually listening to my words and were raising their thunderbolts to strike at me once more. "They are clearly giving me signs," I said to his fearful expression. "But I cannot work out what they mean. I wish they would give me simple clues to this mystery and not these complicated labyrinths," I said slowly to his nodding head. He sniffed and drew his sleeve along his nose. Despite that act, I was pleased I'd eased the look of fear in his face, though I still felt as if the gods were laughing at my pathetic efforts.

"This Acco could be important," said Graccus. "If he had the swords and other objects from the Vulcanal then he must have been there before the fire." I'd already worked that one out and was pleased that he had been keeping up with events too. "But how can he have been hiding all these years and how is he involved in this?"

I looked around the room wondering if Scavolo had any of my wine left and started searching some of his cupboards, which I found annoyingly tidy and well-ordered. "What worries me more is that Hiscus said he was leaving Rome in the next day or two. If he has the silver then we need to find him."

I opened the last door of the cupboard to find my precious amphora looking back at me. I grinned.

"How? Hiscus didn't know where he lives, just that he comes to the Forum every few days and that today he sold him those weapons and accosted Albinus Fusus. There are hundreds of Gauls in the city, slaves and freedmen alike. We'd never find him." I poured a cup of wine and looked at Graccus as he wiped a further silver line across his sleeve with a sniff. "It could also just be another blind alley," he said. "The slave has confirmed that the silver was stolen by Athitatus and Titus, so at least Fusus will get his hands on their houses in recompense for the silver he's lost."

It was an astute observation, and far too simple and quick a solution to this problem to my mind. Torture usually led to the answer you wanted to hear, not the answer that solved the dilemma. It was all very convenient. I sipped at my cup of wine. It was good and so I swirled it around my mouth for a second, at which point Maximus arrived and dropped a wooden bowl of fruit and some hot bread on the table. I ran through what I thought we knew in my mind for a moment as we all sat and ate. I watched Maximus pick at his nose for a second before inspecting whatever he'd found up there and then flicking it into the corner of the room. It was a bad habit for sure and I wondered if there was a small pile of nasal detritus growing against the wall in his room at his home. The lad then picked up some hot bread and tore off a chunk. I reached across and pushed the whole piece toward him with a nod, at which he picked it up and thanked me.

"You may be right Graccus," I said after a short while. "This Gaul could be a blind alley, but we need to check it out. If he took the weapons, then he was at the temple before the fire was set as surely nobody could have taken them after the fire had been started." I chewed at a small fig. "And how did he know that Athitatus was dead? And" I was on a roll with my questions now, "how did he know enough about this case to search out Fusus and let him know this fact? And why did he do that? He *must* have known that Fusus would react as he has done, setting his own man on the case and stopping our search."

"He must have known about the silver being stored in the temple too." It was Maximus who spoke, his eyes wide at his revelation.

"Indeed." I stood and circled the room slowly, still chewing the fig. "What do we know so far?" I asked.

"Titus, his father and the Flamen were working together to steal the silver. Titus got greedy and killed them all," said Maximus.

I looked at him slowly, realising that I still didn't know much about the lad or trust his tongue. He'd jumped to the obvious conclusion that Albinus Fusus had wanted everyone to see. "I'm not sure," I said slowly, bringing furrows to his forehead as he frowned in response to my words. "Athitatus was a clever man, but I never got the impression that he was hiding anything from us. Why would he employ a private investigator if he was the murderer and the thief?"

Graccus agreed with a nod before adding, "He was certainly unlucky." He rubbed the phallus as he continued speaking, stroking the figure of Bacchus gently. Then he stood and pulled a small wax tablet from his pocket and read from it. "We know that the silver was probably moved from the first night that Albinus delivered it. We know that the man found dead in the temple is Flavius Aetius. We think that Titus and Athitatus might have been working together, but we're not sure of that," he looked up at this comment. "We think that Titus moved the ingots each night to somewhere along the road, and that a man and two boys were seen carrying sacks from behind the wall across the road from the Vulcanal." He let out a slow breath. "Then Titus sent a note to Athitatus saying he'd double-crossed him and then lured him into the trees and killed him" he added tapping his bottom lip. "And now we have this Gaul, Acco, who had some of the old swords and weapons from the Vulcanal but we don't know why or where he got them from and neither do we know how he is related to Titus in all of this. And he's leaving the city. And we have Spurius Maelius, who had been at the temple on the night of the fire and is linked to Flavius Aetius and the missing wagon."

I looked at him expecting more, but the truth is that there is no more, anything else we know is just supposition. The facts are few. And then I realised something else. "Fuck!" I said. They stared at me. "We don't even know *if it is* Flavius Aetius," I said slapping my head. "I jumped to that conclusion. It could be anyone. It could as easily be just another gang member who they dressed up in the robes of the temple and murdered." I was shaking my head at my own ignorance and stupidity.

"Father and son. They wanted us to think that Aetius or Titus or both are dead," said Maximus as he stuck a finger up his nose. "Clever bastards," he added as he dug his nail in deeper.

Graccus was used to my ramblings and so stood and circled as I had sat down. "You're right Secundus. What we know is that a man was found dead at the Vulcanal, that the ingots were stolen, that Athitatus was killed, probably by the same people who killed the man at the temple and stole the silver. Whoever it was left a message to implicate Flavius Aetius. We know that three people moved some sacks from across the road, but we don't know that it is related. We know that Maelius has a missing wagon, but nobody knows where it is or why it is missing. And now we have this Acco who had the old weapons from the Vulcanal." He came to a stop and pushed out his bottom lip.

We all sat in silence.

"Maybe it doesn't matter." It was Maximus who spoke into the silent room. "If the slave has accused the priests then Albinus Fusus has solved the case." His shoulders rose as he shrugged.

I stared at him in the realisation that he was right. And yet I didn't believe it was true. There was too much happening within this case for it to be true. I thought through several options and then stood. "I'm going to the Vulcanal to make an offering" I said. "If Albinus has solved it, then that's fine. If not" I rubbed at my eyes, which were feeling very heavy. "Then we need some inspiration. Maximus take some of this wine to the temple of Minerva and ask for her blessing. Graccus, you come with me."

****

"It still doesn't tell us where the silver is," I said to Graccus' nodding head as we strode past Milo's. He glanced across and waved a friendly hand to which we both responded. I noted that he was quite busy and most of his tables were full even though it was past the middle of the day, he really was growing his clients well. "We've searched everywhere and there is still no sign of it. And where would that priest Titus hide, and his father if it isn't him in that room in the cellar," I threw a thumb back over my shoulder. "We really need to get someone to identify the body."

"Who?"

I pondered that question. "His slave. Is he still locked up?" He shook his head in response. "Can you check that out once we're done at the Vulcanal. It's another part of this mystery that needs solving. And" my mind was on fire with questions today. I wondered if the promise of devotions to the gods was giving me divine intervention. "I'm still puzzled as to how Aetius and Titus made up enough to be working on this robbery together. Every priest told me that Titus and his father did not get on and wouldn't speak to each other despite the father trying to make reparations."

"Are they all in on it?" asked Graccus. "Maybe they took the ingots on the night they visited Ostia."

Another thought came to my mind at that, but I answered. "They travelled lightly from what we know. No wagons or carts, just a few shoulder bags. I can't see them being involved at all. I'm still convinced that Titus is at the bottom of this, but where are those ingots?"

We turned the corner at the Clivus Capitolinus and Jugarius junction and were met with a throng of people singing and dancing. We stepped to the side of the roadway as my father and his priests, Scavolo prowling behind with a group of his men, passed by on their return journey to the temple. A small crowd followed singing and praying. Mother's carried sick babies in the hope that the gods would cure their ailments and cripples hobbled past in the hope of a few scraps of food or coins. It was everything I hated about the festivities. My father would have another few hours meeting individuals and groups and listening to their requests before blessing them or giving them some payment so that they went away happy. I watched the last of the crowd turn up the hill, a crippled man missing a leg struggling with crutches as his wooden support slipped on the flagstones. I noted that nobody stopped to help him as he half-fell. So much for piety and support, it was everyone for yourself when it came to gaining the favour of the gods. I clutched the wine in my hand more tightly and set out again for the Vulcanal. I had my own problems which needed seeing to.

The temple wall had grown by a foot or so and the shape of the old site was now quite restored, the piles of broken timber and stone all removed or at least piled up to be re-used. I looked for the old guard but he was nowhere to be seen and so we walked across to the Lotus Tree and then turned into the site and within a minute we were at the altar. There were no priests in sight, only two workers who had their heads turned to the wall they were reconstructing. I shrugged to Graccus and placed my cup on the altar, Graccus dropping the remains of the food we'd had in the room next to it.

"Where is everyone?" I asked quietly. Looking around I saw that the gate was now hung back on the vault and so wandered across and looked down the steps, which were cleaned. I nodded. "Looks like they are getting things sorted quickly," I said, turning to look around the site. "Graccus," I added quickly. "Let's act out what we know now that nobody is here and it is clear. If I took a silver ingot from here," I stared walking slowly and took about fifty seconds to reach the low wall across the street from the temple. "Then I could do one or two every couple of minutes. And that assumes that nobody else was out on the street and saw what I was doing."

People looked at us as we stood by the wall staring back at the temple of Vulcan and then up and down the street.

"I see," he replied. "If three people then moved these ingots," he was tapping his lip with his forefinger and glancing back up towards the Capitol and then along the Jugarius. "The most sensible place is the house of Flavius Aetius" he added. "Look, it's only a few minutes' walk."

"But we searched it and there was nothing."

He agreed but continued with his lip tapping, which made the small blob of snot that was building on his nose start to glisten. His head turned left and right as mine had done a day or so earlier as I'd contemplating the same thoughts. "I can see why you thought the ingots were still here," he said. "The only place that is big enough to hide anything near the size of the pile of silver is that," he lifted his chin to the altar of Vulcan.

"I've checked it," I shrugged, but he was off before I'd finished my words.

We poked and prodded the ancient stone, looking for gaps in the carved images or other areas which could have been moved. We poked at the flagstones, pushing fingers into any gaps and seeing if the stones moved, but nothing. We stood and looked up and down the road but no flashes of light came and no new ideas formed.

"I'll make the devotion," I said pouring the wine into the small groove by the altar and handing Graccus the cup. "Go and find that slave and confirm that it is the body is Flavius Aetius and I'll meet you back there in an hour at the most. I'm going to go along the road again and see if there is any place that the thieves could have stored those ingots."

Devotion made, I set off once more along the Jugarius, stopping at the intersection of the trees where we'd found Athitatus' body. I gave a moment's thought to the old priest as I looked into the thick-trunked foliage. He'd been lured to his death with the initials FA. Why had he rushed out without any comment to anyone. Was there something I'd missed in their relationship that meant that the old priest felt he could meet this potential killer without fear? I rubbed at my eyes and shook my head. I was over-thinking it again. Athitatus wasn't involved, I was certain. He was just unlucky. I'd thought it before the realisation of what I'd thought hit me. I chewed that thought for a while as I stood looking into the trees. People walked by and glanced at me with strange looks. Was he *that* clever? A new idea was forming in my mind and I wished I had a wax tablet with me to write a note but sighed as I pushed on along the road. After a few minutes I approached the house of Metilius and stopped outside. It was closed tight. The old man from next door was not at his seat and so, seeing the clothes shop a few moments along the road I headed there.

"Good day, sir," it was the shopkeeper, his large eyes looking me up and down as I stood and looked at his wares. "New sandals?" he said with raised eyebrows and a furtive movement of his eyes to my feet. I was abashed at the state of my sandals once again and ignored his question, though I did consider that I needed new shoes as it would soon be winter and my old pair were leaking badly. The thought of having no silver ran across my mind like a startled rabbit and I closed my mouth to the thought that I should ask for a price.

"Just looking," I answered amicably as I nodded slowly looking at his cloaks and tunics. There were clothes for men and women as well as children. The cloth was weighted, heavier was more expensive and lighter was cheaper. His board suggested he would trade for barley, corn, wheat, various meats and bronze or silver coins. I remembered Micus' words and so decided to act cautiously. The cloth-seller was a small man, high forehead and thinning hair. I noticed a woman at the back of the shop stitching some tunics and lifting her eyes to see who was with her husband, for she was too well-dressed to be a slave. I looked down at a rack of sandals and boots and nodded approval. He was watching me like a hawk and lifted a pair of dark leather ankle boots which were very well put together.

"Best deer leather, just right for a man of your standing," he suggested. I guessed he didn't know that where I was standing was in a pile of shit as deep as the Cloaca Maxima and that if we didn't find Fusus' ingots them I would likely not be able to afford the cheapest tunic on his rail. "I soften them for two weeks before we stitch them together," he added to explain the process but also to set the bar for the price as the longer the softening process the higher the price would be.

I was nodding thoughtfully and wondering how I could ask him if he'd seen anything on the night of the fire of the Vulcanal when the woman at the back of the shop stood and placed the tunic she was sewing onto a nail. I noticed a small fleck of gold on the collar and then several thoughts tumbled into my mind like an avalanche, the boulders growing as they fell into place. His face seemed to soften as much as his leather at the change in my expression as he clearly thought he'd landed his sale. The devotion to Vulcan was working. Suddenly I'd found a new lead and one that would prove that Albinus Fusus was wrong. It was time for a little name dropping.

"Secundus Sulpicius Merenda," I said, giving him my best patrician glare, the one which suggested he was so low below my status that he should be proud to have me even acknowledge him.

"Merenda?" his eyes widened and his lips curled slightly as he glanced to my hand to see the thin gold ring on my finger. He knew my father by name at least. I was off to a good start.

"I like those," I said, pointing at the tunics that the wife had hung at the rear of the shop.

He turned quickly, a frown on his face turning to a smile as he understood what I was pointing at. "Ah, the blue," he said jovially. The wife was as quick witted as him, her full lips beaming back as she picked the tunic she'd just sewn and handed it across the table at which she sat. "These are for the priests of the Vulcanal," he said proudly. "I have had the contract for many years and they have always been more than pleased with the quality" he was saying as he handed me the tunic. "This is the heavier cut. You will know that they lead a hard life and work most days so need a hard-wearing weave," he was off on his sales pitch but I was looking at the fleck of gold at the collar. "These six items are nearly ready to deliver," he was saying as I turned the sleeve to the light and noticed something which brought a flash of memory. My mouth dropped open. He noticed it and stopped talking for a second before he narrowed his eyes and then set off again. My mind raced. I wasn't listening. "The cut would need to be lighter but the colour, sir," he was pursing his lips now and looking me up and down with a nodding head to suggest that blue was definitely my colour.

"I like it," I said. "I've just been to the temple and spoken to Caelius," I said with a look to his deep brown eyes. "Do you know him?"

"Why of course, sir. We measure each man and have an excellent relationship with them all. I am sure he would speak highly of me and recommend..." he was off again but my mind was still working through what I'd suddenly realised.

"And sandals," I mumbled, almost cutting him off. "They have very good sandals for the work they do at the Vulcanal, I have seen them and often wondered where they got them. Hard-wearing?" I was asking him now in the hope that he'd place another link into place for my chain of thoughts.

"Of course, sir," he was clicking his fingers to the eager wife, who bent below the table to reappear with a pair of sandals in hand.

I now had another clue. The gods were smiling on me once again. I nodded to the cloth-seller. "I didn't ask your name, my apologies," I said slowly.

"Sextus Tullianus," he said quickly. "Master tailor and cobbler. My family have worked here for four generations, sir. We are proudly linked to the tribe Esquillina and support the festival of Mercury each year."

It was a good family name and his suggestion that he supported the festivals brought a nod of approval. "Tullianus, I am impressed. Measure me and I will place an order and send my man around later today with a promissory note."

He couldn't have smiled more broadly, and I was also smiling. I now had a clue that gave a seed of an idea to what may have happened. There were just a few small gaps now in my thinking, the largest of which was where those damned ingots were hiding, and I considered that I might have actually been standing next to them and not noticed.

XVI

I met Graccus on the steps of the temple where he was standing waiting for me now that we had no room of our own since Fusus had taken it over. Maximus was with him, finger up his nose as I approached. "The slave was still locked in the cellars and cried when we showed him the body. It's definitely Flavius Aetius," he said. I knew it would be and nodded at his words. "Novius said we were lucky to come today as he was sending the body to be burned. It stinks," he said, screwing up his face.

I was about to tell them both what I'd learned when a face appeared at the door and called out, "You. Get in here now!" Scavolo was at his charming best as he marched us across the temple to my father's room. "Keep your mouth shut and agree to everything your father says," he snarled with a dark look at me. "You lot wait outside," he added to Graccus and Maximus, dismissing them as he pulled open the door.

Inside I wasn't surprised to see Fusus senior and his son turn their faces to me along with my brother Sul, who I'd not seen for a while, assuming he'd been doing his own work. He nodded and I replied with a brief smile. Fusus sneered and Albinus simply curled his lip with an air of distain. "About time you arrived," said the son.

I ignored his jibe and bowed to my betters, sitting on the chair to which Scavolo pointed me. I noted that he stood formally at the rear of my father's chair. I didn't like the look of this and so allowed my features to loosen and took a few seconds to slow my breathing so that I could appear, at least, to be playing the game as best I could.

A pot-bellied man stepped forward slightly. I guessed he was Fusus' head man. He nodded to us all. His thick beard was greying at the edges and his eyes darted around the room shiftily, but his voice was firm and steady as he spoke. "The slave has confirmed that the priests were at the heart of this crime. The priest Titus and his father had organised to move our ingots via the wagon that Maelius had loaned them but they fell out and Titus murdered his father for some unknown reason. The Flamen Athitatus then fell to swords in dispute, no doubt greed over the ingots, and the Flamen was killed. The house of the priests and any assets they have are therefore forfeit as their guilt has been proven and my Master will lay that claim today." He nodded to Fusus, who nodded in response.

It was a neat solution and all based on the testimony of a single slave under torture. I glanced to Scavolo, who was looking serenely at the wall. Sul had his face fixed in that perpetual stare. I did the same. I felt the urge to speak but tightened my jaw and decided to do as I was told, keeping my breathing measured and my thoughts to myself. They'd ducked the issue of Flavius Aetius' house as they knew that Maelius had a claim for that property.

"Therefore," the shifty-eyed head slave was continuing now that we had all realised that Fusus would reclaim any losses via the case against the priests and forfeiture of their house on the Capitol. I wondered what was coming next. "My Master would like agreement that this course of action is legal and he can proceed."

Scavolo looked to my father, who inclined his head. "It will be done," he replied. I knew enough about the Twelve Tables to know that they would call-out the claim at his house and he wouldn't appear because he was dead. This would lead to claim against his family, of which we knew there were none, and then without any objections the house would be legally forfeit if nobody came to the Comitia at the appointed hour and counter-claimed against the action. It was neat and would be quickly dealt with. I wondered what the value of the house on the Capitol would be and how it related to the lost silver ingots, which were a small fortune and the cost of the house was much less than his losses.

Fusus nodded, Albinus nodded. I sat still and watched the pot-bellied man as he nodded to a raised eyebrow, a predetermined signal for sure, and then continued speaking. "However," he said, and at the look on his face I felt a chill and a foreboding. I was about to twitch when I saw Scavolo's eyes turn to me and I quickly stiffened and sat straight in my seat before adopting my best stoic pose and looking serenely at the wall.

"The value of the loss has been greater than my Master can bear." It was a bad start. "His son has been magnificent in both speed and resolution to close this matter," it was getting worse. Albinus' face showed no emotion as he was credited with finding the murderer and solving the case. I bit my jaw tightly and tried not to tense my face as I flinched at what I now knew was coming. "And yet your search to find his ingots has been pitiful." It was an axe blow to our necks. I felt the weight of the blade slice at my skin as his words hit my ears. "The value of the house is only a half of the lost silver." His statement was met with a dramatic pause. I tried not to glance to my father, who sat quietly and effortlessly dealt with the emotional carnage that was going through my mind and I was sure was crashing through him as well. "As your efforts have been so poor in resolving this case, and the magnificence of Albinus Furius Fusus in gaining a confession and confirmation of the cause, my Master demands reparation."

The death blow was coming. The patron was calling in his debts. My thoughts of the house on the Jugarius, new tunics and sandals from Tullianus and even my slate at Milo's came flooding into my mind. Even the stupid pin that was stuck to my tunic and to which I owed a bronze coin to Graccus hit me like a bolt from Jupiter. Had the gods played me once more? Had their giving me more and more complex avenues to investigate distracted me from the simple truth that Albinus Fusus had found in a few strokes of the lash?

The slave lifted a wooden tablet that he'd placed on the chair behind where he stood and opened it. "My Master wishes to note his displeasure." He glanced to Fusus, who looked as bored as a child in a mathematics lesson. "You had claimed provenance from the goddess Minerva, but he has seen no evidence of this." There was sneering glance from Albinus at this statement. I drew the slowest breath I could to retain my calm exterior as I felt Scavolo's rebukes at my pathetic attempts to remain stoic wash over me. "Your investigations have found nothing," he said with a low sigh. The bastard was enjoying this. "And my Master fears that his ingots have been lost forever because of your delays and incompetence."

He was building up to the climax in which he asked for everything we owned and I sensed the chasm of debt opening. In my mind I saw Fabia turning away from me, her bright eyes closing in tears. I sensed Graccus Porcius' gifts being given to Fusus, the horse farm having to be sold. I needed a drink.

He cleared his throat. Here it came. "And so my Master feels that the house of Merenda should repay the shortfall in lost ingots."

It was a hammer blow from Vulcan himself. A crashing, thundering blast of fire and ash. I tried not to gape. I tried not to speak as I glanced to Scavolo, whose eyes turned slightly to me with a glare telling me I shouldn't speak. But I couldn't see how I could cock this moment up any more than it was already cocked up. My mouth parted slightly and I drew a breath, but the slave continued.

"The debt will be added to the loans already given to the house of Merenda," it was all very impersonal. "The total claim is therefore given as detailed here," and he picked up another slate and handed this to Scavolo, who took it with a firm grip. "You have the remains of the day to confirm the amount owed," at which he nodded to the slate "and five to pay," finished the slave.

Scavolo opened the slate and handed it to my father, who looked at it coldly. Sul glanced to me with a frown.

****

The door closed and Scavolo stood with his back to the wood, looking up at the ceiling. "Bastard."

My father sighed and glared at the slate before closing the two wooden halves together and placing it on the table at his side. His head was shaking. Sul's head was shaking. He placed his hands on his temples and started to rub vigorously.

"What do we do?" asked Scavolo.

"I don't have that much readily available," said my father with a tap on the wooden cover to the debt. "We will need to give him the land deeds Gaius. I'm sorry," he said as Scavolo's head dropped. "You will have to resign your position Sul. I wish there was some other way."

"How can he claim against us for this?" I blurted out aghast at what I'd heard. "The theft was nothing to do with us, he can't claim his losses are *our fault*. It's ludicrous and will not stand in court." My father turned a dejected face toward me. I could see the look in his eye, the look that suggested I had failed, that the goddesses patronage had led us to this point and now she had turned her back on us. "He can't do this to us father," I added angrily.

"You don't understand a thing do you?" It was Scavolo who spoke now, his voice rising. "Your father has always put the family first. Placed his head in the noose more times than I can remember to advance his cause for every single one of his clients. Fusus can do what the fuck he likes. He has the right of patronage to do so," he added, specks of spit forming on his lips. I was shocked at his outburst and turned my face to my father, who sat and stared back at me as if he didn't know me. "And we agreed to find his ingots for a fee. How the fuck do you think we got involved in this. Did your small little brain think that we just accepted the role of finders without thinking, without consideration that his losses could ruin us. Your father saw an advantage and moved to take it. Your fucking god-given skill was our crutch, our rock on which we could base a future with ready cash to build the farms and the future. And now..." he was shaking his head at me. Sul's head was shaking.

I wanted to tell them both to piss right off but realisation hit me hard. I'd been played by both Fusus and my own family. They'd banked on me solving the case quickly and finding the ingots so that they could profit from the situation. Their gamble had gone wrong and they'd lost everything.

"What?" My voice was almost a whisper. "You gambled that I would find his silver." It was a statement, not a question but it raised more anger in Scavolo.

"Oh, get it now do you?" he snapped, his arms flapping and slapping on his thighs. "The fucking clever bastard has worked it out. Only took him three days," he was saying as I stared at my father. I glared at Scavolo, who had come back to face me. "Go on, get out. The grown-ups have things to do."

It was a curt dismissal and I almost saw sorrow in my father's face before he let out a deep sigh and nodded for me to go.

"You can't let this bastard treat us like this," I said angrily, my jaw tightening as I stood. "This isn't the end," I said. "He can't do this."

"He can do what the fuck he likes. We agreed to find those ingots or be forfeit. You've found nothing and that bastard Albinus has done what I wanted to do on the first day," shouted Scavolo his anger boiling over. "And we've lost everything," he added with an accusatory glare. He turned to my father and bowed slowly. "Marcus, I will collect my things and return later with the deeds for my farm. The lads deeds are in my room, I'll bring them all. It's good for about ten or maybe twenty but the rest..." he was shaking his head.

"I'm sorry Gaius." My father's voice was as dejected as I'd ever heard him.

"It was a good ride," said Scavolo in a friendly tone and a quick smile. "While it lasted" he added viciously with a glance to me.

****

My head span.

I sat on the steps of the Comitia, the stone of Lapis Niger looking as dark as my thoughts. What had they done? Why had they kept me out of their plans? My father and brother had left the room behind Scavolo without even a backward glance, the evident disappointment at my failure to find the ingots written in their movements. I hadn't the energy to argue so I'd left the room soon after and wandered down the Clivus with Graccus and Maximus following and asking questions, which I completely ignored. They pestered me and pestered me until I snapped at them and told them to go back to the temple and wait for my return. I was too ashamed to speak to them, to let them know of my failure. All that I'd learned of this case was forgotten as I'd contemplated the loss that my family would feel, by the look of anger and disappointment from my father and from Scavolo. Why did Scavolo's anger bother me? I didn't know, but it did.

The new knowledge I had from the tailor burned in my mind. Thoughts closed in and darkness seemed to surround whatever it was that was intruding into my deepest thoughts and trying to spark light into what had become a day of storms.

I looked up to see Graccus standing in the shadows across the road, trying to hide by the row of low-roofed shops. My anger was dissipated as I watched him drag his sleeve over his nose and turn to Maximus, their heads bent together. It was then that I remembered the sandals and I looked up and waved to them both. There was something there. I had a hunch that needed chasing to its conclusion. Maybe I could rescue something from this day. I looked up at the sun, which was starting its decline towards the horizon. The day had flown past. If my timings were right then my father would likely put his plans in action today and confirm tomorrow morning to Fusus. As I had waved I saw Maximus' grandmother approaching from their left with another lady. They had a slave in tow who was burdened with several bags of goods but his grandmother saw his movement into the street at my beckoning and called out to gain his attention. His face fell. I wandered across, considering how I could apologise to them for my surly behaviour but also tell them that they had lost whatever roles they thought they had supporting me at the temple. It would be a hard conversation but one that I knew I would have to hold if the next few hours drew nothing.

"And why are you out here instead of at your labour?" the old lady was asking with an expression of disappointment which matched that of my father.

Maximus' look in my direction changed her features to one of benevolent friendship as she bowed and fussed for a moment as soon as she saw me approach, introducing me to the lady at her elbow. This lady was dressed in dark mourning clothes which befitted my mood, but I nodded and asked after their health as a good patrician should do before I answered her question to her grandson.

"Maximus and Graccus were looking over some of the prices on the stalls for me. It is my mother's birthday soon and I am looking for a present," I lied, turning the pin I'd bought earlier and adding, "I have this, which isn't much but I thought was quite pretty."

"Oh my dear boy, what a good son you are," said grandma with a look to Maximus which suggested he wasn't. If only she knew the truth. "You should visit the stall of Lurcius, just along by the three trees," she gestured back along the road to where a stall sat under the shade of three prominent pine trees. "He has the most exquisite scarves and gloves. He's a master of his art," she added as both ladies nodded in the surety that they knew one when they saw him. I thanked them and was about to leave when I turned back as a thought suddenly struck me.

"Might I ask what may seem an odd question?" Grandma gave me a shrewd look but inclined her head. "Did you know Marcus Metilius?"

"Well of course we did," she had turned to her friend as if I'd asked the question to both of them. "Poor man," she sighed.

"Yes. I hear he died at the Lupercalia, drowned in the river drunk to the heavens" I was shaking my head slowly.

"Strange affair," said her friend.

"Oh?" I offered wide eyes for her to continue.

"Well I was friends with his wife before he married that..." she looked at me and then to Graccus before she could say the word she was going to use. "Well," she blustered. "Before Lucretia died he never touched a drop of alcohol. Never was there a more pious man than Marcus Metilius. Poor Lucretia," she added with a faraway look in her eyes.

"Why do you ask?" It was Grandma now asking the questions. Her narrowed eyes suggested she was trying to understand what I was looking for in my questioning them about such a thing.

I tried a simple tack. Glancing left and right as if I was worried that people nearby would be listening to what I was about to say, and thus dragging them closer to me as I leant forward slightly, I said, "I have made a bid on the house. I wondered why they were selling?"

Both elderly ladies eyebrows rose at this, stretching their skin into long lines which suggested that they now had some juicy gossip that would soon be shared. To be honest it was not much of a gamble now that I had been told that the mistress had decided not to sell the house. "Well," it was the friend who was speaking again. "*That slave he married,*" her chin receded into her neck as she spoke and the obvious shaking movement of her head suggested that even uttering the word was difficult for her "is moving out as she is bringing down the tone of the neighbourhood with her late night goings on." That surprised me. "And since Marcus bought that man Cursius there has been nothing but trouble. They should never have bought him. He should have died in prison." She huffed at this and Grandma agreed with a curt nod.

"Prison?" I was still reeling at the mention of late night goings on, but now that prison was involved my poor mind was spinning faster than a top whipped on the end of a string.

"Yes," came the surprised answer. "Cursius. He was bought by Agrippa Fusus about ten years ago and then sold to Marcus Metilius, what three years ago?"

"Yes about that," came the reply from her friend.

Graccus sniffed. We all turned to him for a moment before he shrugged.

"I'm sorry," I said slowly. "Cursius was in prison?"

"Yes, he was captured in the war many years before but had been put to work in the quarries. He was sold to Fusus to work on his farms and then Marcus paid far too much over the odds for him. It was that girl," said the friend with a nod which set her hair, which was piled high on her head, to shaking.

"What girl?" It was Maximus who asked. He was also struggling to keep up.

"The slave. His new wife," whispered the friend conspiratorially.

Links began to click and I felt the goddess start to shine her benevolent light on me again. "So, the gardener Cursius was captured in a war and then sold to Fusus, who then sold him to Metilius because the new wife, the slave," even I looked around and whispered the word, "asked for him to be bought."

"Well why wouldn't she?" We all looked like we'd been slapped in the face with a wet fish as she stared at us for our stupidity. I shrugged. "Well she's his daughter of course," she added.

"Daughter?"

"Yes," she answered forcefully as if we were as thick as an olive tree.

Grandma now took over the story. "There was talk that Lucretia was," she pouted and drew her chin to her chest with widening eyes, "you know?" I didn't and my confused look led her to continue. "She developed this dreadful sleeping sickness and then one night simply passed away in her sleep. Poor thing." Her friend was nodding at this. "And Marcus was married to the..." she pursed her lips again and couldn't bring herself to say the word as I looked to the female slave stood five yards away and carrying all of their goods. I hoped she didn't hear what they were, or were not, trying say out loud.

"So, his wife died and he married the slave girl?" They nodded in unison. "And then they bought Cursius from Fusus?" They nodded again.

"And then poor Marcus died," said the friend. "All very odd if you ask me," she confirmed. "He never touched more than a cup of wine each kalends. I couldn't believe it when they said he'd been rolling around the streets drunk and then fallen into the river."

"I can vouch for that," said grandma with a nod. "I'd not seen that man drunk in forty years or more of knowing him," she answered.

"And what complaints have the neighbours had?" I asked, remembering what had been said earlier.

"Well that priest was always there at night."

My brows creased at this and I glanced to Graccus, who was as sharp as a pin and had caught this information too and looked to me at the same moment.

"What priest?"

"The one who burned to death at the Vulcanal. The mad one," she replied. "There were rumours," she said with that chin recession which suggested strange goings-on that could not be spoken out loud. We all looked about us lest someone be closing in to hear what we were saying.

"I don't understand?" It was Maximus again, but I was glad of his question as it gave me a moment to gather my own thoughts.

Grandma sighed and glanced to her friend with the withering look of someone who had to explain something simple to a child and the lad still didn't understand after several attempts. It made me grin for a moment. "Marcus had the priests at the Vulcanal broker a contract to link his sewer system to the Cloaca," she said. I listened closely as I knew this from my visit to the house. Her friend nodded at this as if it was common knowledge. I understood what she meant. As with sales of houses and most land deals the signature of a temple priest was needed to confirm the contract. "Well afterwards, that," at which she pursed her lips once more in disgust "slave was always visiting the temple to *pray*," at which her brows rose to suggest that praying was the last things that was happening "at strange times of the night."

"And then Marcus died," I added, to fill the silence.

They both inclined their heads. "And then that priest, the mad one who was up and down the street at night, was there even more often. He said he was sorting the transfer of the deeds of the house of course," said Grandma, although her meaning wasn't lost on any of us. "But... well you know what I mean," she added with wide eyes and tight lips.

I took a moment to think through what they'd said. "And now the house is for sale," I said quietly, lost in my own thoughts.

"Yes. It went up for a sale about two days before the fire at the Vulcanal if I remember rightly," said Grandma. "It's a nice place. He was a Master builder was Marcus. Incredibly talented man. Such a shame," she said earnestly.

I looked at them both and bowed deeply. "Might I thank you for your sincere thoughts," I smiled. "I can honestly say that you have been a greater help than you can know." Graccus was nodding at this. "Maximus is doing a fine job," I said before they could leave. "I hope tomorrow that I will have more news for you on that front," I said with hope starting to fill my veins as I placed a paternal hand on the boys shoulder. I considered that the devotions to Minerva and Vulcan were starting to work in my favour and chided myself for not giving more libations as I had been too busy to think about it. I'd negated my duties and immediately thought that I needed to drop off at the shrine of Janus and thank him once more. The ladies babbled with excitement as they turned to leave, but then something else struck me.

"Oh ladies," I said to their turned heads. "One more question please. Was Cursius red haired in his youth?"

XVII

Maximus listened as I told him what I wanted him to do before he went home for the day, I didn't want him involved in what I was now planning. He repeated it as I asked, just to be clear and he raced off. We'd returned to the temple and taken a couple of daggers from the store which I knew was held at the back of the altar just in case we needed them. Philus gave us dark looks but I informed him that we were working with Scavolo and he could check our story if he wished. Which he went to do and we scarpered.

"I can't believe it," said Graccus as we strode through the turning at the end of the Forum, turning right.

"I can," I said in reply.

"And you think they'll be leaving now?"

"Or as soon as they can," I said with a shake of the head. "Gods they were clever," I added. We passed the house of Lucius and Fucilla and I pressed back the urge to stop and say hello as our need was more urgent than a social call but I told myself I needed to visit them as our paths were closely linked. *Pay the plebs and the plebs will pay you back* those were the words that ran through my mind.

I thought through my plan. Would Scavolo come as I asked? I wondered if I should have sent Graccus to run the errands, but I shook away the thought as we headed down the Vicus Tuscus to the Forum Boarium. The roads were busy, the crowds making their way home as the day was starting to close. If the thieves were going to leave Rome as I was gambling they would then they had to go soon and I had made a wager with myself that the spy in Fusus' home would inform Titus that the case had been marked as closed and the Merenda family had been forfeit for the missing ingots. As such I could not see any better time than now for the thieves to try and escape Rome as I was certain that they must be growing more and more fearful of being found as every day passed. Of course it was all guesswork, but I could see no other way of getting out of this quagmire. If it fell to further levels of shit, then it was no worse than the levels of shit I was in right now. A gamble in which there was no loss other than the loss of face, which I had already lost. I cracked a wry smile at my logic. My father would be proud of me.

The shrine of Janus was a small affair but I took another two of Graccus' bronze coins from his shaking fingers and pressed them to the water with my eyes closed and a prayer that my plan was good. I hoped that this night would mean that I didn't have to tell Graccus that he'd lost his patronage and his job, but fear still pierced my heart like an arrow of guilt shot from the bow of a crossed lover. Janus looked at me from both sides of his stone and I smiled at his worn face. "All or nothing" I said to both of the cold faces that stared back at me.

"What?" asked Graccus.

"Nothing," I replied, slapping him on the shoulder. "Come on, we have a gate to watch."

The Porta Carmentalis held two gates, the unlucky and the triumph. The unlucky was the gate through which people exited the city and headed into the Campus Martius. It was always called the unlucky as it led to the place where most of the funeral pyres for the dead were held, but its name had grown even more significant as it was the gate through which the accursed Fabii led their family to lose the battle of Cremera. This was also called the Scelerata gate and we placed ourselves just outside and sat with a small bag of food which I'd borrowed even more coins from Graccus to purchase. The gates were old but wide enough for a cart and two good oxen to fit through easily. On the other side was the triumphal gate through which people entered the city. That was also just as wide and had several reliefs of the Etruscan kings defeating their enemies carved into the stone as it was the gate used by conquering generals in triumph.

"Do you think they'll come this way?" asked Graccus.

I shrugged. "If I'm right they will head this way to leave the city. If wrong then I hope that Maximus can convince Scavolo to send men to the other gates. That's assuming they do leave tonight," I said with a slow exhalation which showed just how tired I was.

Graccus drew his sleeve over his nose. "Wish I'd brought a cloak," he said, opening the bag and digging into the food inside.

The light faded. People gave us odd glances as they left the city and headed out towards the bridges across the Tiber, to the Janiculum and other places where they probably lived. The Campus Martius was the only place near Rome that held no houses. Traditionally it had only the one temple, a small affair dedicated to Mars and Jupiter and used when the campaigning season started at the turn of the warmer months. That thought reminded me that I was due to start my military training and I then wondered if I would fall in grace and stature so far that I wouldn't even be able to buy my own spear. It was at this point that we heard a wagon rumbling along the flag-stoned road. My heart jumped and I was on my feet, instantly thinking I needed a piss. I cursed Scavolo as I expected him to be here by now, but there was no sign of him. Braving the expected tirade of abuse as I stepped out I bit down on my fear and prayed to Minerva, Vulcan and Jupiter for support.

The wagon appeared, two people sat on the bench and a third walking. It was smaller than I had expected. I waited until they had passed through the gate and stepped forward purposefully, pulling out the dagger but holding it at my back.

"What do you want?" It was an aged voice and one that I didn't recognise. I looked at the old woman sat beside the man who had spoken and a slave stepped out from the far side of the oxen and quickly made his way across.

"Why are you stopping us?" said the slave, a small, thin, man with long greasy hair.

Graccus pulled out his tablet and held it up quickly, the seal of the temple of Jupiter pushed out at the slave and then to the man up on the cart, who had half-pulled a spear from at his feet. They didn't get a clear look, just as we'd agreed, and he answered the question. "We are checking carts and wagons that leave the city for a missing item from the temple of Jupiter," he said to a frown from the old man.

"It's alright, sir." I added with a wave. "We can see that your wagon is empty and you are not to be held. Please carry on. Sorry," I said, waving him on as the small wagon held nothing more than a few sacks of flour and two amphora of wine. It wasn't who we thought it might have been.

"Pricks," he said with a scowl. "Stopping the fucking oxen. Come on you bastards," he was shaking the reins now and the slave was pushing at the beasts which had come to stop and munched hungrily at the grass.

"Sorry," I said again as I stepped over and started to push at the closest ox to help get the animal to move again. I heard a squelch and felt the heat of a pile of shit that the animal had just done land squarely on my foot.

"Serves you right," said the driver as the beasts started to move once more and he saw and smelled the crap as it ran down my leg.

I was shaking my head as the wagon headed out onto the dirt track. "Bastard" I said as I shook my foot which was soaked through and stank of soddy dung.

I tried to remove as much of the ox shit as I could as we waited, the sky getting ever darker. Whatever I did the smell remained. It was eerily quiet and we'd seen nothing moving for a good half hour before my friend jumped up. "There's another one coming," said Graccus who was listening out, the light fading quickly. We stepped back a bit so that we were out of the gateway and waited until we could see, and hear, the wagon coming through the opening. The wagon seemed to take an age to arrive at the gate and I immediately saw my folly as it came into view.

"Shit!" I said.

Graccus looked to me. "What?"

Then he looked back and realised he and I had made the same mistake. Cursius and another man strode along beside the heavy wagon, with three females aboard who all turned their red haired heads in our direction as we stepped out. Cursius drew a long sword from his belt and looked shocked at our sudden appearance but then simply scowled at the sight of two boys who appeared to have no weapons and no other support but had stepped out into the road to stop them. The other man, who by my reckoning was Titus, turned a confused face to us and then drew another long sword which grated the iron ring at the mouth of its scabbard and flashed in the dying light of the sun. It was a poignant moment and it foretold of our quick deaths. At least it was only a short hop to the Campus Martius and our funerals. One of the girls was asking questions and I heard and saw Bravia hush her. I saw in that split second that the third redhead was the slave from Fusus' house, whom I had assumed correctly was the spy and clearly some relation. If only I'd explored that angle that I had closed early in the investigation. What a fool I was.

"Well well, if it isn't that prick from the temple of Jupiter," said the man I assumed was Titus. Cursius glanced over his shoulder and then peered around the darkness which surrounded us quickly, alert to any other movements to stop them, but there were none. "You are as clever as they say," he grinned. "But not clever enough," he said lightly with a glance to Cursius. The man on my right stepped forward and despite the limp he lifted the sword with the ease of the warrior he had been.

I gambled a few words as he closed on me. "I know that you are Acco of the Gauls," I said quickly, pulling my pitifully small dagger from my back as I noticed Graccus attempt to do the same and snag his tunic as he pulled too quickly. The brute took another step forward. "And that you are Titus from the Vulcanal." I turned to Titus as I guessed he was the leader of this gang of thieves. "Tell me why you did this? Why kill your father and Athitatus?"

"Why?" he roared. "Why?" Acco or Cursius as I had called him stopped his prowl and turned a baleful eye to the ex-priest at this angry question. "For a new life. For them," he waved his sword at the wagon, the three ladies who stared down at us. "Get out of the way or we'll gut you where you stand."

"No, we need to kill them. We can't leave evidence." It was Bravia who shouted at Titus and I turned sharply back to Titus as he hesitated.

"Why kill your father? Why tie him to the altar?"

This caught his attention. He held out a hand to Acco, who had moved menacingly close now. "Ha," he laughed. "You noticed that" he was appraising me now. "That bastard tried to make up with me after all those years of abuse. The years he made me pull at his cock and grease him. The years of telling me it was all my fault, that mother had died because of me and so I had to please him. I was glad he sold me to the temple to get away from his fucking groping hands." he snarled. A horrible picture flew in my mind. "Why kill him? The fucker turned up in the middle of one of the nights when we were moving the last of the silver. He had been every night for a week, telling me he was dying and wanted to make peace with me. Bastard"

He spat on the ground at his feet.

"He saw the silver, so I saw a chance. I told him it was Fusus' and that he could leave with us, start a new life. He spread the rumour as I knew he would." He shrugged. "He came to the temple that night and helped us move the ingots. The girls were wrapped in dark cloaks which made them almost invisible and Acco and myself playing the drunken priest. You'd be amazed how people think they see only one loud man in the street when in fact two or three are moving up and down at the same time but hiding in the shadows."

So that was how they'd done it. Four of them moving ingots as I guessed that Fusus' slave could not get out of his house but as spying on her Master and feeding back information.

"On the last night he turned up just as we had the last of the silver out. He'd changed his mind. Said it was against the gods and called out. But Acco had him by the throat so we forced the lotus juice down his throat and drugged him. Then we dressed him in one of the cloaks. It was fortuitous. Or so I thought at the time," he grinned slowly. "And then I tied the bastard to the altar and sacrificed him to Vulcan. A parting gift for his years of abuse," he smiled coldly and then started to walk towards us, sword out.

We stepped back slowly. "Go. Run," I hissed at Graccus before turning back to the predator at my front. "And you knew about the silver from her," I lifted my chin towards the wagon where the redhead I'd seen at Fusus' house glared at me. "And I guessed she told you that the case has been closed and you could sneak out tonight if you were quick. Well I guessed that part but I am right, you are here," I said.

"Shut the fuck up!" snarled Acco as he raised his sword and leapt at me. I dived to the right but in my stupidity I crashed into the curb of the road and fell headfirst, my dagger flying out onto the grass. The Sword slashed past my head and clanged dully into the hard packed earth at my feet, scattering stones.

Acco laughed as I heard Graccus running. To be fair I couldn't blame him, I'd given him the cue to do it and I guessed he realised that he could act as a witness. Acco's sword rose and I tried desperately to scrabble away, my shit covered foot slipping on the grass as I tried to kick out.

"Oh no you fucking don't," said a voice I knew well.

The movement of his sword arm was impressively fast as Acco changed the direction of his strike from a killing blow to me to swing it at waist height to his left and circle his whole body in a defensive blow. The resounding crash of iron on iron stung my ears. Scavolo was inside the cut and pushing his man backwards as all three of the girls screamed from the wagon and I heard another clang from a sword strike which must be that of Titus fighting one of Scavolo's men. Another scream rang out as Acco turned his face to Scavolo.

"You."

"We seem fated to be together," smiled my former boss, his features as calm as that statue I had seen him become so many times. "I thought you were dead?" he added, lifting his lips into a smile.

"No fucking Roman will kill me," he screamed, levelling his sword and charging straight at Scavolo.

I was trying to stand as they hit each other, the two bodies thrashing blows as they circled and entwined like snakes writhing in a sack. An arm grabbed me, bringing sudden fear as I turned my face sharply to see Graccus. He'd not run after all. Ahead I saw two men take down Titus, a blow to his midriff doubling him over. A voice screamed and a flash of red hair jumped from the wagon. The noise grew as I heard Scavolo goading Acco, calling him names, telling him he had grown old and useless, saying that his daughters would be his playthings when he killed him, shouting any abuse that might cause him to make a mistake. Acco was jabbing as he stepped forwards, Scavolo striking the sword away effortlessly. A dagger appeared in his spare hand, the blade glinting in the half-light as the sun started to drop below the horizon.

Clashing swords brought a grunt of pain and Novius called out as a girl screamed and I saw a body fall as another yelled and ran forward. Acco turned at the noise and yelled something, anguish and pain in his eyes as he sprinted towards the fallen girl. It was Bravia, blood seeping through her fingers as Novius pushed her away from the kneeling Titus, his face contorted as he'd taken a deep wound to his side and tried to hold back dripping blood. Acco twisted as Scavolo's sword burst through his shoulder, a blow designed to hinder not kill. The Gaul cried out in pain and turned, his left shoulder drooping uselessly at his side.

"You will not take me prisoner again," he said, throwing himself into a flurry of blows and sword strokes. He screamed obscenities with every step. Scavolo skipped and twisted, parried and struck to aim to disarm the Gaul but he kept up his relentless attack and they worked around the rear of the wagon.

Another scream and I was running over to Novius and the other man who had come with Scavolo. I didn't know him but he had the youngest girl by the hair and was trying to avoid a blade that she thrust at him again and again, kicking and screaming as her blows missed time and again. Bravia seemed motionless and I could hear Titus calling her name through the grunts of pain as he clutched at his belly. The remaining red head, the slave from Fusus' house jumped onto Novius' back from the wagon and bit his ear, the blood seeping as he yelled and screamed. Novius was too fast though and punched her to release her grip. The girl held by the hair then dug her knife into the man's thigh and earned a hefty kick to the face for her efforts. She fell like a sack of flour, her neck clearly snapped as her head landed at the wrong angle and her eyes stared out in shock. I turned back to watch Scavolo twist his blade into the guts of Acco, who simply did not stop attacking and had to be dealt with. The Gaul fell to his knees and turned with tears in his eyes to look at the fallen women.

"No," he croaked with his last breath. His lifeless body fell to the ground and Scavolo placed a foot on his back and shook his head.

Titus groaned and tried to stand but was pushed back by Novius. The remaining red-haired girl screamed and grabbed the long sword that Titus had dropped. I lifted my dagger in the expectation that she would run at me as I was closest to her. Instead she screamed at Titus, "I will never be a slave again. That bastard Fusus will never see my body again. He raped my mother, he will never rape me again." She stared at Acco's dead body. "Goodbye grandfather. I am glad I knew you briefly. You are a good man Titus," she said with a long look at the hurt priest. "The gods will repay us all in the next life."

She promptly up ended the sword to place the point at her heart. Before I could shout or move forward she'd fallen onto the blade. It ran through her heart and burst out of her back as she fell. Her eyes turned to mine as she hit the floor and her mouth moved without words. I knew my dreams would haunt me again as I stared at her dead face.

"Bastards!" grunted Titus. "Bastards. Why couldn't you just let us go." He looked at his fingers and the blood continued to pour through as he pushed hard against his leaking guts.

I knelt at face level and looked at him. "Why? Tell me. I have to know," I said slowly and quietly.

His eyes were drooping but had a spark behind them. His head rolled from side to side as he ground his teeth against the pain in his ruined belly. I heard Scavolo giving orders to his men but I ignored them.

"Why?"

Tears flooded his eyes as Titus looked at Bravia. "I love her," he said. "We need to be together," he added with his face turning to mine. I understood instantly what he meant and I shoved my arm under his arm pit and dragged him forward.

"You will die together Titus. It is all I can do," I said.

He looked at me and a sense of resignation seemed to flood through him. "My father was a bastard" he said. "For years I was his boy, his plaything. Behind closed doors he'd force me to..." he grunted and blood formed on his lips. "And then.." He let one hand go so that he could stroke the red hair of his lost love. "She came along and I was fulfilled. She is his daughter," which I had guessed. "She talked Metilius into buying him. I arranged the contract for them. It was easy to confuse him, he was losing his mind."

"The others?" He looked at me but grimaced with pain and could not answer. "Children of the other daughter." He nodded.

"She is dead. Fusus has many children from his female slaves. Saves buying them," he grunted.

"Did you use the berry juice on Metilius?" I asked. He looked at me with sad eyes and nodded with a deep sigh. His gasps started to become laboured. I felt Scavolo at my shoulder. "And you tried to confuse us by killing Athitatus in a bid to place the murder onto him and your father?" Again he nodded. "It was very well done and convinced everyone."

"Except you," he replied ruefully. "Bravia said you had the goddess in your eyes," he said unexpectedly. "She could see it."

I stayed silent. He rubbed her hair and started to cry, the breath that was in him coming in deep lungful's of pain as blood spattered onto his face and the ground below him with deep coughs. "I'm sorry," I said.

He looked at me and through tears he half-laughed. "The gods are bastards," he said. "Take it while you can, they will make you pay for it one day."

At that he fell to one elbow, placed his head next to that of his love, Bravia, and I heard his last gasping breath leave his body before he died.

Scavolo gripped my arm and pulled me up forcefully. Novius came across and looked down at Titus.

Scavolo sniffed, looked at me and said, "have you shit yourself?"

XVIII

Sul stared at me.

My father stared at me.

Scavolo grinned.

"What? You think it'll work?"

I looked to my father whose usually stoic face had gone out the window at what we had shown him and my words at his questions. "It's the lads idea," said Scavolo. "Fucking good one if you ask me."

My father circled the enormous pile of silver and bronze ingots that we'd unloaded from the wagon and placed in the small room at the front of the house, one that was rarely if ever used. There were at least sixty silver and fifty bronze ingots and two of gold, plus a hoard of silver coins which sat in three jars and five leather bags of bronze coins. It was a fortune.

"People will have seen you, they'll report back that there was a fight at the gate and people killed? They will have seen you coming here in the wagon," said Sul.

"We can shut that down," said Novius. "Nobody got close enough until we'd piled the bodies in the wagon and covered them up. I don't think one person saw what happened and Secundus told them that a thief had been killed trying to steal the wagon. They left after that. The wagon is just a consignment of flour and barley. I can take it out and dump the wagon later."

"Maelius taught me something," I said with a smile to my father. "He taught me that if you start a rumour and spread it quietly but with conviction it spreads. He told us that Athitatus was an unlucky man and so we all assumed he was. I found myself saying it as well. He wasn't unlucky. He was just in the wrong place at the wrong time." I looked at the ingots and coins and shook my head. "If we all start the rumour that an unlucky thief was killed, then it will be forgotten in a week."

Scavolo laughed at this. Novius joined him.

"What about the bodies?"

"I'll burn them," said Novius with a shrug. "Nobody will ever know."

"And that is why we should do what I have suggested father," I added.

He looked at me for a long moment which suggested he was considering my words but also a modicum of what I thought might be pride. "You think he will buy it, Fusus? That he'll take his own ingots for payment without knowing they were his?"

"We can place our mark on them tonight," said Sul. "He'll never know."

I shrugged. "What else can he do but accept that we have called in our own loans to pay him back. There will be no evidence that the ingots were found. They disappeared the moment Albinus Fusus turned the screw on us and our family and said that Athitatus was the thief." I glanced to Scavolo, Novius and Graccus as I spoke. "It was Albinus who saw profit in the house on the Capitol and decided to hang us out to dry. We owe Fusus nothing, father. Now is the time to break the yoke of his patronage. Give him the ingots, keep the rest."

Sul nodded.

Scavolo nodded.

Novius and Graccus nodded.

My father looked at all the items in the room and his head was shaking. "Do it," he said to Sul. But first, tell me how you knew it, how you solved it?"

I closed my eyes for moment. "I'll try and put it in order. In truth I'm not really sure how it all fits, but I think I know most of it now." I looked at Scavolo. "It starts with you," I said. "You captured Acco. His son was old enough to be strangled and gutted. His daughters sold to slavery. One to Fusus and one to Metilius. Acco was held prisoner for years until he was bought by Fusus, or his head man, to work on the farm. By then I guessed that nobody knew him as Acco and he'd taken on a new name, Cursius." I rubbed at my left eye, which was hurting for some reason. "Whatever happened it seems that both of his daughters had given birth to girls after a short period. I guess Metilius enjoyed the company of his slaves too," I shrugged as it was not something I knew to be true but it was a logical guess.

"But the daughter Fusus owned died and left the girl who became a spy in their household. At some point later Titus did some work for Metilius and fell in love with Bravia. They seem to have had a long affair and somehow they convinced Fusus to sell Acco to them. At that point they started to plan how to kill Metilius so that Bravia could inherit the house and lands. He had no other heirs as his wife had also died of a sleeping sickness, which I guess was lotus berry juice and a plan between Titus and Bravia to get her out of the way." Novius nodded at this and my father grunted. "Titus had set up this scheme of him being alone in the temple at night so that he could continue to see Bravia, whether at her house or in the temple I don't know. But it went on for some time. And then Titus learned of the silver from Acco's granddaughter in Fusus house. I guess she was being used by Albinus and he had a loose tongue in bed. That's what she said before she threw herself on that sword," I added. "So Titus and Acco set a plan to steal the silver, sell the house and leave Rome for a new life. All of them. Acco would get his family back and Titus would be a free man with his new love. I think that Titus' father was an addition to their plan as he started asking for them to become close as he was dying, what of I don't know. Titus hated him because he had been abused as a child and saw no ill in hurting him the moment he had the opportunity. I guess he somehow tricked him into taking loans from Maelius, including the wagon, on the pretence that they could try to repair the ill-feeling between them but in reality it was so that he could implicate him in the theft. It was well thought through. Titus, Acco, Bravia and the girl moved the ingots each night under cover of darkness and with Titus wandering the streets shouting and calling. People got used to seeing him outside and so stopped looking. It was a good ruse.

Your guard even saw them on the day after the fire moving the last sacks from that place across the road" I said to Scavolo.

"He saw a man and two boys, when it was in fact Acco, Bravia and the other girl. And then on the night of the last delivery things changed. I think that Titus had planned all along to leave his father as the suspect and steal away with the silver, though he had promised to take him with them. But then his father appeared at the Vulcanal unexpectedly and they killed him to silence him because he started to shout that he had changed his mind. Titus told me that he dressed him in the robes of the priests and then tied his father to the altar after filling him full of Lotus juice. He slit his throat in mock sacrifice and they stabbed him to make it look like he'd try to defend himself. Dressing him as a priest made everyone suspect it was Titus who had died. They set fire to the Vulcanal to hide the fact that it was Flavius and not Titus who had died. It was genius, until I discovered that the priests all shaved daily and the dead body wore a beard. And Micus visited the house of Flavius Aetius and found that he had been talking of silver ingots in the Vulcanal and had disappeared on the night of the fire. We assumed he had been a party in the plot to steal the goods. At this point the stories crossed and so it got confusing for us as well as Titus who had now planted two stories, the one where his father was the thief and the one where Titus had died defending the temple but it was in fact Flavius that was dead. That was why Titus had to keep low and couldn't leave Rome. His cleverness had back-fired slightly because his plan to implicate his father was mixed with the death of Titus and as he was missing, it caused more people to be out looking for the missing wagon and his father than he'd set as the original plot. That is my guess though as I am unsure if it is true, but it fits. Titus and Acco just had to lay low until the noise died down. If Titus was presumed dead and his father the thief then they would be able to sneak away when the noise quietened. But then they got greedy and decided to sell the house. At that point I came along and started asking questions."

I looked at their silent faces and they seemed to be keeping up with my rambling.

"But how did you solve it?" asked my father.

I laughed mirthlessly. "Sandals, cloaks and red hair," I said. "I visited the house of Metilius as I saw it had a for sale sign outside and had presumptions of a town house. At the house I saw blue cloaks which looked like those of the priests, I assumed they were just commonplace. But there were also sandals, numbered, which I assumed were for days of the week and used by the gardener Cursius, who was also Acco. Then when Acco accosted Albinus in the Forum, he wore a blue cloak and I started to guess there was a link. Later I visited that tailor shop on the Jugarius," I turned to Graccus at this point and he nodded recognition. "And he was just finishing the latest order for the priests. Guess what? Numbered sandals and numbered cloaks. One for the first priest, Titus. Two for the second and so on. I'd seen those sandals and cloaks in the house of Metilius and I made a link. And then Maximus' Grandmother and her friend told me that Metilius never drank and that his wife had died of a sleeping sickness. Caelius had told me that too much berry juice caused drowsiness and it wouldn't take much to over-dose someone." I shrugged at that. "They also told me that Acco was red haired as a youth. It all linked as all the main houses involved in this mystery had a red-haired slave. Understanding how they were all linked was a bit of a guess."

I took a moment to gather my thoughts.

"And then I played a gamble," I said as my father looked at me more closely. "Once we'd lost everything to Fusus' scheme and I was armed with this new information I assumed that the spy in Fusus' house would know about the case being closed. It made sense for them to cut and run as quickly as they could. It's what I would do and so I guessed it is what they would do too. Scavolo told me that you have to think like the thief to catch the thief," I said with a look to his smiling face at being credited with this wisdom. "They'd closed the sale of the house to me as I was getting too close to finding out the truth and I now guess that they had the silver and Titus hidden in a locked room just off the kitchen. I saw it when I visited the house and saw the dirt under the door as they must have carried it into the house straight from the road at night and hadn't cleaned up. I should have asked them to open it."

I looked to my father once more. "It was a gamble. I didn't know the answers but we had nothing to lose. If they didn't run I would probably have visited the house today with a few men and demanded to open that door. But I took the risk and until that wagon came to the unlucky gate and Titus told me his tale as he lay dying I wasn't sure. But I was almost right in everything that I had considered."

"A marvellous tale and one for telling again. I'm for a hot bath, join me and tell it again," he added jovially.

The words of Titus rang in my ears as Sul and Scavolo agreed to his suggestion that they join my father in the tub.

It was the priest Drusus' final words that had put the thought in my mind regarding the ingots. *Take it while you can*. Whether he meant I should take the love of the gods whilst I could or take the ingots, I would never know. And yet it seemed the right thing to do. I felt sorrow for the Gaul and his family and the loss of the priest, but his words were prophetic and I acted swiftly on them the moment I'd replied to Scavolo's jibe that I had shat myself. I'd moved swiftly, ordering the men to cover the bodies and drive the wagon back here. We'd unloaded in silence and called every hand we could to move the ingots indoors. Mother had gasped at the state of us, covered in blood and dishevelled, but she had put down her wine and joined us in moving the treasures as soon as she realised what was happening.

Graccus broke my thoughts as he came to stand at my side. He rubbed the phallus that was hanging from a chain at his throat and spoke quietly. "Thank you" he said with a longing in his voice.

I glared at him with furrowed brows. "What for?"

"You know," he said with a dip of his chin. I shook my head. He placed a hand on my shoulder and looked at me for a moment. "I won't forget it, however humble you may be. You stood there to protect me," he smiled and then gripped me in a hug which lasted a few moment's too long for my liking.

"I should get home," he said with a look to my father.

"Wait," I said as I still didn't understand what he had done and why. "I think these men deserve some reward father, if I may."

"Yes. Scavolo, you do the honours," he said with a wave and a brief glance to me before departing, my mother on his arm looking tenderly back over her shoulder doe-eyed.

Scavolo lifted his shoulders and waved a hand slowly to me to suggest I choose what the men could have. I looked at the piles. A silver ingot was more money than a man like Novius would earn in his lifetime, and at the same time it would cause questions if he was found with one. I said as much as I looked at the three men, Graccus, Novius and the man who had a bandage around his thigh where the girl had stuck her dagger, who was named Aulus. It seemed to have penetrated only an inch or two into his flesh and was thankfully more painful than damaging. They all nodded understanding at my words but looked eagerly at the treasure.

I looked to Scavolo. "Men, I give you this for your service to the family. You know that we will always honour and support you, so see this as a gift but not the *final* gift. Tonight has brought us together more than any other, but it must also remain our secret. Patronage can free you as much as bind you," I said with true feeling as I was already considering sacrifices for Janus, Minerva, Vulcan and Jupiter. I took two handfuls of the silver coins and gave them to Aulus. His thanks and broad grin were enough to make any man happy for the giving. Novius and Graccus got the same. For both of them it was ready cash that they might have earned in the course of their daily duties and they would live on it well for years if they spent it wisely. And then I bent down once more and picked up three coins that I'd seen in the pile.

"I owe you these for lunch, and this," I said, taking the pin that I still had attached to my tunic. I handed him the small bronze coins and he took them with a grin.

I turned to Scavolo and shrugged. "I owe you my life," I said.

"Don't get soft on me lad," he said with a stern face. "I saved the bosses son who'd shit himself in the face of danger."

"I did not shit myself!" I said indignantly.

Novius, Graccus and Aulus burst out laughing.

XIX

"Fusus is here," said Graccus, appearing at the door with wide, fearful, eyes.

I reacted by smoothing out my toga, we'd decided to give a show of our patrician status and noble blood however many levels Fusus thought he was above us. Scavolo and my father had taken the gold, silver and bronze as dictated by their request this morning to the house of Fusus and returned to tell how Fusus and his son were shocked that we'd collected the amount so rapidly. In truth it was less than half of the enormous amount that Titus had collected and stored in the house. We'd assumed that what remained in our front room was the private wealth of Metilius added to the stolen hoard from the temple of Vulcan but we'd never know that for sure. It gave me great pleasure to hear that Fusus was 'out of sorts' that my father had requested a receipt and the formal closing of the patronage that the *great man* had given over the years. Indeed it was Scavolo who had made comment that Fusus even raised his voice to ask how we had come by such an enormous amount in such a short time. My father had, of course, told him that our business affairs were nothing to do with him and we had paid the debt that he called-in at the first opportunity despite our family loyalty and support given freely over a decade. The slur had been clear. At that my father had played the silent stoic that he did so well and Fusus had turned red-cheeked in his anger. When they returned I had laughed, but Scavolo said it wasn't over, adding that the bastard will be back for certain and that men like him never forget. And he was right, because he was now at the door of the temple seeking an audience.

The Fusus clan stomped into the temple, ignorant of the rules as they pushed past Philus and pointed angrily towards my father as he appeared and greeted them with a solemn bow. I dragged Graccus with me as the party snaked across the back of the great altar and into the largest room at the rear.

"Agrippa." My father used his most charming voice. "What can we do for you?"

Albinus Fusus stared around the room as if he expected it to be full of missing silver. His eyes landed on me with such hostility that I almost laughed to provoke him as I knew he no longer had any hold over our family. I noted that my father remained sitting and looked quietly at his visitor with fingers interlaced and hands resting on his desk. It was a statement that he no longer held Fusus as higher status and I could tell that this irked his former patron as there were no chairs within the room on which he could seat himself; another of my father's tricks.

"Cut the bullshit," said Agrippa Fusus angrily. "We hear that a wagon was stopped at the unlucky gate last night and there was a fight. Do you know about this?"

My father's lip protruded as his head shook in surprise. He turned to Scavolo, who was wearing his centurions sash, medals shining like stars. "Last night? Have you heard of this Gaius?"

"I heard a thief was caught and killed," he shrugged. "Nothing more." He turned a frown back to Fusus.

"Then you know nothing about a rumour that several people were seen fighting and that all the bodies were removed?" I stared at the wall and my head movement suggested I knew nothing. He turned back to my father. "And a large wagon was seen entering and then leaving your house late last night" he snapped.

My father narrowed his eyes for a moment before he spoke. "I'm sure that you know that a large wagon entered my property because I had to call in all my debts from several sources to repay the loan that you demanded. As you gave us such a short time in which to pay it is quite obvious to anyone that we would be transporting goods at night."

He looked to his son, whose face was growing redder with frustration. "And one of my slaves is missing," he added sharply. "What do you know about that?"

My father stood, slowly rising like a Titan from the depths of the sea. He never moved his gaze from Fusus once as he spoke. "Under the eyes of Jupiter I ask you to explain why you have come here Agrippa Fusus. *Are you accusing me of stealing your slave?*" he said indignantly. He turned quickly to Philus, who was standing by the door with his mouth open. "Philus, fetch a tablet, write down every word that this gentlemen says so that we can respond in the proper manner," at which his eyes returned a cold glare to his former patron. "The manner in which a patrician deals with his equals," he finished.

The insult was not lost on Fusus, whose teeth showed as he flinched. I placed my thumbs into the folds of my tunic and lifted my chin. Albinus noted the movement and scowled. "Something has happened here Merenda, and I'm going to find out what." His anger wasn't abated. "I know that there is no way you could get that much silver in one night. I demand that you tell me if you have recovered my ingots and found more," his voice was rising as he spoke. "If you have and they were found with mu ingots then they belong to me..."

Like a bolt from Jupiter my father spoke, his voice booming over Fusus. "My affairs are none of your business. If a greater patron wishes to support my family because they see good things in an alliance with the Merenda clan then it is your loss." The great man seemed to recoil at that suggestion and it was a good trick to suggest that a new patron was funding the family and his eyes flicked to me for a moment. "We are rising Fusus. Rising with the love of the gods," at which his eyes came to me. "And if you cannot see that there are men in Rome who would support us in our hour of need then you are a fool. Secundus has a new bride," at which the man's head lowered and he seemed to glare at me with even more loathing than I had sensed previously. "He starts his military training with Cincinnatus in a week. His star is glowing. Yours is fading. It is the will of the gods," he said slapping the tabletop with both hands.

Scavolo stepped across the table and stood in front of Fusus, anger in his eyes. "Unless you wish to make a formal statement against Marcus Sulpicius Merenda then I think your time here is ended."

It was an order.

"This is not finished," snapped Fusus, his head whirling toward me. "You don't have the love of any gods boy. If it's true that you didn't find my ingots then this story is full of more shit than fills the Cloaca after the festival of Bacchus. I've seen nothing in your supposed god-given skills. Albinus solved this case, not you."

My eyebrows rose. "Well if the case is solved then I am sure your son knows where your ingots are," I stated.

"What?" snatched Albinus, realising after a second what I had said. "I didn't find them."

I shrugged.

Scavolo stepped in before Albinus, with white spit forming at the edges of his lips, could speak again.

"I'll be watching you," snarled Agrippa Fusus as he was marched out of the room.

****

Fusus and his entourage left the temple like a thundercloud ploughing its way across the heavens, a dark mood seemed to follow them like a swarm of flies. I'd followed them out into the main room of the temple and allowed myself a smile as they disappeared out of the large doorway into the lowering sunlight of what remained of the day. I felt relief. Was that it, was this over? I considered my fortune and how I'd nearly lost my life to the towering Gaul and his family, to the priest of Vulcan. A sudden chill blew through the doorway and caught me, creasing my brows. I was deep in thought about what this sudden change in the air could mean when I saw Philus waving to Scavolo and showing him a series of scrolls, the former centurion taking one and unrolling it to peer at the contents. They began to discuss something within the document at great length and I felt that change in the air once more as I watched them, the two faces turning to me momentarily before they bent their heads back over the scrolls. Scavolo glanced in my direction and I caught his usual disapproving sneer as he turned back to the slave and continued to ask questions.

A slight movement caught my eye and I turned to look at the altar of Jupiter, but it seemed unchanged, no different to usual. Slaves and priests busied themselves with cleaning duties, replacing candles and boxes of offerings. A lone man stood looking up at the statue of Jupiter which adorned the rear of the temple, the flashing eyes of the greatest of the gods staring down at him as he made his plea for a better life. I grinned. It reminded me that I needed to pay a visit to the shrine of Minerva to offer my thanks. I thought about Athitatus and his spirit. Would he forgive me for thinking he was a murderer? Maybe I'd better go to the Vulcanal and offer a coin too? As these thoughts ran through my mind I saw Scavolo slap Philus on the shoulder and turn to march away towards his room with the scrolls in his hand. I wondered for a moment what it is that they had been discussing and yet I don't really care. The case is closed and I can go home and relax. I need a drink.

Returning to my room to get my cloak I notice that Graccus has left and I closed the shutters to the window, still deep in thought. For some reason I could not get the image of Athitatus out of my head. Had I done something wrong? Offended his spirit? I racked my brains. Surely I had done everything I could to support the man and find the solution to the case at the temple of Vulcan. If he'd asked for help in those final hours maybe things would be different? I turned to the door to see Scavolo standing at the entrance with a broad smile on his face. It unnerved me.

"You'll want to hear this I am sure," he said and was gone.

I followed, frowning. He turned into my father's room and I was instantly wary. Inside, my brother Sul stood by our father's desk with the widest smile I'd ever seen spread across his face. Scavolo stood across from him, arms behind his back and chest out like a cock in a henhouse. My father had both hands holding a scroll and Philus was at his shoulder holding a bag of coins in his hands with the appearance of a man who'd bet his life savings on Green and they'd romped home at odds of twenty to one. I looked at Sul and then to my father and then to the document. I recognised something about it and frowned.

"Ah, Secundus." It was my father who spoke and his eyes turned to me with joy written in them. "Great Jupiter is surely smiling on us today and so is your goddess Minerva" he tapped the scroll with his gold-ringed finger. "This is incredible luck," he turned to Philus with a nod. The slave glanced to me but couldn't maintain eye contact. My frown was growing. "Philus brought us this from the records." My father was looking up at me now. "It's the house of Metilius, on the Jugarius just as you mentioned," he said as my stomach clenched and I felt the blood run from my veins. "You said that it was for sale and nobody has bought it but the records show that the house of Merenda had been and made enquiries. You had been there and discussed options."

He glanced to Scavolo who stood like a statue at the side of the desk, didn't blink and didn't move a muscle. I felt that chill return to run up my back like a cold blade.

"And we have both documents related to the property. In law we can prove we now own this property as there are no heirs," he added with a grin. "Jupiter and Minerva are smiling on us today," he laughed aloud as Sul joined him.

"Father, I..."

"I know what you did."

Philus backed away, the bastard.

Father stood and placed his hands flat on the desk, covering the scroll. "And it was *brilliant*," he said, causing me to frown more deeply. "Scavolo has told me everything," he added as I turned to the statue-like man on my right. "It is fabulous."

My head turned from man to man and ended up looking down at the scroll. I didn't understand.

And then Sul gripped my shoulders. "I knew you were a clever bastard, but this." His head was shaking and his whole body was radiating happiness. He hugged me like a lover. "I cannot thank you enough little brother. Scavolo has told me all about it."

"What?" my mouth was drooping and my eyes wide. "I don't..."

"The house," it was Scavolo who was taking over the conversation. "I told your father how you suspected that the priest and the widow of Metilius were somehow involved and that you'd created a ruse to get into the house and look around. Philus told us all about his part in it," he added as Philus looked like he was going to shit himself but clutched at the bag of coins like it was an only child. "And now we have both documents here in the temple and the house has no legal owner."

He turned to my father who was beaming.

"I..."

"Don't be so bashful," replied Sul. "I never thought you would do this for me," he punched me lightly on the shoulder. "Honestly," his head shook and he couldn't let his gaze move from me, his joy brimming over into another bear-like hug. "Thank you."

I turned to Scavolo. The ex-centurion grinned but his eyes were hard. "You did well lad," he said slowly, daring me to disagree. "You knew your brother needed a good house for his family and you sorted it for him," he was nodding slowly to suggest I had done a great service to my family. "The house of Metilius will be perfect for him for his next step on the Cursus Honorum. This gift you have been given from Minerva," he was shaking his head in disbelief now too. "Well, I cannot believe it, but we are all grateful for it."

He stepped across and hugged me, squeezing me a little too hard and staring hard into my eyes with a look which suggested that if I disagreed with his words he'd squeeze every drop of life out of my body like a snake crushing its prey.

My brother hugged me again.

My father stepped across, held my shoulders in his hands and then dragged me into his arms like a babe.

Philus scuttled from the room with a fearful look over his shoulder.

Scavolo bared his teeth in a half-smile with a triumphant gleam in his eye.

I felt like crying.

Janus had turned against me. I hadn't given him a second thought and the two-faced bastard had dug his knife into my back with glee.

The end

I hope you enjoyed this book.

Please can I ask you to add some stars to Amazon as this encourages me to keep writing as well as for others to consider a purchase. Also, please leave a written review if you enjoyed the book.

Below is a section of the next book, The Case of Libera.

The Case of Liber

(please note that this section may have changed in the editing process when Book 3 is published)

The widow continued to sob with her hands over her face her back arched and her head bent to her lap. She'd started with a great wailing sound and quickly fallen into the position in which she now sat, her distress evident to each of us as we stood over her, unsure what to do next.

Scavolo made miniscule head movements which suggested he'd had his fill of listening to the woman's grief-stricken cries before his eyes caught mine and his lips tightened into that grimace which I knew meant he wanted to get on with things. I saw his chest rise and fall slowly as he inhaled and exhaled waiting for the woman to get a grip of herself. He glanced to me once more and I lifted my shoulders in response, I didn't know what to do either.

Graccus stepped forward and knelt in front of the crying lady before asking, "are there any other women in the house?" It sounded like a good suggestion as we were clearly incapable of helping the poor woman in her moment of grief.

She fumbled at her waist and with wet eyes staring up at my friend she thrust a small bunch of keys at him and answered in a gurgling voice, "out the back" before further sobs began. Her head fell to her knees once more as she rocked backwards and forwards in the chair wrapped in the personal distress at the news we'd brought.

I looked to Scavolo, who continued his small head movements before placing his balled fists on his hips and glancing around the large entrance space. The room was square in shape, had two large, shuttered, windows and a fireplace which held the remnants of a fire that seemed to have gone out some time earlier, although there were one or two white glowing embers still visible in the semi-darkness that struggled to light the room. The two exit doors from the room both stood open, the one that Graccus had disappeared through and another which seemed to lead to the remainder of the house. We were stood in the atrium, she had sat on one of three chairs which were placed against the back wall, obviously set up for visitors to await the Master. The Master, though, was not coming back to greet anyone as we'd found him hanging, naked, from a tree near the crossroads of the Vicus Tellenae and the Vicus Patricius. It Hadn't taken us long to get his body to the floor and to take the mask from his face so that a member of the gathered crowd could identify him. Several bystanders had told us who he was and we had hurried to the house to inform the widow whilst Philus, who had been the finder, took the corpse back to the temple of Jupiter.

I looked down at the crying figure, her ringed fingers wrapped across the top of her head were all that I could see as she continued to wail at the loss of her spouse, rocking back and forth as she wept.

To be fair to her it had been a shock as Scavolo had banged on the door, Novius, Manius, Graccus and myself in tow and demanded to speak to the mistress of the house without any other formal announcement of who we were or why we had arrived at such a late hour. We'd assumed the pretty woman, well-dressed in a brown tunic like everyone else who had been at the festival and wide-eyed with surprise, was a slave or daughter as she had opened the door a crack to Scavolo's hammering and peered at us with fearful eyes. We were also dressed in the brown tunics of the Festival of Liberata and carrying our masks in our hands as we'd not yet had a chance to fix them to one of the fig trees as was the festive custom. Five strange men hammering at the door was not usual and this showed in her reaction. She informed us that she was the mistress of the house and expected her husband back at any moment. I wondered where the door slave was but could see nothing within the darkened interior of the house that was visible over her shoulder. It seemed odd that she was answering the door herself, it was a well-positioned and expensive house and we all had some knowledge of her husband as he had been, until tonight, one of Rome's most distinguished slave traders. As such we'd assumed a boy or at least a burly door-slave would greet us.

We had entered, placing the oil lamps we'd brought with us on the table which stood on the left of the doorway as Novius and Manius waited at the door with the bright burning torches we had lit to walk home. Scavolo had announced that we had come from the Festival and had bad news, quickly explaining who we were despite our very unusual appearance. A small crowd had also gathered and followed us to the doorway and her eyes had flicked to the faces which peered in through the half-open gap, nosy buggers all trying to get a little gossip for the street corners. Scavolo turned to his men and lifted his chin. Manius understood at once and pushed the door shut with his foot before I heard him telling the crowd to go home. I guessed they'd still be there when we came out. The temple head-man had returned his gaze to the panic-stricken face of the woman and told her to sit down and that we had bad news. She did so meekly, her hands coming to her face and her eyes darting between us in fear. I noticed several heavy gold rings, a bracelet with an Egyptian scarab etched into a stone of a light blue colour at her wrist and thin braids of gold sewn into her tightly bunched hair. This was certainly a very wealthy woman. "Your husband is dead" Scavolo had announced as soon as she had sat. It was blunt but he'd told me on the way to the house that there was no easy way to tell the wife that her husband was dead and that it was best to just *get it out*. I was as shocked as the wife by the suddenness of his comment as I'd expected at least some sort of preamble. She'd stared at us for the briefest of moments, her deep brown orbs shifting between us and then her head had fallen to her lap and she'd started to wail like a babe. Un-used to such behaviour we had stood and stared at her for several moments.

Graccus returned with two waif-like slave girls dressed in the most meagre of clothes which gave away too much of their nakedness through the thin cloth which was backlit by Graccus' oil lamp. Scavolo's eyebrows rose with interest as I simply stared at the scene with an open mouth. "Look after your mistress" said Graccus with authority. "She's had bad news."

The two slaves, fear written in their faces, turned to each other before they knelt at the feet of the mistress and placed placating hands on her back and shoulders, whispering to her and asking what had happened. The woman wailed more loudly and

Scavolo shook his head dramatically. Both slave girls appeared to be in their teenage years, closing on twenty if I was any judge. Fair hair suggested they had northern heritage and their slim features also gave a hint that they weren't over-fed by the mistress. My eyes kept dropping to the naked backs which faced me as the thin cloth that covered their bodies was like a morning mist which hid the valley but allowed you to see the trees. Scavolo coughed lightly and I turned to see his nod towards the widow. I understood at once that he wanted me to question her. I rolled my eyes and jutted my chin towards the distraught creature that sat before us. His disapproving scowl told me that he wanted me to get on with it.

"Mistress" I said, stepping forward and looking down as one of the slaves turned her head toward me with wet blue-grey eyes. "We must speak to you about what has happened" I said, unsure if this would get her attention. The slave turned back to the mistress and wrapped a protective arm around her knees, placing her head next to the mistresses. It was very familiar but I knew many women treated their slaves like sisters, although the lack of decent quality clothes indicated otherwise. I was shaking my head now as the widow ignored my words and continued to weep into her hands. Scavolo was almost jumping on the spot as his deep breath of exasperation caught my ears. I pulled one of the chairs closer to the mistress, both slaves turning their gaze to me and flashing their breasts as they made defensive adjustments to their positions which put me off my stride for a moment. I caught Scavolo leering and Graccus, true to form, was wiping his nose on a sleeve. "Mistress" I said again but more loudly. "We were the ones who found your husband and our men have taken him to the temple of Jupiter Optimus Maximus. Do you understand?"

The mistress looked up at us once before she broke down in further fits of tears.

Also by Francis M. Mulhern

The Dictator Of Rome series

Dawn of the Eagle (Book 1)

The Fall of Veii; part one (Book 2)

The Fall of Veii; part two (Book 3)

Vae Victis (Book 4)

The King of Rome (Book 5)

The Last Battle (Book 6)

Also in this series

The Ancilia Shield (prequel to Book 1)

The Thracian; a short story

In Fantasy Adventure Fiction (as Fran Mulhern)

Witch Hunt

In Murder and Mystery

Secundus Sulpicius Series

The Case of Minerva (Book 1)

The Case of Vulcan (Book 2)

The Case of Libera (Book 3)

The Case of Fama (Book 4)

The Case of Mercury (Book 5)

Printed in Great Britain
by Amazon

26026141R00106